Christie Barlow is the number one international bestselling author of seventeen romantic comedies including the iconic *Love Heart Lane* Series, *A Home at Honeysuckle Farm* and *Kitty's Countryside Dream*. She lives in a ramshackle cottage in a quaint village in the heart of Staffordshire with her four children and two dogs.

Her writing career came as a lovely surprise when Christie decided to write a book to teach her children a valuable life lesson and show them that they are capable of achieving their dreams.

Christie writes about love, life, friendships and the importance of community spirit. She loves to hear from her readers and you can get in touch via Twitter, Facebook and Instagram.

facebook.com/ChristieJBarlow

twitter.com/ChristieJBarlow

bookbub.com/authors/christie-barlow

instagram.com/christie_barlow

Also by Christie Barlow

The Love Heart Lane Series

Love Heart Lane

Foxglove Farm

Clover Cottage

Starcross Manor

The Lake House

Primrose Park

Heartcross Castle

The New Doctor at Peony Practice

New Beginnings at the Old Bakehouse

The Hidden Secrets of Bumblebee Cottage

Standalones

The Cosy Canal Boat Dream

A Home at Honeysuckle Farm

A SUMMER SURPRISE AT THE LITTLE BLUE BOATHOUSE

CHRISTIE BARLOW

One More Chapter
a division of HarperCollins*Publishers* Ltd
1 London Bridge Street
London SE1 9GF
www.harpercollins.co.uk
HarperCollins*Publishers*
Macken House, 39/40 Mayor Street Upper,
Dublin 1, D01 C9W8

This paperback edition 2023
2
First published in Great Britain in ebook format
by HarperCollins*Publishers* 2023

ISBN: 978-0-00-841319-4

This novel is entirely a work of fiction. The names, characters and
incidents portrayed in it are the work of the author's imagination. Any
resemblance to actual persons, living or dead, events or localities is
entirely coincidental.

Printed and bound in the UK using 100% Renewable Electricity
by CPI Group (UK) Ltd

For me.

Now, a strong independent woman who will never settle for anything or anyone less than I deserve.

This chapter in my life is now called my turn.

Loveheart L

Primrose Park

The Lake House

CLOVER COTTAGE ESTATE

The Old Bakehouse

Bumblebee Cottage

The B

Starcross Manor

Scott's Veterinary Practice

THE GREEN

HIGH STREET

Primary School

Post Office

Callie's apartment

Peony Practice

Solicitors Office

Dolores' apartment

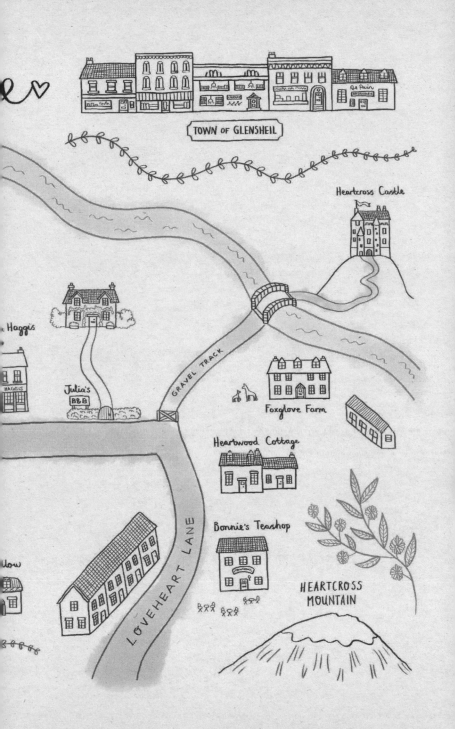

Chapter One

This had been the best idea Bea Fernsby had had in the last eight years.

She wasn't known for taking chances but here she was following the mountainous roads up into the Scottish Highlands. According to the satnav she would reach her destination in approximately seven miles. It was the beginning of August and her whole world had come crashing down. The man she'd trusted her future to since the age of fifteen had let her down, again. Her memories had been shattered, her engagement was over and the future was scary.

Bea wasn't a confident driver – the furthest she'd ever driven was to the nearest town – so she tried to concentrate as the roads became more winding. She shuffled her numb bum in the seat and took a quick glance at the spectacular view out of the window: wall-to-wall mountains under the wide cobalt sky, with a few scattered clouds. Her phone rang, causing her to jump, and when she looked at the flashing screen, she saw it was Emmie. She knew her sister would be worried about her so she picked up the call.

'Where the hell are you?'

'The Scottish Highlands,' replied Bea.

'Don't be ridiculous. That's miles away!'

'I'm not being ridiculous. I actually am in the Scottish Highlands. I just needed to get away for a couple of weeks.'

'Look, running away isn't going to help the situation.'

Bea wanted to be anywhere that didn't remind her of *him*. She carefully manoeuvred the next twist and turn. 'I'm not running away. I'm taking time for me.'

'Yes, he made a mistake, but he's sorry and wants to put it right.'

Bea sighed heavily. 'He's cheated. *Again*. And this time he had the audacity to blame the death of his father for his lack of self-control. There's nothing to work out.' She really didn't want to talk about this anymore or she'd arrive at the B&B close to tears.

There was a heavy silence.

Bea swallowed and hoped her voice didn't falter. 'As hard as it is – because it's so easy to fall back into the same routine – I know my worth and what I deserve. I'm just thankful we didn't get married or have children, otherwise this would be a right holy mess.' All Bea had ever wanted was to settle down with the man of her dreams, have a family and live the fairy tale with the happy-ever-after. But she was beginning to think she wasn't destined to find the one.

'And anyway, this might be a good thing for me.'

'How do you make that out?'

'It will give me time to breathe. I've always been good, dependable Bea. Always putting others first – and where has that got me? What exactly am I doing with my life? Unlike you, I don't even have a decent job that inspires me to get out of bed in the morning.' Although at times their relationship was strained, and Emmie's way was always the right way, Bea admired her sister. Not only did she have a family but she was also a highly successful midwife. 'I need to figure out what exactly my dream is. I want to make a difference in life and all I've been doing is standing still. It's time for that to change.'

'But you're going to be by yourself.'

'I'll be fine. I'm wearing my big girl's pants.' Bea *wanted* to be by herself. She wanted to take time out where no one knew her or looked at her in that sympathetic way, knowing that she'd been cheated on, and she certainly didn't want to have to talk about it. 'Emmie, I need to concentrate. I'm literally driving on a single-lane mountain track and I need to follow the satnav.'

'Okay, but you call me as soon as you get to... And where exactly are you staying?'

'A village called Heartcross, and I promise I will.'

As Bea hung up the call, she looked down at her engagement ring and gripped the steering wheel. He was her past and all she could do now was concentrate on the future. She was more than mad at herself for letting him consume her thoughts for even a moment. She needed to think about herself now, not him. She snaked around the coastal path as the satnav led her through a town called Glensheil, which was joined with Heartcross by a bridge. Coming around a corner, Bea got her first glimpse of the River Heart, glistening in the sunlight. Taking a moment, she pulled into a small layby just next to the bridge and, with the engine still running, stepped out of the car and breathed in the fresh Scottish air. She looked down at her finger, pulled off her engagement ring and turned it over in her hand. Damn that man. Bea screamed 'URGHH' at the top of her voice, surprising a few passers-by, before hurling the ring into the river. Lowering her arm, she exhaled, smoothed down her top and climbed back into the car.

Feeling better, she began to drive over the bridge then bumped along a gravel track and noticed the sign saying, 'Welcome to Heartcross'. She was so glad she'd stumbled across this village on social media. 'Heartcross village is a tranquil place off the beaten track, surrounded by majestic mountains, heather-wreathed glens and beautiful waterfalls – a place untouched by time,' she'd read.

She decided that the internet had described this place perfectly as she took in the magnificent view and slowed the car, coming to a stop at the bottom of Love Heart Lane, which Bea couldn't help thinking was an ironic name, given she'd just well and truly had her heart broken.

The whitewashed terrace houses a little further up the narrow lane looked utterly gorgeous with their potted plants guarding the duck-egg-blue front doors with tumbling blooms full of colour. There was a sign for

'Bonnie's Teashop' and Bea smiled at the comical-looking alpacas grazing in a field alongside. To cap it all, a majestic mountain stood tall at the top of the lane, backed by the beautiful blue sky. This was just what Bea needed – a change of scenery to change her life. She checked the piece of paper that was lying on the passenger seat, on which she'd scrawled the address for 'Julia's B&B', and saw that, according to the satnav, it was only a few hundred yards off the main high street. With the hope of a shower and food in the next hour, Bea couldn't wait to check in and start exploring the village. She began to drive on, still staring up at the mountain, when she heard the screech of tyres followed by the long beep of a horn.

Bea slammed her foot on the brake, her eyes darting over her shoulder. Time slowed and her seatbelt tightened as she watched a Union Jack-roofed Mini mount the kerb and plunge into the hedgerow. She squeezed her eyes shut and felt her chest tighten. Her body trembled as she put the car into neutral, pulled on her handbrake and switched off the engine. Unclipping her seatbelt, she pushed open the car door.

'Oh my gosh, I'm so sorry,' she shouted, tripping over her own feet as she hurried towards the Mini. The driver's side door opened and a woman stepped out of the car.

'I'm really sorry, that was my fault. I wasn't looking where I was going. Are you okay?'

'Yes, though a little surprised,' replied the woman.

Bea was taken in by her appearance. Her hands were wrapped in fingerless gloves, her wrists laced with bangles and her bony fingers stacked with silver rings. Draped around her shoulders was a black shawl and from her tiny waist hung a black skirt with gold crescent moons. Bea knew she was staring, but she couldn't take her eyes off the woman standing in front of her.

'I might be a psychic but I didn't see this coming.' She gave a little chuckle, much to Bea's relief. The last thing she wanted was to anger anyone on her arrival.

'But are you okay?' Bea asked again. 'How's the car? Do we need to swap details? I'm Bea.'

'Martha Gray,' replied Martha, who was looking at the Mini. 'I think we're okay as there seems to be no damage.'

'Thank God,' replied Bea, still trying to calm her beating heart. 'I've only just arrived in the village. What a way to make an entrance.' Her voice wavered and she felt like she was about to burst into tears.

Martha's face softened. 'It's okay, these things happen. As long as you're fine too?'

'This was meant to be the first day of the rest of my life, and now look.'

Martha narrowed her eyes. 'Heartache or running away from trouble?' Martha clearly wasn't afraid to say what she thought. 'In my experience – there's been a lot of that – and at your age, it's usually one of the two.'

'I'm not in trouble, except maybe with you.'

'So, it's a man then.' Martha reached inside her bra and pulled out a card, which she handed to Bea.

Bea looked down at the card, which read: 'Mystic Martha the fortune teller'.

Martha pointed towards a sign wafting in the light breeze, which said "Foxglove Farm". 'You'll find me up there, the vintage caravan. Five pounds to have your fortune told.' Martha checked her watch. 'I have somewhere I need to be. Where are you heading?'

'Julia's B&B.'

Martha pointed. 'It's just down that lane. Don't give that man any more headspace. He was never good enough for you. Chalk and cheese. Any man who has had a fungal nail infection since the age of sixteen can't look after himself, never mind a beautiful soul like yourself. Punching above his weight, I'd say.' Martha tipped her a wink.

Bea's mouth dropped open. 'How would you even know that?'

'You, my dear, have had a lucky escape and one day your ship will come in – and believe me, you won't be making him wear socks in bed.' Martha gave a small chortle. 'And how long are you staying in Heartcross?'

'Two weeks.'

Martha stared at Bea as though in deep concentration. When she spoke, her voice was low, causing the hairs on the back of Bea's neck to stand up. 'That's what you think.'

Bea gave a nervous laugh. She'd never really believed in psychics but there was something mesmerising about Martha. Her gaze didn't leave the older woman as she turned on her heels and climbed back into her car, leaving Bea spellbound by their first meeting. She stuffed the card she had been clutching into the back pocket of her jeans and watched the Mini slowly reverse out of the hedge. Martha nodded in acknowledgement as she drove past.

Bea was thankful that after her lack of concentration no one was hurt and there was no damage to either car. Despite the bad start to her arrival, the weather was glorious and Heartcross felt a good place to be. She wondered exactly what Martha meant by saying, 'That's what you think.' Bea knew she couldn't stay longer than two weeks – she had a job back home, and at some point would need to move her stuff out of the rented flat she shared with her ex. She didn't relish the thought of that.

But in the meantime, despite everything, she was determined to enjoy her time in Heartcross and couldn't wait to explore.

Chapter Two

Arriving at the B&B, Bea parked the car and grabbed her suitcase from the boot. She knew from the website that the elegant three-storey country-style house dated back to the mid-1800s. She was thankful she'd rung ahead to secure a room, as a 'No Vacancies' sign hung on the gate.

Inside, a woman behind the reception desk gave her a welcoming smile. 'Good afternoon, I'm Julia, do you have a room booked?'

'I do, Bea Fernsby,' replied Bea. 'And you must be the owner of this lovely property.'

'Did the name give it away? "Julia's B&B",' she replied, still smiling, whilst tapping on the computer in front of her. 'And thank you, I do agree it's lovely but I'm a tiny bit biased. That's an accent from not around these parts.'

'Staffordshire.'

'Are you here for a holiday?' asked Julia, opening up the key cupboard at the back of the reception area.

'I think so,' said Bea, thinking about Martha's words then noticing the look of confusion on Julia's face. 'Mending a broken heart,' she shared. 'Assessing my life and wondering what the heck is next for me.'

'We've all been there and you've certainly come to the right place. Heartcross is the best place to mend a broken heart.'

'I'm hoping so, but I nearly didn't make a good first impression.'

'Why?' asked Julia.

'I've just had a tiny incident. I ran Mystic Martha off the road, but she's okay.'

Julia's eyes widened then she chuckled. 'Well, she should have seen that coming!'

The door to the B&B swung open and Bea was greeted by a younger woman whose facial features resembled Martha's. Unlike her, though, this woman was dressed in khaki overalls and wellies and there was a faint whiff of cow dung around her.

'What's my granny been up to now?'

'This is Isla, grand-daughter to one psychic and dating guru,' said Julia by way of introduction.

'I'm Bea, arrived ten minutes ago, broken-hearted, and may just need a dating guru.'

'Don't go asking my granny, otherwise Tinderella you will become and you will go to the ball with every right swipe and your love life would be more of a mess than it is now.'

'I'm not sure that is even possible.' Bea grinned.

'But as much as my grandmother is as mad as a box of frogs, her psychic powers are off the scale. Honestly, she knows what is happening in your life before you do!'

Julia laughed. 'I can vouch for that. There are no secrets in Heartcross.'

'Martha might be worth a visit. I need to find out what direction I'm heading.'

'Third van on the right up at Foxglove Farm.' Isla thrust her hand forward. 'Isla, wife to Drew, mother to two, and owner of Foxglove Farm.' She shook Bea's hand. 'And Martha is the reason I'm here.'

'Tell me more,' encouraged Julia, folding her arms on the counter and leaning forward, giving Isla her full attention.

'Grandmother Martha is soon to be eighty years old.'

'NO way!' chorused Julia and Bea, causing Isla to laugh.

'Yes way!'

'I would never have said she was eighty, more mid-sixties,' exclaimed Bea, genuinely surprised. 'It must be the mountain air.'

'More like Botox in three areas,' replied Isla. 'I kid you not.'

Everyone laughed.

'We are holding a surprise birthday gathering – an afternoon at The Lakehouse. It's also the River Festival and the magnificent firework display will end the night perfectly.'

'Or with a bang, you mean,' joked Julia.

Isla leaned forwards, looked behind her and lowered her voice. 'And this is top secret.' She looked between the two of them. 'No one is to breathe a word.'

Both Julia and Bea automatically put up the three-finger salute. 'Scout's honour,' they both whispered.

'Were you in the scouts?' asked Bea, looking towards Julia.

She shook her head. 'No, were you?'

Bea shook her head too, laughing. 'No, never.'

'As I was saying… My mum is coming back from New Zealand for the occasion!'

'Woah!' exclaimed Julia. 'That is going to be a tearful reunion. How many years has it been?'

'Too many to count.' Isla handed Julia an invitation. 'For you and Flynn, and that's the second reason I'm here.'

'Flynn?' replied Julia.

'The Little Blue Boathouse. I believe Wilbur has finally retired and Flynn is looking for help over the summer. He said you have some posters advertising the vacancy that we could put up around the village? I can pin one up in the farm shop.'

'Perfect. Thank you.' Julia pulled open the drawer of the filing cabinet behind the reception desk and took out a couple of flyers. 'The summer is the busiest time for the Boathouse and with the River Festival fast approaching the boats will soon start to sail in.'

'River Festival?' chipped in Bea, listening to the

conversation. 'And what exactly is The Little Blue Boathouse? It sounds absolutely divine.'

'The River Festival is like a mini festival on the water. Yachts and vintage houseboats sail into the harbour from far and wide. The most amazing firework display sets the sky alight to music and there's numerous stalls on the banks of the River Heart,' explained Isla.

'It's an amazing sight, a mini St Tropez,' added Julia, 'and The Little Blue Boathouse is owned by my partner, Flynn. His father, Wilbur, was in charge but has finally agreed to take well-deserved retirement … with a little bit of persuasion. It's the hub of all water sports for the tourists – wetsuit hire, kayaking, paddleboarding, rowing boats, et cetera. It's a massive hit with the locals too. There's also the river taxis, which provide excursions and a direct taxi to The Lakehouse.'

'I've heard of The Lakehouse. The famous celebrity restaurant.' Bea had stumbled across it on social media.

'The very one,' replied Julia, handing over the flyers to Isla. 'No real experience is necessary, just good people skills and the willingness to work their backside off for the summer.'

Hearing those words, the cogs quickly turned over in Bea's mind. 'Could I possibly take a look at one of those?' She gestured towards the flyers.

Isla handed one over whilst Julia chatted away. 'I'm going to have to leave Eleni in charge of this place for the next couple of weeks whilst I try and help Flynn find the perfect candidate.'

'But surely this is your busiest time with the tourists and the summer holidays?' probed Isla.

'It is, but with the River Festival, that water will be packed, especially in this gorgeous weather. It can't afford to stay shut and lose income.'

Bea suddenly felt a wave of excitement. 'I could help! I know I've only just arrived and I really don't want to put anyone on the spot but...' Bea glanced between the pair of them. Their eyes were on her.

'What are you suggesting?' asked Julia.

Bea placed both hands on her chest. 'I could do it,' she enthused, knowing this could be exactly what she needed to throw herself into in order to get over her current situation. A busy couple of weeks would be perfect for helping her take her mind off things.

'We can't ask that of you, you're here for a holiday,' declared Julia, reaching across and touching her arm. 'But thank you, that is such a kind offer.' She smiled warmly at Bea.

'A two-week working holiday may be just what I need though. What if I say you would be doing me a favour as much as I would be doing you one? If I'm being honest, it will keep me occupied. Otherwise, I may be left sitting around, wallowing and thinking about the reason I'm here.'

Isla looked puzzled. 'What have I missed?'

'Heartbreak,' replied Bea. 'A cheating fiancé. In fact, I should say ex-fiancé. I've just tossed the ring in the river.'

'You haven't,' exclaimed Isla, giving a tiny gasp.

'I have, and I was planning on taking this time to work

out what to do with my life and where I go from here. I'm good with money and I have customer service skills as I've worked in a supermarket since leaving school.'

Bea realised the second she'd said those words that she felt a little disappointed in herself. Why had she settled in a job that didn't excite her? She was once ambitious, made plans to travel and work abroad. There was a time she'd wanted to stretch her wings from the town she'd been brought up in, but Carl had squashed any ambition in her, always telling her she didn't really want to do that, and a nice steady reliable income was what they needed. The supermarket had been within walking distance of their rented home and came with the bonus of a hefty discount on food and alcohol. Bea had worked long night shifts. It was very rare that she saw much of the day.

'And your grandmother did say one day my ship will come in. Maybe this is a sign. I'm destined to find love on the water,' joked Bea, who had no intention of going near a man anytime soon, unless Harry Styles fell across her path and declared his undying love for her, of course. He was the only exception to the rule and, realistically, Bea knew she had more chance of winning the lottery.

Still pleading her case, she continued, 'Honestly, I'm a hard worker. Maybe I could do a trial shift for free?' Bea put her hands together in a prayer-like pose. 'Please, give me a chance.'

Isla nodded towards Julia. 'What have you got to lose?'

Julia thought for a moment. 'Are you sure? I really would feel bad putting you out.'

Bea held both hands up and crossed her fingers. 'Absolutely sure!'

'Okay, a free trial it is and I won't be offended if you change your mind.'

Bea clapped her hands. 'I don't think there's much chance of that. This is just what I need.'

'But take the next day to settle in and go and do some exploring. The Little Blue Boathouse is open from 9am to 6pm but has extended hours on Saturday evening. It also closes for an hour over lunchtime.'

'Perfect, that's no problem at all.'

'And it comes with a room above. It's tiny though, and basic. It's essentially just a bed with a small bathroom and cooking facilities, but there's a comfy chair by the window, taking in a view that spans for miles.'

Bea couldn't think of anything better than waking up to a view of the river for the next two weeks. She could already picture herself sitting in the chair, curled up with a good book whilst watching the river flow by. A huge beam spread across her face. 'I'm going to just love the next couple of weeks, I can feel it in my bones.'

'You may change your mind when you see the place – and I need to warn you it will only be minimum wage, and cash in hand if it's just for two weeks.'

'That works for me.' She held out her hand towards Julia and they shook on it wholeheartedly. Bea wasn't doing it for the money – this was going to be a brilliant distraction whilst she worked out her plan of action.

'Welcome to Heartcross! You've arrived at just the right time.'

Isla leaned on the counter and whispered, 'There is something I do have to warn you about, though.'

Bea's eyes widened. 'Go on.'

'The Heartcross curse.'

Bea noticed that Julia was chuckling.

'Once you arrive in Heartcross, you never leave!' Isla said sagely.

This was the second time today that Bea had heard that, and she was beginning to wonder if there was any truth in it. She gave a nervous but excited laugh.

'Maybe Heartcross is just the place to heal my broken heart.'

Julia and Isla gave her a knowing look before Bea held out her hand and took the room key from Julia.

She was going to embrace the next two weeks with everything she had. She was beginning to wonder if uprooting her life for good was indeed a possibility.

Chapter Three

After Julia had given Bea directions towards her room, she walked through reception and down a winding hallway. She stopped and admired the walls, which displayed intricate artwork. The whole place had such a good feel about it. At the end of the hall were small steps leading to a cosy reading corner where a pew, arrayed with soft cushions, overlooked the gardens. She passed the communal sitting room and made her way up another small flight of stairs. Bedroom two was straight in front of her.

It was a simple, rustic room featuring a beautiful four-poster bed, which stood out against the white walls with their minimal decoration. A goose-down duvet with Egyptian cotton linen added elegance and charm, and the bed was dressed with dusky pink scatter cushions. She placed her suitcase on the luggage rack and peered out of the open window at acres of lush grasslands, and the proud beauty of the mountains in the distance. As much as the

B&B felt warm and cosy and was perfect for her stay, Bea was keen to check out the room above The Little Blue Boathouse.

Feeling exhausted after the long drive, she kicked off her trainers and lay down on the bed. Her thoughts immediately turned to Carl and the relationship she'd thought they'd had. Throughout her late teens, he'd convinced her their future was filled only with loveliness, which was a promise he hadn't kept. She'd given him a second chance years ago, after discovering his relationship with Philippa, a family friend, but now, after the death of his father, he'd become withdrawn. It was understandable that he would need time to deal with his grief alone, but Bea had discovered it wasn't the whole truth. He'd struck up another affair with yet another friend of the family, Nicola. Bea was frustrated with herself; she should have by now been able to recognise the signs of his betrayal. He'd continually told her he was very much in love with her but with his infidelities all lines had been blurred, and she couldn't be sure if he'd ever told her the truth about anything. Bea didn't know what to believe, but she knew she didn't want or need to resolve that uncertainty. That was in her past, and making a promise to herself there and then, she vowed to never let a man make her feel this level of anxiety again. She was ready to stand up for her own self-worth and say enough was enough.

Pushing herself off the bed, she wandered into the bathroom and risked a tentative look in the mirror, studying her reflection. The puffiness around her deep hazel eyes indicated to everyone that she'd been crying. After splashing cold water on her face and patting it dry with the towel, Bea gave herself an encouraging smile. 'You've got this, girl,' she murmured before applying fresh makeup and pulling a brush through her hair.

Ten minutes later, Bea declared herself ready and, despite feeling tired after the long drive, she was ready to explore and see everything that Heartcross had to offer. Her first stop? The Little Blue Boathouse. Picking up a tourist leaflet from the welcome pack on the desk, she studied the map. There were two routes that led her towards the river. One through the high street, past the green and along the public footpath of the Clover Cottage Estate, or she could head back down the gravel path and cut through to the footpath that took her right along the riverbank towards The Little Blue Boathouse. Bea opted for the route along the riverbank but first with a detour to Bonnie's Teashop. Hearing her phone ring she rummaged in her bag and looked at the screen. Her ex's name was flashing. She declined the call, switched her phone onto silent and threw it back into her bag.

Five minutes later, Bea found herself following the delicious aroma filtering from Bonnie's Teashop to the top of Love Heart Lane. Feeling a rumble in her stomach, she realised she was ravenous, so her plan was to pick up a takeaway pasty and a coffee and head down to the river. Taking in the trendy chalkboard standing on the pavement with specials written on it, and the yellow and white striped awning already shielding the front of the teashop from the glorious sunshine, she smiled. This place looked like a slice of delightful happiness, she thought, as she pushed open the small wooden gate and ambled up the path. The first thing she noticed was the poster in the window advertising the River Festival and right next to that Mystic Martha advertising her psychic predictions at five pounds a reading. Bea stopped and looked over the poster.

'Highly recommended,' the girl behind the counter said, looking in Bea's direction and smiling. 'Are you thinking of having a reading?'

'Maybe,' Bea replied. She didn't know if she even believed in that sort of stuff but since crossing paths with Martha that morning, she had to admit she was intrigued by her. 'She's a very interesting character.'

'You've met our Martha then?'

'You could say that. I only arrived in Heartcross this morning, and soon afterwards I ran Martha off the road.'

'Then you must be Bea.'

'I am! Don't tell me everyone around here is psychic.'

The girl behind the counter stretched out her hand and shook Bea's. 'Not quite.' She grinned. 'I'm Felicity. Isla's one of my best friends and nipped in here after meeting you at the B&B. But nothing gets past anyone in this village. Mark my words.'

'It seems so,' replied Bea with a smile.

'And I believe you're doing a trial at The Little Blue

Boathouse? According to the forecast, the weather is going to be sweltering over the next month and I can't think of a better place to be working than right next to the water. Two weeks, Isla said you would be around for.'

'Yes, I've planned a two-week holiday. I needed a change of scenery.'

'That's a shame it's only two weeks as you'll miss the River Festival. It's spectacular. Soon the river will be littered with houseboats, yachts and basically anything that floats. The village gets very busy and the atmosphere is amazing.'

Bea began to turn Felicity's words over in her mind: *You'll miss the River Festival.* As a teenager she'd always fancied taking off during the summer months and disappearing to the coast with only her rucksack for company. She imagined herself landing a summer job then returning home for autumn. But now, exactly what did she have at home? A job that she didn't really enjoy and a rental property with a man she never wanted to see again. This might be the push she needed to walk away from the mundane routine that had been her life for so long. Sunshine and water were just what she needed to blow away the cobwebs and mend her broken heart.

'But Julia and Flynn will be chuffed for your help, even if it's only for two weeks. It'll give them time to interview,' continued Felicity. 'If we weren't run off our feet here, because of all the tourists that flock in for the summer, I could imagine myself waking up in that attic room overlooking the water and living my best life. Sometimes the simple things make us happiest, don't they?'

Bea couldn't agree more. Even though she'd shed a few tears in the last twenty-four hours, the heartfelt and welcoming ambience of Heartcross was uplifting – not to mention the splendid views.

'Look at me babbling on. What can I get you?' asked Felicity, rolling her eyes. 'I could chat for Scotland.'

Bea laughed. 'Could I take a pork and apple pasty? They look delicious. And…' Bea perused the glass counter in front of her, which was filled with all things sugary and looked divine. 'So many choices. I'll take one of those chocolate gingerbread men. I've not had one of those since I was a little girl. And a takeaway coffee, please.'

Felicity placed the pastries in white paper bags, handed over the coffee and rang up the bill.

'Thank you,' said Bea as she paid. 'I'm going to wander down to The Little Blue Boathouse and eat these by the river.'

'You enjoy it. You've certainly timed your arrival well, as I believe the first houseboat has recently arrived for the festival. They start sailing in a few weeks before and, like yourself, make a holiday of it.'

***

Walking back down Love Heart Lane, Bea was already thinking she couldn't wait to explore what the village had to offer. This place was just a different way of life. She'd been here for only a few hours and could already feel Heartcross was going to be good for her. There was a sense of calm and, strangely, she felt quite settled already. All the villagers who had crossed her path had instantly made her feel welcome.

As she joined the path along the riverbank, the sound of a motor caught her attention. Bea watched a speedboat thump across another boat's wake. Music blared and a group of friends talked and laughed as the gentle lap of the water hit the riverbank. Bea took in the sight. She could see why tourists flocked here – it was spectacular. There were children in wetsuits playing in a shallow bay further up the river, fishermen dropping lines into the water, jet skis racing back and forth under the bridge that separated the village from the town, and Heartcross Castle looked magnificent in the distance. Bea walked to the water's edge and stood under the shade of a tree, the leaf-dappled sunlight hitting the water and making it sparkle. She smiled at the kids swinging from a rope out over the river, watched by their parents, who were enjoying a picnic on a blanket. Noticing a large, flat pebble, Bea picked it up and skimmed it across the water. It bounced three times before hitting some knobby driftwood. Skimming stones was something she'd always do as a youngster on holiday with her father. She smiled, thinking about her dad. He'd never been keen on Carl, though he hadn't said so in so many words, and she remembered now when he'd asked her whether he was the one. She'd hesitated and replied, 'How do you even know?'

Her father's words still rang in her ears, four years after his death: 'If you're asking that question, then he isn't the one.' He'd been right.

Bea took a moment and swallowed a lump. She missed her father and wished she'd listened to him back then.

Somehow the relationship with Carl had shifted to autopilot. She should have recognised the signs sooner – men rarely go off sex without good reason. Feeling a stirring in her stomach, she realised it was a sense of relief. Even though the betrayal had hurt, part of her was glad he'd been unfaithful, as it was the push she'd needed to begin her own adventure.

Turning, she exhaled and stared at the craggy cliffs behind her. Impulsively, she tilted her face up to the sun before stretching out her arms wide, then shouted at the top of her lungs, 'I'm free to do what I want!' Spinning around, she felt happy-go-lucky. This holiday was the start for her – her time to shine and laugh again.

Still spinning, with the light breeze in her face, Bea giggled and finally came to a stop. It felt good to let go and just be by herself. Hastily taking a step back to steady herself as the spinning caught up with her, she wobbled. Losing her balance, she gave a tiny squeal and then nearly jumped out of her skin as a hand steadied her. Startled, she looked up. The hand belonged to a man with a look of amusement on his face.

'Sorry, I didn't mean to make you jump. I just thought it would be a bit too soon for you to go falling at my feet when we've not even met yet.' He had a glint in his eye.

'Thank you' were the only words she could muster. She had no idea where he'd sprung from. Goodness, he was attractive with his huge hazel eyes, flawless olive skin and mass of chestnut hair. His white, short-sleeved shirt complemented his tan perfectly and was clinging to every muscle.

Smiling, he let go of her arm and offered his hand. 'Hi, I'm Nolan.'

Bea was still staring at him. She couldn't help it. 'Bea,' she said, finally taking his hand and instantly feeling a tiny flip in her stomach, completely taking her by surprise.

'Are you from around these parts?' he asked.

Bea shook her head. 'Just here for a two-week holiday, but I may stay a little longer. I've not quite decided yet. And you?'

'Just staying a few weeks,' he replied. 'Maybe I'll see you around?'

'Maybe you will.'

'And whatever you're free from, I really hope you do what you want.' He gave her a warm smile before heading off in the opposite direction, leaving Bea catching the aroma from an aftershave that oozed class. Nolan was drop dead gorgeous. Daring to glance back over her shoulder, she saw he had the perkiest bum she'd ever seen. Nolan also snatched a quick look back just then. Damn, he'd caught her looking. She bit her lip to suppress her smile. There was an air of confidence about him and a twinkle in his eye that caused Bea's heart to instantly race. Astonishingly, he tipped her a wink, and she couldn't stop her smile from growing wider. He soon disappeared around the winding river path and was out of sight, leaving Bea wondering what the handsome stranger was doing in Heartcross.

As she carried on walking with a renewed spring in her step, she noticed a huge rock, which was a perfect place to eat her lunch, and so she perched on the edge. The pasty tasted as good as it looked and Bea devoured it quickly whilst watching two seagulls on a nearby rock squabbling over an abandoned piece of bread. Their grey and white bodies were quite enormous and the clacking of their beaks could be heard as their boisterous antics continued. One soon flew off when it noticed a small boy throwing stale bread into the water at the end of the jetty. As soon as she finished her lunch, she tossed the paper bag into a nearby bin and carried on walking.

Turning the next corner, Bea gave a tiny gasp. The Little Blue Boathouse was in sight and it was exactly how she imagined it would look. It was a small stone building with a timber roof that was painted in a watery pale blue, and large windows looking out over the river.

'Could this place get any more idyllic?' she murmured to herself. Breathing in the fresh air and listening to the river lapping against the jetty and the tiny shingle bay where all the kayaks lay in line, she could tell this would be the perfect sanctuary for the next couple of weeks. She had every intention of passing her trial shift. Up ahead, there was a bright yellow water taxi heading towards the jetty with its engine humming away. It was packed with tourists and Bea guessed there were approximately fifty passengers on board. She noticed a small metal sign advertising today's excursion; hopefully, in a couple of days' time she would be selling tickets for those very trips.

Excited to see inside, Bea stepped through the door, which was propped open with the perfect anchor doorstop. Whitewashed panelling gave the whole place an authentic nautical feel and the walls were covered with paintings and photographs of what Bea assumed was the River Festival, along with boat races and the scenery that surrounded the River Heart in all the various seasons.

'Welcome, what can I do for you today? Great day for kayaking, or a rowing boat for two?'

The man standing in front of her was a jolly-looking fellow with charm. His welcoming smile was huge. Even though it was a glorious day outside, he was wearing a flamboyant blue velvet suit, sporting a bright-red checked cravat and leaning on a cane. Bea loved his dress sense, which certainly stood out in the crowd.

'A kayak for one would be good. And I'm Bea. Pleased to meet you. I have a trial here in a couple of days.'

'Oh yes, Bea! I've already heard. Lovely to meet you, I'm Wilbur. You're around for two weeks, is that right?'

'I am, but from what I've seen so far, I already feel like I could stay for ever. It's so beautiful.'

'Believe me, this place has that effect on people. And if your trial is successful, are you ready for a busy two weeks?'

'I was born to be ready,' she said, remembering hearing those words in a movie once.

'You'll need to be. It's the busiest time for the Boathouse, especially with such glorious weather and the River Festival coming up. It's been going for sixty years, this year. How incredible is that?'

'Very incredible. Julia mentioned there's a little attic room available too. If I'm successful at my trial, of course.'

'There is, would you like to go and have a look?' Wilbur gestured behind him. 'It's vacant.'

'Would I? That would be great!' enthused Bea.

'It's very basic but I don't think there's anything better than waking up with a view of the water.'

Bea couldn't agree more. Wilbur pointed to the door at the back of the room. 'Through there and up the ladder.'

Excited to see the room, Bea headed through the door and spotted a rope ladder straight in front of her. It reminded her of a story that her father used to read to her as a child, with a rope ladder that led to a secret tree house. She balanced on the wobbly bottom rung and climbed up, pushing open the hatch door above her head. Placing both hands on the tiny wooden handles each side of the opening, Bea pulled herself up. Once on her feet, she gave a tiny gasp. What a beautiful space. The first thing she noticed was the view of the river and the cliffs, which seemed to go on for miles and miles. The room was minimalist but perfect. The floorboards were covered with a wool rug in blue and rose, creating a striking first impression and bringing warmth and colour to the room. There was a bed with a small table and lamp beside it, and a small basin in the corner of the room with a mirror. The beautiful green velvet armchair positioned in front of the window was adorned with a crocheted blanket and a cushion, and the small writing desk and chair on the other side of the room were positioned next to a vintage clothes rail with wooden hangers. There was also a small counter with a kettle, a portable hob and a small freestanding fridge.

Walking across the creaky floor, Bea smiled up at the attic beams that met in a series of arches, absorbing the beauty of deep brown hues. Taking a seat in the armchair, she gazed at the paintings and pictures of boats that covered the walls and the series of classic books piled on the shelf, before looking out at the view. Felicity was right, the first houseboat had arrived. Bea hadn't ever seen anything quite like it. The handcrafted cedar boat had a massive deck with sofas and a hammock that hung over the water. The elegance, panache and charm of the houseboat bobbing on the water blew her away. It was very different from the gleaming white yachts that you saw in movies and magazines. Daydreaming, she thought about how wonderful it would be to live on a houseboat and sail all over the world, with a different bay to wake up in every morning. That would be something Bea thought she would never tire of. Wondering who lived on a boat like that, she noticed a pair of binoculars hanging at the side of the window and a selection of birdwatching magazines strewn across the table. Bringing the binoculars to her eyes she focused on the houseboat and the bold lettering on the side, which read: 'The Hemingway'.

Hearing Wilbur call her name, she took another quick look around before descending the ladder. Bea's face was stretching into a huge smile and she felt a positive shift in her feelings and mood. This place was just what she needed to concentrate on herself and her own well-being. This was an adventure she couldn't wait to start.

'What do you think?' asked Wilbur, handing over change to a customer who then disappeared into the changing room with a wetsuit.

'I love it! I want to wake up to that view and the room is utterly gorgeous.' She crossed her fingers in front of Wilbur. 'I'm hoping I pass my trial.'

'I'm sure you will sail through it. No pun intended.' He gave a little chuckle. 'And there's no charge for your kayak today. If you would like a wetsuit, they're just there.' Wilbur pointed to a rail. 'And life jackets are over there, lockers for your personal items too.'

Within five minutes, Bea was tightening up her life jacket and walking down to the shallow bay. The river was full of kayaks and with the weather as sunny as it was Bea was going to take the opportunity to spend an hour on the water. The spare kayaks were lined up, all in bright solid colours, and Bea chose yellow. The front end of the kayak was planted on the shingle and the rudder in the water, so she found a rock-free area to enter the water from the shore. As she waded in, the cool water splashed against her legs, her feet squelching inside her now soggy trainers. With the drag marks already half erased by the waves, the banana-coloured boat was soon bobbing in the water. Bea strapped her helmet under her chin and scooted slowly into the cockpit, extending one leg at a time. She began to use sweeping strokes to pivot the kayak and soon she was heading out into the middle of the river in the direction of the houseboat. She soon got into the rhythm and shouted 'Good afternoon' at everyone who crossed her path.

The water was a little choppy at times but overall surprisingly calm – nothing that Bea couldn't handle. Enjoying the views, she glided for a wee while. She could already imagine the exciting atmosphere of the River Festival. Beginning to paddle again, she hit shallow water. With the sun reflecting on the water, Bea could see darting fish below the surface. This made a lovely change. If she was back home, she would be trying to grab a few more hours' sleep ahead of the no doubt mundane night shift she would have to take on later.

After five minutes she changed direction and headed for deeper water. It wasn't long before she was paddling close to The Hemingway, wondering who lived on a boat like that and where they had travelled from. The hammock looked divine and she could imagine herself lying there, soaking up the rays with a cheeky bottle of pinot grigio chilling in an ice bucket at the side of her. 'That's the life,' she murmured to herself.

'Well, if it isn't Bea, the woman who is free to do what she wants.'

Immediately, Bea swung a glance to the deck and met the gaze of Nolan, who grinned at her. He was standing with a paintbrush in his hand and wearing just a pair of grey lounge pants. Her hands poised on the paddle, Bea couldn't help admiring his tanned torso. And there it was, a feeling she'd forgotten – that tingle, the goosebumps and the flutters in her stomach that had been missing for so long.

'Pleased to meet you again,' she said, flicking her eyes over the boat. 'Are you the captain of this amazing vessel?'

Nolan threw his head back and laughed. His eyes flashed with instant warmth as he winked then rescued her from the embarrassment. 'I'm just about to crack open a beer, do you fancy one?'

'The sunshine, a beer and an almighty vessel – an offer no one can refuse,' she replied playfully, looking up at the boat and wondering exactly how she would climb on board.

Nolan must have read her mind and threw a rope over the side. 'Attach the clip on the end of the rope to the metal ring behind you,' he instructed.

Bea swizzled her body round, located the metal ring and did exactly that.

'Now pass me up your paddle.' Nolan lay on his stomach, reached over the side of the boat and grabbed it from her.

The kayak was bobbing from side to side and, feeling a little jittery, Bea slowly wriggled backwards as much as she could, praying the kayak didn't tip over. Nolan then unravelled a rope ladder, which hung down the side of the boat.

'Okay, as you stand up, there's a fair chance you may end up in the water if the kayak tips over,' he shared.

Bea had already worked that one out for herself but, determined not to end up in the water, she made a swift move and grabbed the rope ladder like her life depended on it. The kayak tipped but luckily Bea was already climbing towards the deck, where Nolan was standing waiting with two beers in his hand. Only forty-eight hours ago her life had been doom and gloom as she packed her suitcase and readied to flee. Never in a million years could she have envisaged this – standing on the deck of a houseboat with a handsome stranger, and drinking beer in the sunshine. Could life actually get any better than this?

'Cheers.' He handed her a bottle and clinked his against it. Immediately she detected his divine, spicy masculine fragrance, which sent a tingle down her spine. Knowing she was blushing slightly she couldn't stop her eyes flitting over his body. Then full-blown embarrassment hit her as she realised she was wearing a life jacket along with an unflattering wetsuit, her legs resembling black puddings hanging in a butcher's window, and on her feet were sodden trainers that felt all squelchy and stank to high heaven.

'Do you want to take off your jacket and trainers?' Nolan asked, as if reading her mind.

'Thanks,' replied Bea, handing back the beer while she unclipped her helmet, hung her life jacket on a nearby hook and kicked off her trainers. Holding them over the side of the boat she promptly poured the water back into the river before placing them on the deck to dry out in the sunshine.

Taking back the beer, she took a sip. 'It's like a log cabin on the water,' she said, admiring her surroundings. 'It's truly amazing.'

'Because that's exactly what it is.'

'And everything is so olde-worlde. Do you actually live on here?'

'I do, at the minute,' he replied, gesturing towards the bamboo cane seat with plush soft cushions. Bea sat down. 'And I can't see it changing any time soon. I've been sailing the seas for the last six months. This was my grandfather's boat and it's been part of the family for many years. He passed away last winter…'

'I'm sorry to hear that,' Bea offered warmly.

'Thanks,' Nolan replied, sitting down in the chair next to Bea and taking a swig of his beer. 'I've spent the winter months renovating the boat. It was hard work, took a lot of blood, sweat and tears, but it's been well worth it. It had been moored outside my grandfather's house for many years and it was only when he passed away that I came to realise there's more to life than a nine-to-five job and answering to someone else.'

Bea could relate to that but it took some guts to give up the security of regular work on a whim. She'd never been one for taking chances. This was the first daring thing she'd done for many years.

'Where did your grandfather live?' asked Bea.

'On the coast of Cornwall.'

'That's a lot of water you've covered to get here.'

'And worth every second. Me and The Hemingway

have bonded. I'm glad I took the decision to renovate it, otherwise it would have been scrapped.'

'You've renovated this entirely by yourself?' Bea was amazed. 'It's a thing of beauty.'

'Isn't it just,' replied Nolan, holding her gaze, and there was that feeling again, the flutter of a hundred fireflies swirling around her stomach.

'Would you believe I've never actually been on a boat before? This is a first for me.'

'And I've never had a visitor on my boat before, so this is a first for me, too.' He held up his beer bottle and clinked it against Bea's. 'Welcome!'

'It's such a grand name for a boat, "The Hemingway".'

'Named after my grandfather, Morgan Hemingway. Would you like a tour?'

'I thought you'd never ask.' Bea was curious to have a look at all the nooks and crannies and discover what the boat had to offer, and it was soon clear that The Hemingway was not just a run-of-the-mill houseboat. She thought it would be all mod cons and leather upholstery but was surprised to find it was littered with paintings on the walls, and old velvet settees with crocheted blankets and brightly coloured cushions. In a corner there was a bar stacked with bottles of different spirits.

Nolan pointed to it. 'I'm not an alcoholic,' he said, smiling and holding up a bottle. 'Each one of these bottles tells a story… Look.' He handed one of the bottles to Bea and pointed to the handwritten label. 'At every bay my grandfather sailed into he purchased a bottle and labelled it with the place he bought it.'

'What an amazing collection.' Bea handed the bottle back and began to look at some of the others. 'Salcombe. St Ives. Oh my, look at this one…' Bea picked up the bottle of Glensheil Gin. 'Heartcross. The Hemingway has frequented these waters before!'

'Yes, that's right. I'm retracing some of my grandfather's voyages.' Nolan picked up a leather-bound book. 'This is the Hemingway's logbook. My grandfather logged every voyage he ever sailed.' Nolan carefully opened the book and Bea saw how precise it was. There was entry after entry with the date and voyage details, and all in such neat, precise handwriting.

'Just look at that. All the history, the places your grandfather has visited. And are you sailing all these trips?'

'Just a few,' shared Nolan, closing the book. 'When I was a little boy, my grandfather shared his stories from his latest adventures on the water whenever he returned. He convinced me he'd fought pirates, tackled sea monsters and fought sharks. He was the best storyteller. He told me his princess lived in the tiny village of Heartcross up in the Scottish Highlands and worked at The Little Blue Boathouse. One day she would be his queen. That story always stuck in my head and I suppose that's why I'm here. I wanted to see this place and it's exactly how my grandfather described it.'

Bea brought her hands up to her chest. 'How romantic,' she said, taking another glance at the bottles.

'Very,' replied Nolan. 'You never know, history may have a habit of repeating itself.'

Bea lifted her head and gazed towards him. 'Single?' she asked calmly, even though her heart was hammering in anticipation of the answer.

For a brief second the question hung in the air.

'I am,' he replied.

Goosebumps prickled every inch of her body. 'That's good then.' The words left her mouth before she could stop them. He looked directly into her eyes. Neither of them faltered.

'And yourself?'

'Single, for about forty-eight hours … since I discovered my fiancé has been sleeping, yet again, with an old family friend. I stumbled across his Facebook messages, an app which he claimed he didn't have or use.'

'Yet again?'

'A different family friend from last time.'

'Ouch! What an idiot he is.'

'I can't disagree with you there.'

'Together long?'

'My childhood sweetheart. But not such a sweetheart anymore. Hence the reason I'm here. I'm taking time off work to heal my broken heart.'

'And how's that going?' asked Nolan, watching her closely.

'Funnily enough, it seems to be mending pretty fast,' she replied with a grin, taking another look around the cosy living room. 'I wouldn't be able to spend months sailing around the seas,' she said, changing the subject.

'Why ever not?'

'I suppose because I'm not financially secure. You'd need a few quid in the bank.'

'I beg to differ. Why do you need to be financially secure? Make money as you go. There's a whole world out there. Why would anyone want to be stuck in the same place day in and day out, when you can wake up in a different bay each day? You get two lives in the world and the second one begins when you realise you only have one.'

Bea admired Nolan's thinking. 'But isn't it scary, not having a routine? Not knowing where you're going to end up?'

'Taking chances and living a carefree life is the best feeling in the world. Life is for the living and if you don't live it, what's the point?' He put his hand in the small of her back. 'Come on, I'll show you the rest.'

In the whole of her life, Bea couldn't remember when she'd done anything out of the ordinary – except for now. This was the first time she had been away from her town by herself and, if she stopped and thought about it, it felt quite liberating. Her mother and father had worked the same jobs since they were sixteen years old. They had a sense of pride working for the same company for so long and looked forward to receiving their gold-plated carriage clock for fifty years of dedicated service. She supposed that's what had been expected of her. She could remember her father's words: 'Jobs are hard to come by. When you get one you work hard and work your way up the ranks and you will be valued.' Bea felt far from valued in her work and her home life. There had been no room for promotion for the general staff that stacked the shelves and worked the tills, yet graduates were brought in and put straight into management positions without understanding what it was like on the shop floor. The hierarchy in the supermarket reminded her a little of the House of Commons; those at the top had no real clue how to do the jobs that kept the company going, and those that did were paid the national minimum wage. Listening to Nolan, she thought him brave and carefree. His way of life sounded fun. But Bea wasn't that brave. She liked a plan and a routine and that's what this two-week holiday was about, planning the rest of her life.

Taking a few steps forward, Bea noticed an easel with fresh paint on a palette. She took in the newly painted picture on the canvas. 'Wow! That's the view from the boat. It's magnificent.' The watercolour captured the steely blue river and the bridge with Heartcross Castle towering in the distance. There were kayaks bobbing on the water with gulls swooping in front of the white-washed cliffs.

'It's a magnificent view to paint.'

'You painted this?'

'I did.' Nolan pointed to numerous paintings stacked up against the wall. 'That's what I do, I paint pictures and sell them in the bays I visit; make some pocket money, and sail on. When I finally finish my adventures, my dream is to moor The Hemingway and turn it into a floating art gallery, maybe even teach some classes.'

Bea was in awe. 'You're super talented. These are just amazing. Both the villagers and tourists would snap these up.' She glanced through the paintings. 'I love this one.' It was a painting of the shingle bay with the kayaks lined up, the jetty and The Little Blue Boathouse. The detail was unbelievable. 'I would love to buy this one from you.' This painting was everything the next two weeks of her life represented.

'Have it as a present,' he said with a warm smile.

'I couldn't possibly. I've only just met you.'

'That's true, but knowing you like it and it's going to a good home is more than enough payment for me.'

Bea didn't chip in that actually she had no clue where her home was anymore. She knew that as soon as she did, she would hang the painting in pride of place.

Nolan picked up the painting and turned it over. Reaching for an old-fashioned ink pen, which was lying on a nearby desk, he dipped it in an ink bottle then wrote an inscription on the back of the painting.

For Bea
She's free to do want she wants,
Nolan x

'I suggest you don't try and take it back in the kayak. Let me know where I can drop it for you.'

'Thank you. I'll treasure it, I promise.'

'I'm in no doubt.' He smiled warmly.

Bea looked down at the final painting in the pile. 'And who are they? They look like royalty.'

'My grandfather's Heartcross Princess, and that is my grandfather. He was an artist too.'

Bea couldn't take her eyes off the woman in the painting. 'She's such a natural beauty ... and look at their faces, they look so in love. What's her name?'

'Patsy, and according to the stories of my grandfather, they were exactly that, in love.'

'And do we know what happened to her?' asked Bea, interested in their love story.

Nolan shook his head. 'Unfortunately, I'm not quite sure of all the details. But remembering the story he told me when I was a little boy, I think my grandfather was here for the summer. Years later, he told me he'd come back looking for Patsy, but I'm not sure what happened.' He picked up the painting. 'Maybe, whilst I'm here, I could ask some questions. There must be some villagers who are still around from that time, though I only have her first name to go by.'

'There has got to be someone who knows something.'

'Before my grandfather passed away, he was very weak. My hands were cupped around his and he murmured "Patsy" and "Heartcross".' Nolan's voice faltered. 'Whoever this woman is, she was on his mind before he passed away.'

'That's beautiful but a little sad too. Did you have a grandmother?'

'My grandmother upped and left a long time ago and

my mum was a single parent who passed away over ten years ago, leaving just me and grandfather. I always wondered what it would be like to be a part of a big family.'

'I have a sister. She's married and I have a niece and nephew. Sometimes she can be a little bossy – offering her opinion an awful lot and being overbearing – and she thinks I'm mad for coming away on my own.' She rolled her eyes. 'But of course, I love her.'

'Sometimes, we need space from what we know and from the norm. And no one is mad who comes to this place. I mean, just look at that view. The whitewashed cliffs, the bridge, the castle, the mountain…'

They both looked towards the bridge.

'When my grandfather told me stories about this place, he spoke with such happiness – and the second I sailed in, I could see why. It will be difficult to leave.'

'How long are you staying for?

'Just until the River Festival and then I'll head wherever the logbook takes me next. But before that happens, if I could find Patsy and tell her how much my grandfather thought about her, wouldn't that be fantastic?'

'It would. There must be something really special about this woman for him to still remember her years later.'

'I believe so.' Nolan looked at the painting and for a second Bea thought he was going to say something else, but he changed his mind and they stepped into the small kitchen area, which was fully equipped and had large windows with a view of the craggy white cliffs.

'Waking up and making a brew to that view must be … just wow!'

'It's something else, isn't it?' Nolan pointed. 'Through there is the bathroom and then the bedroom.'

Curious to see what the bedroom looked like, Bea took a quick peep. The room was small, the double bed filling the space almost wall to wall. There was also a small bedside cabinet with a lamp, and a line of built-in wardrobes.

'Small but very cosy,' said Nolan. 'I spend most of the time out on deck, painting.' They walked back out into the sunshine and sat down on the chairs.

'I couldn't imagine ever living on a boat but after seeing what it has to offer, I can see the appeal. It's like something out of a romance novel, tranquil and peaceful.'

'I absolutely love it. Waking up to the sound of water, the gulls flying high … and there's something cleansing about the fresh air. Rain or shine I sit out with a cuppa first thing in the morning and live for the moment. Then I spend my day fishing, or there's water sports, or walking through scenery that would never have crossed my path otherwise.'

'You're living the dream.'

'I am on a day like today, but it can be a different story in winter and it's no fun if it's lashing down.'

'Do you get lonely?' asked Bea.

'I'm completely happy in my own skin, love my own company and my painting. And every time I sail into a new bay there's a whole village of fabulous folk to chat to.'

'But don't you want to put down roots and find a

permanent base for your life? I can see the attraction of this for a short-term holiday but to do this for ever…'

'I'm all about taking chances, living life to the max. What would you choose – constant shifts in a supermarket or waking up with a view to kill and scenery to paint?'

'When you put it like that,' answered Bea, still thinking she would never be brave enough to take the plunge into a constant unknown.

'And what do you do for a job?' asked Nolan, stretching out his legs in front of him and leaning back in the chair.

Bea laughed. 'I work night shifts in a supermarket.' She watched as Nolan swallowed hard, then brought his hand up to his mouth.

'I'm so sorry, I didn't mean to—'

'You didn't.'

'And how do you find it?'

Bea exhaled. 'Mundane, rarely challenging, the same old, same old, but I know when I get paid and how much goes into my bank account.'

'But does it make you happy?'

Bea considered the question carefully. 'Do you know, this is going to sound a little sad when I say it, but I'm not exactly sure what happiness is.'

Nolan sat up in his chair and rested his arms on his knees. 'It doesn't sound sad at all. It might be you've lost your way.'

'I was thinking about this earlier. I can't remember the last time I had a proper belly laugh or thought, "That was a damn good day," and I can't remember the last time I had anything to look forward to.'

'We can't have that. Laughter is a must. Life is so much better when you have a smile on your face and there's nothing better than that ache in your stomach when you've laughed hard. What are you doing tomorrow?'

Bea raised her eyebrows and smiled. 'What are you suggesting?' she asked in anticipation.

'That Bea…' He waved his hand around in a circle of enquiry.

'Fernsby,' she said, filling in the blank.

'That Bea Fernsby, who is free to do what she wants, spends the afternoon with me and there's one thing on the agenda.'

'And that is?'

'Laughter!' Nolan reached out to hold her hand. The second his fingers brushed against hers, there was that quiver through her whole body again.

'Deal,' she replied, with a wide grin on her face before sitting back in her chair.

'And what is Bea's ambition in life?'

Thinking about Nolan's question, Bea's heart sank. She had no idea. Life had become comfortingly familiar, surrounded by what she knew, but now a tiny niggle was beginning to fester inside her. Why had she settled for the life she had? The whole world was full of opportunities and she was beginning to recognise that everything in her life since becoming Carl's partner had revolved around what he wanted and he thought she should do. His ways, combined with her parents' traditional views, had stifled her own aspirations. Carl George had indeed done her a favour by cheating on her again. It was the kick up the backside she needed. It was about time she made her own way in the world.

'I actually don't know what to say,' she admitted. 'I've no clue what my ambitions are. I always thought I'd be married in the next couple of years and have children and that's exactly what my parents wanted for me too.'

'That's a good ambition to have – but make time for you. You can always be a wife and a mother but do something for you, that makes you happy.'

Bea listened to Nolan's words carefully. He had a point.

'Like what?'

'You have to follow your heart,' encouraged Nolan. 'That's half the fun of being free to do what you want.'

Bea laughed.

'You have a beautiful laugh, and there should be more of that in the world.' Nolan's smile was warm, his eyes fixed on her.

'Thank you.' Sitting next to him, Bea felt strangely relaxed. Maybe this was her time to shine, to find a purpose in life.

'I've always been a realist,' she admitted. 'I work to pay my bills and if I can afford a night out that's a bonus, but for these next two weeks I'm going to have a think about what I want to do with my life. Maybe Mystic Martha will give me some insight in the morning.'

'Who is Mystic Martha?' Nolan raised an eyebrow.

'Mystic Martha is known for the best psychic readings in the Scottish Highlands. She's based up at Foxglove Farm and it's only a fiver for a reading.'

Nolan laughed. 'For a fiver she is going to tell you all about your future?'

'Hey, don't knock it until you've tried it.'

Nolan held his hands up. 'If you want to waste your money, who am I to argue.'

'Why don't you come with me?'

'I'll leave that one to you and look forward to hearing all about it tomorrow afternoon.'

'I may have the whole of my future mapped out by the time I see you next.' Bea swigged the last of her beer and stood up. 'I best get this kayak back but I'm already looking forward to tomorrow.'

'I'm looking forward to it too. I'll have my best joke book ready.'

'Really?'

'Absolutely not. I'm just naturally funny.'

Bea shook her head in jest, thanked Nolan for the beer, squeezed her feet back into her trainers and reached for her life jacket and helmet.

'Here, let me help you on with it,' offered Nolan, holding out the life jacket so Bea could slip her arms into it. She turned to face him, her heart pounding. Nolan leaned in extra close and with a short tug zipped up the life vest, then grabbed the buckles and pulled the first one tight. Bea inhaled. She noticed a small scar just above his right eyebrow and that, when he was concentrating, he bit his lip lightly, which she found incredibly sexy. He was standing so close that she tried to avert her gaze but was unsuccessful. She couldn't take her eyes off him. The scent of his aftershave wasn't helping in the slightest, either, but was again stirring up feelings inside her. 'There you go. All done. And you best let me know where you're staying so I can drop your painting off.'

'I think you'll have no problem in finding me.' She gave him a mischievous smile. 'What time shall I meet you tomorrow?'

'Say 1pm? End of the jetty?'

'It's a date!' she replied. Nolan cocked an eyebrow. 'I didn't mean a *date* date. I just meant a date,' she quickly added, noting her enthusiasm was a little over the top.

'I know exactly what you meant.' He grinned. 'Bring a swimsuit and a towel. I'll take care of the rest. Tomorrow the weather forecast is glorious – though with a chance of a summer shower in the early evening – so hopefully the water will be calm.'

Bea climbed carefully back down the ladder and gratefully manoeuvred herself back into the kayak without rocking the boat. She unhooked the rope and Nolan passed her the paddle.

As she began to manoeuvre her way back towards the riverbank, Bea knew she had a huge smile on her face. Grabbing two weeks away from everything she knew was going to do her the world of good. Carl was already becoming a distant memory. She felt excitement zipping through her veins. The water might be calm, but right now there was nothing calm about the way her heart was beating.

Within ten minutes she was wading through the shallow water in front of The Little Blue Boathouse and pulling the kayak back onto the shingle. She dared to look over towards The Hemingway and glimpsed Nolan sitting back at his easel. He had such a happy-go-lucky lifestyle and wasn't bound by mundane routines. He was certainly living his best life, doing whatever he wanted each day. Bea envied that and couldn't wait to spend more time with him. Tomorrow couldn't come soon enough.

Chapter Four

The next morning, when Bea woke from her slumber, she took a moment to remember where she was before rolling over and checking the time on her phone. She couldn't quite believe that it was past 10am and she'd managed to miss breakfast. Her stomach rumbled at the thought and even though she was ravenous, she couldn't help but feel happy. This was the first time for as long as she could remember that she'd slept over twelve hours. Her shift pattern of working nights at the supermarket had played havoc with her sleeping routine, as she'd always found it difficult to sleep in the day. Last night her head hit the pillow just before 10pm and the last thought on her mind was Nolan … and even just a couple of seconds after waking up, he'd already crossed her mind. With a big smile on her face, Bea pushed back the covers and swung her legs to the floor. After making a cup of tea she pulled back the drapes in a corner of the room and to her surprise discovered a tiny balcony with a couple of wrought iron chairs and a table. The perfect setting to start the day.

Bea twisted the key that was in the lock of the balcony door. It clicked open and she stepped out into the sunshine. Tilting her face towards the sun, she could already tell it was going to be another warm day. All she could think about was what Nolan might have in store for her this afternoon. Just thinking about the time they were going to spend together activated a tiny flutter in her heart.

Surprised to hear a knock on the door, Bea hurried to answer it. Standing on the other side was Julia, holding out a tray.

'You missed breakfast and I knew you hadn't gone out so I just assumed you must have had the best sleep ever, as the mountain air tends to knock everyone out for the count,' said Julia, with a smile.

Bea couldn't argue with that; she felt refreshed and hungry. 'You're a superstar. I've only just woken up and this is fully welcome. Thanks so much for thinking of me!' enthused Bea.

'You're very welcome.' Julia handed over the tray. 'Any plans for today?'

'This morning, I'm going to take the plunge and be brave – I'm going to visit Mystic Martha for a reading. And this afternoon I'm in for a treat but I'm not sure what it is just yet,' replied Bea, not giving any more away.

'That sounds intriguing!' Julia tilted her head, encouraging Bea to say more, but she swiftly changed the subject.

'I met Wilbur yesterday, such a character. I hope you don't think I'm jumping the gun but I took a sneaky look at the attic room.'

'And what did you think?'

'It's adorable, and that view!'

'It's amazing, isn't it? Throughout the years, in fact I'd say at least … sixty years ago, the very first member of staff took the room for the summer – the perfect room for the perfect summer job. Now, eat that breakfast before it goes cold and we can catch up later.'

'Thank you again for this.'

After the door was closed, Bea made her way back out to the balcony. Lifting up the silver cloche she found a full Scottish breakfast accompanied by buttery granary toast. This would definitely keep her going until this afternoon. Then a sudden thought crossed her mind: should she eat lunch before she met Nolan or would they grab something whilst they were out? Whichever way, she was looking forward to her afternoon of laughter.

An hour later, and with a full stomach, Bea was walking towards Love Heart Lane. Hearing a rustle in the hedgerow, she giggled as a comical-looking alpaca stuck its head through a hole in the hedge; she was convinced it was smiling at her. Looking down at the card Martha had given her she remembered she needed to locate a vintage caravan which was located at Foxglove Farm. Spotting the long driveway, she ambled down it. A magnificent farmhouse stood at the bottom and there were cows dotted in the fields, alpacas and sheep grazing on the lush green grass, and a huge line of milking sheds. There were three signposts telling Bea that up ahead was the farm shop, to the left was Foxglove Camping, and to the right a caravan set aside from the rest… Mystic Martha.

If someone had even suggested to Bea at the start of the month that she would be taking a break in the Scottish Highlands and be about to pay to have her fortune told, then she would have thought they were bonkers. Even though she was intrigued by fortune tellers it wasn't something she'd ever believed in – so what exactly was she doing here? She stopped walking. This was daft. No one could predict your future because that was in your own hands, based on the decisions you made. Turning around, Bea was wondering whether her reluctance to step into the caravan was because she was worried Martha might tell her something she didn't want to hear.

'Curiosity got the better of you, didn't it?'

Bea stopped in her tracks. She'd been spotted.

'I've been expecting you,' Martha added.

There was no escaping now. Bea turned around again. The beaded curtain was parted and Martha was standing in the doorway of the caravan. She stepped aside and beckoned Bea towards her. Suddenly nervous, Bea slowly headed towards the vintage van, which looked picture perfect with its terracotta pots of cherry-red geraniums either side of the doorway happily lapping up the sunshine.

There was a small paved area with a painted cream rocking chair and a table littered with magazines and a small bowl housing coins and notes.

'Put your money in there.' Martha nodded towards the table before disappearing inside.

After rummaging in her purse and throwing five pounds into the bowl, Bea stepped inside the caravan and was amazed to see it was all things vintage, with floral triangular bunting draping the corners, and a beautiful teapot and china cups stacked on top of a small cabinet. She admired one of the paintings on the wall of a secluded sandy bay.

'Is that a real place?' asked Bea, thinking how beautiful and dreamy it looked.

Martha stood by Bea's side and looked at the painting. 'It is,' she replied, her gaze transfixed on the painting.

'It looks a special place,' added Bea, still admiring the canvas.

Martha didn't reply but Bea thought she noticed a faraway look in Martha's eyes as she gestured for Bea to sit in the chair on the opposite side of the table.

'This is a gorgeous van. Very light and colourful.' Bea didn't know why she'd been expecting the place to be dark and dreary – it was the complete opposite.

'It is, isn't it? My grand-daughter and her husband own the farm and a few years ago discovered the vintage vans in the barn and turned one of the fields into a camping area. I thought this one was perfect for giving readings.'

'That would be Isla. I met her at the B&B yesterday. The

farm has such stunning scenery, it must feel like paradise waking up to the views of the mountain each morning. Such beautiful surroundings.'

'I'm not sure you could call this place paradise as it always stinks of cow manure, but I suppose you get used to it after a time.' Martha gave a chuckle. 'But there is nothing better than a brisk walk up the mountain pass or along the river.'

Bea was just about to share that she had a trial at The Little Blue Boathouse tomorrow but something stopped her. She wondered whether Martha would know anything about that when she made her predictions.

'Now, relax and breathe. I can sense you're very tense.'

'I've never had my future told before,' admitted Bea, unable to hide the worry in her voice.

Martha didn't answer. With her eyes cast down she lowered her veil over her face and hunched herself over the crystal ball, running her hands over it. They were wrapped in the same gloves as yesterday, her wrists laced with bangles and her bony fingers stacked with rings.

'Just remember your future is never set in stone.' Martha's voice was low and eerie. 'You're in charge of your own destiny.'

Bea began to wonder: if that was the case, what exactly was she paying the fiver for? But then her mind flicked back to yesterday. There were certain things Martha had said about her ex which there was no way she could have known. Now gripped by anticipation, Bea didn't take her eyes off Martha. Still running her hands over the ball,

Martha remained focused on the object in front of her as she started to speak.

'You, my dear, have been taken advantage of for many years.' Martha briefly looked up and gave her a sympathetic look. 'And you deserve so much better, but I can see you're now starting to recognise your own worth. Honesty and loyalty are important to you and with yet another betrayal under his belt he was never going to be marriage material.'

Bea knew exactly who she was talking about. Even from the early stages, Carl had manipulated their relationship, but it was only now that she could see that.

'He used his father's death to say he wanted to spend more time on his own and that he was grieving. I gave him that space and he used the opportunity to strike up a relationship with Nicola,' Bea blurted, unable to hold back.

Martha was nodding but still focused on the crystal ball. 'Things are changing for you. Happier times on the horizon,' she continued.

This was more like it and was exactly what Bea wanted to hear.

'There's a whole world out there but you have already stumbled across your forever home.'

Bea arched an eyebrow and her heart began to beat a little faster. What did Martha mean by that? Did she mean Heartcross or back home? Bea was unsure whether she was allowed to ask questions and took the plunge.

'And where is my forever home?'

Dismissing Bea's question, Martha waved her hand and

continued. 'You have to take a chance, believe in yourself and don't settle for anything less than you deserve.'

Bea's mind turned towards Nolan for a moment.

Martha's eyes drifted in and out of focus. 'You're going on a hell of a journey and life will not be smooth sailing.' She quickly caught Bea's eye. 'I see water. Danger.' She looked back into the ball. 'And you're going to champion life like you've never done before. A meeting will change the direction of your path and a job is going to unravel a mystery.'

Bea wasn't sure whether Martha meant a meeting with someone, or a work meeting. And what job was going to unravel a mystery? Did she mean the job at The Little Blue Boathouse?

'You're going to be faced with a life-changing dilemma.'

'Life-changing?' probed Bea, wanting to know more.

Martha briefly looked up but didn't answer Bea's question. 'A boat … a different type of boat.' Martha was running her hands faster and faster over the crystal ball. Bea couldn't take her eyes off her. She was mesmerising.

Not knowing what had come over her Bea suddenly blurted, 'Maybe that's The Hemingway,' then instantly regretted giving information away.

Martha stopped dead in her tracks. Her hands hovered over the top of the ball and then she pushed it away. Lifting up her veil, Martha's eyes locked on Bea's. She was staring at Bea in a way that slightly unnerved her. Her eyes didn't leave Bea's. 'Say that again.'

'The Hemingway,' Bea repeated slowly, noticing

Martha's aura had completely changed. 'It's a boat on the river.'

'The River Heart?'

'Yes,' replied Bea.

'Your reading has come to an end,' announced Martha, taking Bea by surprise. She stood up, walked towards the door and held the beaded curtain wide open. It was very clearly Bea's cue to leave.

Surprised the reading had come to such an abrupt end, Bea walked towards the door. Not knowing what else to say, she said, 'Thank you very much.'

Martha nodded. 'And good luck at The Little Blue Boathouse. You'll pass your trial with flying colours,' she added before turning on her heels, the beaded fringe curtain swishing behind her.

Trying to make sense of what had just happened, Bea felt a little bewildered as she headed towards the long driveway. She suddenly realised that she had never mentioned anything about her trial. Going over the reading in her mind, Bea was convinced that something had spooked Martha. But what exactly was it? Bea hoped she was merely overreacting but there was no denying the anxious feeling swirling around in the pit of her stomach.

Chapter Five

Nolan had woken at the crack of dawn to the sound of the gulls circulating above The Hemingway. It was the best sleep he'd had in a long time, which was quite surprising since it was the time of year when he was normally consumed with guilt. He couldn't quite believe another year had passed by and things still hadn't got any easier.

Sitting out on the deck with a mug of coffee in his hand was his favourite part of the day. The waters were calm and there wasn't a soul in sight except for a man walking along the riverbank with the shaggiest dog Nolan had ever seen.

From the small table next to him, he picked up his grandfather's logbook, the reason he'd sailed The Hemingway into Heartcross. Looking at the date, he saw it was the very day he'd taken Patsy to Castaway Bay all those years ago. Just after arriving in Heartcross, Nolan had followed his grandfather's hand-drawn map and discovered the secret bay further downstream for himself. It was stunning, and the beauty of it all had taken his breath away. He spent the afternoon there, sketching the scenery, and could see why his grandfather had spoken about the place with such passion.

Knowing The Hemingway had always been his grandfather's pride and joy, Nolan was also feeling the same and quickly becoming very attached to the boat. In a way, it had saved his life. Renovating The Hemingway had given him the perfect distraction to keep himself to himself. Just the thought of the past few years could bring him close to tears, and he wished his grandfather was still around to help him navigate the most difficult time of his life. It was a strange feeling, knowing that he had no other family to lean on in the world, a thought that made him feel extremely lonely.

His thoughts turned to Bea and the glorious day ahead that he had planned. Castaway Bay would be the perfect place to swim and paint for a few hours. He smiled, thinking about her whizzing around with her arms in the air, screaming she was free. Despite the fact that he'd only been in her company for a matter of minutes so far, there was something about her that intrigued him. She was naturally beautiful, her smile infectious, and she'd put him immediately at ease. That was something that had never happened in the last few years ... He'd surprised himself by inviting her out today. The invitation had tripped off his tongue quite naturally, even though it wasn't something he would normally do. In fact, he usually shied away from making new friends – but he'd been drawn to her and wanted to know all about her.

Today's plan was simple: this morning he was going to sail The Hemingway to Castaway Bay, set up the picnic and easel, then row Bea over to spend the afternoon soaking up the sunshine. He often felt his grandfather was watching over him and today he hoped there was some sort of sign at the secret bay that would make him feel closer to him.

After closing the logbook, he reached across and picked up the painting of his grandfather and Patsy. 'And where are you, Patsy? *Who* are you?' he murmured. Bea was right; the look in their eyes radiated the love between them and suddenly Nolan felt a stab of guilt again. He closed his eyes, took a deep breath and raked his hands through his hair. 'I don't deserve love': Nolan had convinced himself of that over the last few years and even after all this time he knew he was still struggling to come to terms with the past.

Standing up, he carefully placed the painting down on the table. Risking a tentative look in the mirror, he saw his hair was wild, and as he attempted to tame his unruly mop with his hand, he played out a strategy suggested by his therapist. He looked straight in the mirror. 'You *do* deserve to be happy. It wasn't your fault.' He locked eyes with himself but he knew he still wasn't quite believing it.

Chapter Six

Having no clue what Nolan had in store for her this afternoon, Bea packed her rucksack with sun cream, a change of shorts, T-shirt and a towel. Then, feeling suitably embarrassed, she looked down at the two swimsuits that she'd stuffed in her luggage when she'd fled from Staffordshire. One was threadbare and one sported a print of a unicorn, which for some reason that Bea couldn't remember she'd thought was a good idea to buy – at the time. There was only one thing for it. Eeny meeny miny moe… Bea pointed from one to the other, ended up on the unicorn and sighed. Neither of them oozed sexy, and she was beginning to wish she'd updated her summer wardrobe a little sooner. After checking her watch, she saw that if she wandered down to the river now there was still an hour to kill. Maybe the best thing was to ask Julia where she could purchase swimwear – and quickly.

Hurrying down the stairs to reception clutching the

unicorn bathing suit, she waited until Julia had hung up her call. Julia beamed. 'How are you?'

Bea grimaced, holding up the swimsuit in front of her body. 'All good, but I need your help.'

'Ooo, I think that may have lost its sparkle,' teased Julia, giving a little chuckle.

'I agree! What I need to know is where can I buy a new swimsuit within the hour?'

'There's a number of options – there are lots of boutiques over in Glensheil, there's a small shop inside Starcross Manor or there's The Little Blue Boathouse. There's a section at the back behind the wetsuits but they are mainly bog-standard black costumes. What look are you trying to achieve?'

'Head-turning,' exclaimed Bea, before she could stop herself.

'You can't say fairer than that,' replied Julia, giving her a look of intrigue. 'For sunbathing or water sports?'

'Both, I think?' replied Bea, not knowing what Nolan had planned. 'But anything would be better than this.'

Julia got to her feet and sized up Bea. 'Wait there!' she ordered, and disappeared out of the door before Bea could answer.

Bemused, Bea was wondering what she was up to but she didn't need to wait long before Julia waltzed back through the door holding up a red bikini on a coat hanger.

'It's brand-new, still with tags. I bought it last summer but didn't have a chance to wear it. It would look perfect on you.'

'I couldn't possibly.' Bea admired the bikini in front of her. 'I'd never have the confidence to wear something as sexy as this.'

'You could. And you will look amazing.'

There had never been a time when Bea would have thought of wearing an item of clothing like this. There hadn't been any call for it, living in town, and it wasn't as though Carl ever suggested whisking her away to a warm holiday destination. She remembered that he always moaned the second the sun came out and he didn't like the heat at all. All of a sudden, she was beginning to see the life she'd been willing to settle for. No longer. Now it was time to think about what *she* wanted. She loved the sun and couldn't think of anything better than lying on a sunbed, basking in the sunlight and reading a book.

'Do you think? Would you mind if I try it on? Of course I'll pay you for it.'

'You'll do no such thing. It's been stuck in the drawer for over a year and I'm not going away this summer. So be my guest.'

Bea couldn't thank Julia enough. Racing back to her room she stripped off her clothes and tried on the bikini. She twirled around in front of the mirror and stared at her reflection.

'Not bad,' she murmured. 'Even if I do say so myself.'

There was already some colour to her skin, as in the last few weeks Bea had taken advantage of working nights and snoozed in the garden when the weather had been warm. Pulling on a pair of shorts and throwing a T-shirt over her head, she slipped her feet into her Converses. Placing her sunglasses on top of her head, she picked up her rucksack and took one last look in the mirror.

Julia was checking out a couple of guests when Bea arrived back in reception.

'Sorry to interrupt,' apologised Bea, looking towards her. 'It's perfect, thank you.'

'Oh, I am pleased. And whatever you're up to, have a lovely afternoon.'

'I will and thank you again.'

With her hair swishing from side to side, Bea waltzed towards the river oozing confidence yet feeling a little nervous. It was amazing: something as little as knowing you had a sexy bikini on underneath your clothes could make you feel like a new woman. Her face was beaming and her heartbeat racing as she tried to imagine the afternoon ahead. For the first time in ages, she felt good about herself and began to wonder why she hadn't taken control of her life sooner.

It was only a five-minute walk to The Little Blue Boathouse and she was soon ambling along the river path. Lifting up her sunglasses to admire the view, she saw the river was packed with boats of all shapes and sizes bobbing about on the water, along with people enjoying the use of paddleboards and canoes. Knowing that business was booming at The Little Blue Boathouse, Bea was going to enjoy this afternoon before her work trial tomorrow.

With the gentle rush of the river lapping against the jetty, and the crunch of the shingle beneath her feet, Bea felt a rush of happiness as she walked towards the water's edge. There was The Hemingway, anchored in front of her, and she immediately spotted Nolan rowing towards the jetty in a red rowing boat. Darting a glance at him before she broke out into a silly grin, Bea cupped her hands around her mouth and shouted, 'Aye aye, captain!'

Nolan looked over in her direction then stood up in the boat and saluted. Instantly, there was a warm, fluttering feeling in Bea's stomach. She knew she found him attractive but where was that going to get her? She was here to plan the rest of her life and wasn't sure even what direction she was heading in. She'd always had structure and routine, whereas Nolan was a fly-by-the-seat-of-his-pants type of guy. He lived for the moment and any time soon he would be sailing off to a new destination.

'But there's nothing stopping me from enjoying myself while he's here,' she murmured to herself.

'Wait there,' shouted Nolan.

'Don't worry, I'm not going anywhere!' she bellowed back.

Just at that moment, the rowing boat began to rock from side to side. The smile slid from Nolan's face as he began to wobble, but Bea couldn't help but chuckle. She heard him shout 'Crikey' as the boat swayed, before losing his balance and toppling into the water.

Splash.

Bea hurried to the end of the jetty. Still grinning, Nolan's head popped up out of the water. He flicked his hair out of his eyes and swam after his flip-flops, which seemed to be floating off in different directions.

'No one likes a show-off,' Bea shouted good-naturedly.

He threw a mischievous look in her direction before retrieving the oar and pulling himself back into the boat. 'I'm alive,' he bellowed.

'That's good to know!'

He was soon rowing towards the shingle bay then wading through the shallow water of the tiny man-made beach. He pulled the rowing boat out of the water before turning towards her. 'Remind me never to stand up in a rowing boat again.' He gave her a lopsided grin before looking down at his clothes. He was soaked from head to toe, his white T-shirt clinging to every muscle. He peeled it from his body and wrung out the excess water.

'It's a bit too soon to be falling for me, isn't it?' Bea teased, trying to divert her eyes from his tanned torso but failing miserably.

'I don't know about that,' he replied, still grinning, pulling the wet T-shirt back over his body. 'At least, with this sun, I should dry out quickly. Have you eaten lunch?' he asked.

Bea shook her head. 'No, I wasn't sure what we would be doing.'

'That's good because it's all in hand.'

'Are we heading towards The Hemingway?' she asked, noticing there was no food in the boat.

'I can do better than that. I'm taking you to a special place for lunch.' Nolan held out his hand to help her into the rowing boat. The touch of his skin sent shockwaves through her body. 'If you want to sit that end of the boat, I can drag you back into the water.'

Placing her rucksack in the middle of the boat, Bea let go of Nolan's hand before sitting on the wooden seat and holding on to the sides. He pulled the boat back into the water and it rocked gently as he climbed inside and used the oar to move them away from the shore.

'Are you ready to set sail?'

'I am, captain.' She gave a tiny salute and wondered where they were heading.

'There's a life jacket behind you.'

With a few long strokes they quickly moved away from the edge of the river and were now heading upstream. Bea relaxed and looked around. The water taxi was ferrying people on sightseeing excursions and there were children standing on rocks swooping their fishing nets into the water. She noticed that Nolan kept stealing glances in her direction.

'You're looking at me,' she said, noticing his eyes glinting in the sunshine.

'Your face is glowing and those freckles…'

Bea knew that yesterday's sun, when she was kayaking, had brought the freckles out right across her nose. She'd already noticed them this morning when she was getting ready. Usually, they would be covered with make-up, but she'd decided to go *au naturel* for the next two weeks and hopefully catch the sun whilst she was here.

'They always come out in the sun,' she replied. She noticed a string of not so run of the mill boats coming up the river, each oozing expense and class. 'Look at those.'

'They are something else, aren't they? I noticed a couple more boats arriving this morning for the River Festival.'

'It's so exciting. I think I'm going to have my work cut out at The Little Blue Boathouse for the next couple of weeks.'

'I didn't know you were working there.'

'I have a trial shift tomorrow.' She crossed her fingers and held them up. 'The method to my madness was keeping myself occupied so I didn't sit and mope.'

'And look at you now, there's no moping at all.' He smiled warmly at her.

'And it seems I'm going to be successful in getting the job.'

Nolan was still smiling but narrowed his eyes. 'And how would you know that?'

'Because that's exactly what Martha predicted.'

'Interesting, so I'm assuming you told her about the trial?'

'Actually, I didn't.'

'Even more interesting.'

Bea began to think about the other things that Martha had said. 'Apparently, I've found my forever home – though I'm not exactly sure where that is – and my life is about taking chances and not settling for less than I deserve.'

'All very generic then. *I* could have predicted that.'

'Life will not be smooth sailing,' she added with a grin. 'So, I'm hoping this boat doesn't sink before we reach our destination.'

Nolan was still rowing, the oars in sync and his biceps flexing at every turn. 'Still all very generic ... we have nearly reached our destination.'

'That's good because Martha predicted danger and a chance meeting that is going to change my life. Time will tell what any of it means.'

'And did you believe any of it?'

'Obviously, I've taken everything with a pinch of salt. My destiny is in my own hands. Have you met Martha?' asked Bea, knowing that she thought the reading had come to an abrupt end because she'd mentioned The Hemingway.

Nolan shook his head. 'No, I haven't, and unless she can predict the lottery numbers, I'm keeping hold of my money.'

Bea gave a tiny laugh. With her hair wafting in the breeze, she tilted her face up towards the sun. 'I've never been in a rowing boat before. This is a first for me.'

Nolan raised an eyebrow. 'I think I could row before I could walk. My grandfather had me in boats from a very early age.'

Impressed, Bea looked behind her to see how far they'd come. The boat was coping well with the slap of the waves and The Little Blue Boathouse was still in sight. She could even make out Wilbur standing in the doorway. She cast her eyes upwards to the craggy white cliffs behind Nolan and the gulls circulating above them in the clear blue sky. Then she noticed a familiar figure standing on the cliff path: Martha. She did a double-take then narrowed her eyes. It was definitely Martha, still dressed in her mystical outfit, and her binoculars were pointing straight towards The Hemingway. Or was that just Bea's imagination?

Chapter Seven

B ea was sitting back enjoying the view. Everywhere was so peaceful. They'd rowed past children splashing at the water's edge, and dog walkers ambling along the coastal paths, and she was mesmerised by the colourful houses dotted along the Glensheil bank of the river.

She kept snagging a look back towards the cliff, intrigued by Martha, but she'd disappeared now. Nolan's tanned arms had rowed the boat to calmer water where there were expanses of sand and taller cliffs, with impressive views and the coastline becoming more indented by coves and estuaries. 'It's beautiful. It's like something out of a romantic novel.'

'It is, sort of, and that's the reason we're heading to where we're heading.'

'Huh?' replied Bea.

'My grandfather's diary.'

'Your grandfather had a diary?'

'Not so much a diary, but on the back pages of the sailing logbook there were further entries. You'll never guess what today's date is.'

'Is that a trick question?' replied Bea, knowing it was the 2nd of August.

'It's the day my grandfather, Morgan, took Patsy to Castaway Bay on their first date of the summer.'

Bea brought her hands up to her heart. 'Castaway Bay. What an utterly romantic name.'

'And that's exactly where we are heading.' Nolan gave her a heart-warming smile.

'Is this our first date of the summer?' Bea was teasing but also curious to hear his answer. She wasn't even sure how she could think about going on a date so soon after what she'd been through, but maybe a little fun over the summer couldn't hurt. A holiday romance with a drop-dead gorgeous male was maybe just what she needed to boost her confidence a little and get her back on the horse.

Nolan gave her a cheeky wink. 'Ha, you never know.'

For a moment, they stared at each other in contemplative silence, both smiling. Bea could feel the spark between them. She'd felt it the second she'd laid eyes on him. Wondering what his story was, she watched him closely whilst he rowed. Nolan was handsome, his thick chestnut hair wild on top. His lashes and deep hazel eyes were to die for. His face was tanned and he had that unshaven thing going on, which Bea found super sexy, and a beaming smile that showed a perfect set of teeth.

'And according to the log, they spent most of the summer in Castaway Bay. Nights in front of a fire, sleeping under the stars, fishing for their food.'

'It sounds like heaven.' Bea had never experienced real romance. Carl had never swept her off her feet. Before she began to work nights his idea of a romantic night out was to sit in an old men's pub and drink real ale. At times Bea had suggested the trendy new wine bar in town or even a cocktail at the local Slug and Lettuce for a change, but he never took her feelings into account. Bea was beginning to question how she'd stayed in the relationship for so long.

'Do you know why it was only a summer romance? Why didn't they continue to see each other?'

Nolan shrugged. 'I'm not entirely sure. Sometimes you might not be on the same path, or at different stages of life…' He shrugged. 'I do know my grandfather still spoke about her on many occasions. Like I said, she was still in his thoughts near to the end of his life.'

'She must have been a special person. Do you know if they ever met up again?'

Nolan shook his head. 'Not to my knowledge. I would love to know what happened to Patsy. Did she remember my grandfather? That's my reason for being here. I want to find out more about her, if possible. But there's just one problem, I don't have a surname. And who knows, maybe she was only here for the summer with her family.'

'That is indeed a possibility. I never thought of that,' admitted Bea. 'It would be nice to find out more though.'

'It would, so I hope something comes to light before the River Festival.'

'I've got everything crossed for you … and, by the way, this is all so surreal!' She spread her arms wide and rocked the boat.

'Woah, keep still. I'm not going in twice.'

'Sorry!'

This was the first time in ages she'd felt like she didn't have a care in the world. She was enjoying every second of being in Nolan's company. 'Forty-eight hours ago, if anyone had told me I'd be in a rowing boat with a handsome stranger heading towards Castaway Bay, I'd have thought they were dreaming.'

'Did you just call me handsome?' There was a spark in Nolan's eye as he asked the question.

'Maybe…' Bea bit her lip to suppress her smile. 'And I wish I was more like you.'

'In what way?'

'Carefree, flying by the seat of my pants. No worries and happy to see where life takes me next.'

When Nolan looked up and met Bea's gaze, she saw the smile had slipped slightly from his face. 'You never know what's around the corner. As you well know, things can happen overnight and your life changes in a matter of seconds.'

There was something about the way Nolan spoke that made Bea sure he was talking from experience.

'I've learned to take each day as it comes. Live for the moment. What's the point in worrying about the future when the future might never come?' Nolan's voice faltered, leaving Bea wondering what his story was, but he didn't elaborate any further.

For the next couple of minutes, Nolan rowed in silence, then he began to slow down and Bea noticed the boat drifting towards calm waters.

'We're nearly there. Are you ready for this?'

Nolan navigated the rowing boat around a cluster of rocks and under numerous weeping willow trees. Bea was amazed to see a secret waterway. It looked like a private driveway on water. He began to row again, gently, whilst Bea took in the view. Up ahead the white rugged cliffs towered over a tiny secluded beach of sparkling beige sand. Bea breathed, 'It's beautiful. It's so special, isn't it?' Her eyes were wide as she took in the view.

'Welcome to Castaway Bay. And yes, it's very special.' Nolan gave her a sideward glance, a look that caused Bea's heart to race.

As Nolan carefully guided the boat to a tiny jetty, Bea saw directly in front of them a tiny hut with pink roses tumbling all over the roof.

'Oh my, look at that!' she gasped. She was awestruck, looking at the waterfall cascading down the cliff and running into the small bay. Taking in the magnificent view, she held on to the side of the boat as it gently bumped along the bottom of the bay. Nolan threw his oar onto the sand before climbing out and paddling to the edge of the now shallow water. 'How would anyone even know this place existed?' Bea had never seen a view so beautiful. 'Where exactly are we?' She was still taking in the beauty all around. 'It feels like we're on a desert island.' There wasn't another soul in sight.

'This is Castaway Bay,' said Nolan. 'According to my grandfather's log, he and Patsy stumbled across this little piece of paradise by accident.'

He extended his hand and helped Bea to stand up. She looked at the shallow water and then down at her pumps. Nolan must have read her mind and lifted her clean off her feet. Bea didn't put up a fight.

She giggled, placing her arm around his neck. 'Don't drop me,' she said, turning inwards towards his chest.

'Stop wriggling then,' he ordered, holding her tighter.

Their faces were centimetres apart. Feeling her heart race faster, Bea knew there was a wide smile on her face and the moment felt full of warmth, romantic even. She dared to look straight at him. Nolan was looking at her lips and now she was looking at his. Their eyes moved upwards, his sparkling as they lingered for a second, until he cleared his throat and lowered her onto the sand.

'I just need to grab the boat otherwise we'll be castaways in Castaway Bay.'

Truth be told, Bea didn't think she would object to spending a night under the stars here with Nolan. The whole place was just wonderful, and had a romantic feel about it. She'd never done anything so daring in her life, spending the afternoon alone with a stranger on a secluded bay. She watched Nolan swing her rucksack over his shoulder, grab the rowing boat and haul it onto the sand.

Bea had now kicked off her trainers and was waggling her toes in the water.

'Do you think anyone actually comes here?' asked Bea.

'I have no idea.'

'They must have, because look...' Bea pointed to footsteps in the sand. 'They look fresh and there's only one set. Do you think someone else is here?' She quickly scanned the area.

Nolan smiled. 'I think they might be mine.'

Bea had a puzzled look on her face. 'But you've only just got here.'

'I might have been here earlier this morning.'

'Why would you come here twice in one day?'

'I'll show you. Come on.' Nolan reached out a hand and without hesitation she took it. Holding his hand seemed like the most natural thing in the world as he led her towards the hut. It was then Bea noticed the table and chairs overlooking the water. Just inside there was an easel and paints with a couple of blank canvases. 'Lunch will be served shortly ... and I couldn't come here without painting a picture – the scenery is way too beautiful to let that opportunity pass.'

Bea thought back to the painting of Nolan's grandfather and Patsy. 'Do you think this is where your grandfather painted Patsy?'

'I'm sure he did. Maybe you would let me paint you?' Nolan's voice was hopeful.

A tiny thrill ran through Bea's body at the suggestion. 'Maybe I will,' she replied. The intensity of his gaze made her tingle, and her heart was beating wildly. She could feel the raw chemistry between them.

There was a gentlemanly confidence about Nolan as he placed her rucksack on the sand outside the hut and pointed to the table. 'Would you like lunch in here, or on a blanket by the water's edge?'

Bea looked over her shoulder. 'Let's make the most of the sunshine. I don't see it that often, working nights. The water's edge sounds perfect.'

Nolan walked to the back of the hut and picked up a pastel tartan picnic blanket that was placed on top of a large cool box. He handed it to her. 'Go and choose your spot.'

Bea walked back towards the water, the fine grains of sand underfoot warm from the sun beating down. She chose a spot and laid out the blanket then stood on a nearby rock taking in the panoramic sea views and mountain terrain in the background. 'We could actually be in Switzerland.'

'I'm sure I'll go there one day,' replied Nolan, walking towards her carrying the cool box.

Sitting down on the blanket, she asked, 'Do you think you'll ever settle in one place?' She was genuinely intrigued by the way Nolan was living his life.

'I tried that,' he replied. 'But when there's places like this to discover, why would anyone settle in one place?'

Bea could see his point. If it wasn't for their chance meeting she wouldn't be sitting here now and experiencing this spectacular scenery. She wondered what he meant by 'I tried that', but Nolan had already steered the conversation in a different direction.

'Are you hungry?' he asked.

Bea nodded but also brought the conversation back on track.

'But what about putting down roots? Belonging to a place? Making a home?'

'Home is where your heart is and for now that's living onboard The Hemingway. Where is the most amazing place you've ever visited?' Nolan asked, opening the lid of the cool box. He settled himself on the blanket next to Bea and stretched out, his leg brushing against hers, causing her to feel a flush of warmth in her body again.

Bea was thinking and looked towards Nolan. 'You know what? I have no clue. That sounds so lame.'

'Paris, Venice, Barcelona?' Nolan began reeling off a list.

'I've never been to any of those places. The furthest I've ever been is here, and I think this is probably the most amazing place I've ever seen.' Bea could see the same amazement written all over Nolan's face.

'You've really never been abroad?'

Bea shook her head. 'My ex didn't like the sun.'

'And that stopped you going on your own or with a friend because…?'

'Good question. Because he wouldn't let me. Every time I suggested anything he would reply, "You don't want to do that, though, do you?" Which basically meant my idea was kiboshed.'

'That's sad to hear. Couples should encourage each other's growth, not clip one another's wings.'

'I quite agree. I'm now beginning to realise we didn't have much in common at all. For me, the best part of the day was early morning when I arrived home, whereas he never got out of bed before midday on a Saturday. I liked a full cooked breakfast, he didn't even like breakfast. I liked a McDonalds, he didn't—'

'I'm sorry, who doesn't like a McDonalds? That should have been your first red flag.' Nolan was deadly serious then burst into laughter. 'It sounds to me like you've had a lucky escape.'

Bea laughed too. 'I should have known. But I'm here now.'

'That you are.'

'And I'm taking control of my life.'

'There's nothing stopping you now. This is your time. Do what's right for Bea and what makes you happy. The world is your oyster and you're free to do what you want.' Nolan stood up and began to spin around with his arms open wide.

'I'm never going to live that down, am I?' she said, shaking her head good-humouredly.

'You did make me smile,' he said, sitting back down. 'What's next for you?'

Bea thought about it for a moment, 'I've no clue. I've lost myself along the way and my time here is going to be spent figuring out what's next for me. I think I've gone along pleasing everyone else but myself for far too long. I do know I want more than night shifts at a supermarket. I want to make a difference to people's lives, even if it's a small one. Look at me, I'm sounding like I'm running for prime minister.'

'You'd do a much better job.'

'I think I can turn my hands to most things, but my biggest skill is communication. It's just a matter of finding the path that excites me most. I mean, you have your life sussed. Sailing the seas and painting.' Being in Nolan's company felt so easy and natural for Bea and she could feel herself relaxing and opening up. 'Whatever will be will be,' she added, bringing her knees up to her chest. 'And what have we got in there? I'm beginning to feel a little peckish.' She leaned over to take a peep and Nolan gently snapped the lid of the cool box down, causing Bea to bring her hands to her heart before letting out a peal of laughter.

'Only joking! Would you fancy a glass of champagne?'

'We have champagne?'

'We do!'

'Then yes, please, I would love a glass. Are we celebrating?'

'We are celebrating life and the fact you're finally free to do what you want.' He grinned as he took the bottle from the cool box and passed a flute to Bea.

'You've thought of everything,' she said, suitably impressed that Nolan had gone to so much trouble.

Nolan popped the cork from the bottle and it flew through the air and landed by the edge of the water. Bea was up on her feet to retrieve it. 'A keepsake of our afternoon together,' she said when he looked at her with curiosity.

After Nolan had poured the champagne into both glasses, he chinked his against hers. 'Here's to a great afternoon.'

'I'm already having such a great time.'

'Glad to hear it. It sounds to me like you need to be spoilt a little.' Nolan began taking things out of the cool box, laying in front of her the most delicious-looking food she had ever seen.

'You really have gone all out, haven't you?'

'I've always loved a picnic, especially when it's in a secluded bay with a beautiful girl. Of course I'm going to go all out! We have smoked salmon, ham, pasties, super salad wraps, egg and cress sandwiches, cheesecake, rainbow fruit skewers...'

Bea stared at all the wonderful food, still focusing on the word 'beautiful'. She couldn't remember the last time she had been called beautiful or truly felt it. Right at this moment she didn't have a care in the world. Sipping her champagne she stared out across the water. Everywhere was calm and tranquil. All she could hear was the lapping of the water against the sand.

'I could stay here for ever,' she murmured.

'Why don't you then? There's nothing stopping you.'

Bea laughed. 'Could you imagine if I rang my sister and said, "Hey, I'm not coming home, I'm spending the rest of my life living in a secluded bay"?'

Nolan passed Bea a plate. 'You don't have to answer to

anyone anymore. There's no one to put a kibosh on your plans and suggestions.'

They began to tuck into the food and Bea tried a little bit of everything. It all tasted so good. The rainbow fruit skewers were so juicy she had to wipe her chin with the back of her hand. When Nolan finished eating, he lay down on the blanket with his hands behind his head. His T-shirt rose up and Bea risked a glance at his toned, tanned stomach.

'What do you think your sister would say if she could see you now?' He took a sideward glance at her.

'She would think I've lost the plot.' She could hear Emmie's voice inside her head and mimicked her sister. 'Are you mad? He could be a mass murderer! No one would know you're there. What if something happened to you?'

Nolan laughed. 'She may have a fair point.'

Bea was usually the sensible one, always reliable and putting others first. But not today. Today was the first day of the rest of her life – and what a way to start. This was completely out of character for her. In the past she would never have put herself in this position; she was usually shy around men, didn't know what to talk about. She looked over at Nolan and gave a tiny chuckle, thinking, *What exactly did a mass murderer look like anyway?* He had his eyes closed, his face tilted to the sun. She studied him, wondering what it would be like to kiss those lips ... even to sleep with him. She'd never had a one-night stand in her life. In fact, she'd only ever slept with one person and believed in monogamy, but look where that had gotten her.

She glanced back towards the water. It looked inviting. That was something else she'd never done – gone swimming in open water. This was her time now and she had every intention of throwing caution to the wind and having some fun. Looking back towards Nolan, she saw that his eyes were still shut.

'Are you staring at me?'

'How do you know that?'

'I just do.'

Bea was thankful he couldn't read her mind. She was actually wondering what it would be like to have a two-week fling with him. Surely it couldn't do any harm? They were both adults, and maybe a holiday romance would be just the thing to boost her confidence and get herself back on track.

'What are you thinking about?' Nolan opened one eye and glanced in Bea's direction.

'Wouldn't you like to know?' she replied, grinning. 'Tell me, why haven't you got anyone special in your life?' She dug her feet into the sand and looked across at him. He had both eyes open now and Bea could have sworn there was a fleeting look of sadness in them.

'Because that's the way it is.'

Bea thought he was going to say something else but he didn't. He sat up, placed the leftover food in the cool box and balanced the champagne flutes against it.

'Shall we swim?' he asked, peeling the T-shirt from his broad shoulders before throwing it down onto the blanket.

'Is it safe?' asked Bea, looking at the water.

'There's only one way to find out.' Nolan was up on his feet and began running towards the rocks, then he started to climb.

Feeling slightly panicked, Bea stood up and walked to the water's edge. Her heart was pounding. 'What are you doing? It might be dangerous. It might not be deep enough. You could hit your head on something.'

'It's okay, the water is clear!' he bellowed, before gliding through the air straight into the cobalt blue water.

Splash.

Nolan surfaced immediately and took Bea's breath away. His tousled hair was now slicked back as he swam gently towards her. 'This water is refreshing,' he shouted.

'That means cold!' she replied, laughing.

'Maybe just a little, but it's so liberating,' he said, scooping water up in his hands and attempting to splash her. She squealed and jumped backwards. Nolan waded out of the deeper water, his shoulders broad, his skin glistening. Bea couldn't take her eyes off him.

'Are you coming in? Once you get in, it's not that cold.' He sat down in the shallow water and splashed the water over his chest.

Bea was hesitant. She wanted to get into the water, let herself go and have fun, but though she'd felt super confident earlier, now she was slightly nervous at the thought of someone seeing her in a swimsuit. She'd always lacked body confidence and here she was in a situation with a handsome stranger who didn't have an ounce of excess fat on his body. She was suddenly beginning to regret the late night cream cakes on the night shift and the early morning cinnamon swirls. Nolan was now swimming a little further out. When he stood up, the water was up to his middle.

He shouted, 'What's keeping you?' before diving under the water.

Bea took her chance and quickly peeled off her shorts. It was glorious to feel the sun on her skin. She began to walk slowly into the water, the rocky ground underneath her feet soon turning to sand.

'It's freezing!' Lifting her arms up in the air, she gasped as the cold water touched her stomach. She counted to three; it was now or never. Quickly submerging her shoulders, she began to swim towards Nolan. An unexpectedly forceful wave splashed her in the face, leaving her spluttering. Her hair was soaked and she pushed her wet fringe out of her eyes.

Nolan was by her side immediately. 'You okay?'

'I think I'll be washing my hair tonight!'

Like it was the most natural thing in the world, Nolan hooked a stray strand of hair behind her ear and looked at her with such tenderness, causing her stomach to somersault numerous times. The intensity between them was getting hotter than the afternoon sun. Was it wrong to feel these feelings so soon after ending a relationship? Right in that moment, all she could think about was kissing him, and he was looking at her in a way that suggested he wanted the same. There was an attraction, lust, and even if Nolan had a girl in every bay he visited, it didn't matter. He was making her feel special, like she was the only girl in the world, and that was a feeling she hadn't had in such a long time.

Taking both of her hands, he pulled her towards him then spun around and encouraged her to climb on his back. With her arms wrapped around his neck and feeling her bare skin next to his, every inch of her tingled with desire. He waded further in the water towards the rocks, then gently turned around and lowered her onto one of them. He pointed to a rock pool and almost immediately Bea spotted a starfish. 'Look how beautiful that is,' she said as she studied it. With its spiny skin and pincer-like organs and suckers, it crept slowly along the bottom of the rock pool. She soon realised that Nolan wasn't looking in the same direction.

'Red suits you,' he said, his eyes not leaving hers.

'Thank you,' she replied. Bea thought her heart was going to beat out of her chest at any second.

Nolan never took his eyes off her as he grabbed her waist, gently lifting her down from the rock. With the perfect backdrop and the sun beating down on their bodies, Bea took a chance. She leaned in slowly, hoping that Nolan would lower his lips to hers, and that's exactly what happened. His kiss was soft, leaving Bea wanting more.

'I wasn't expecting that,' she said, smiling at him.

'You so were,' he replied, grinning.

Bea pinched her thumb and forefinger together. 'Maybe a little. I had hope.'

'I hope I haven't overstepped the mark, what with everything that's going on in your life.'

'You haven't overstepped the mark. I'm living for the moment and enjoying every single second.'

'As long as you're sure?'

'Very. We're adults.' Bea had never done anything like this before. She felt all grown-up and in charge of her life. If she wanted to kiss an utterly gorgeous man that she'd just met, then why couldn't she? It felt good, her whole body erupting in goosebumps at his touch. 'It's just a shame you're going to sail out of my life almost as soon as you've arrived.'

'Unfortunately, that is the case. I'm here to discover anything possible about Patsy and see whether she's still alive, then I'll be off on my next adventure.'

Hearing those words, Bea felt her mood slump slightly. But Nolan was just being completely honest. He hadn't given her any false hope that that kiss was anything more than a kiss.

Nolan must have noticed her smile slip. 'Let's make the most of the time we have together.' He leaned in again, taking her by surprise. This time, his kiss was long and deep.

Never in her life had she taken a chance like this or been attracted to anyone in this way. As they kissed she turned the words over in her mind: *Live for the moment. Have fun.*

His kiss was like no other and Bea forced herself to breathe calmly, even though her whole body was trembling.

He pulled her in closer and instantly Bea pressed herself against him. Still kissing him, she felt an immense tingle and wanted this moment to last for ever. They started to run their hands over each other's body, and Bea felt truly alive for the first time in ages. It had been a while since she'd touched a man's body – her ex was always claiming he was tired or it was the wrong time, though now she knew why he'd been so reluctant. And besides, what she'd had with Carl had never felt like this. It felt *so good* kissing and touching Nolan. He lifted her off her feet and into his arms, then strolled through the water and onto the sand. He laid her gently on the blanket and then lay down next to her, one arm bent at the elbow, his head resting on his hand. The excitement of the situation electrified Bea's body. Feelings of excitement and trepidation were all rolled into one. Wanting to feel in control, she leaned up and kissed him again, pulling him on top of her. Nolan stopped kissing her for a second and looked at her with adoration. In this moment she wanted him, and despite weighing up the consequences, she embraced the tingling pleasure that flooded her body. All she could think about was having him right now.

'I want this,' she murmured.

'Are you sure?'

'I'm sure.' And then Nolan kissed her again, taking her breath away.

An hour later, Bea was perched on a rock, posing, while Nolan sat on an upturned wooden barrel that they'd found in the hut. His easel was in front of him and he had a palette of paint and a brush in his hands. He was painting Bea's portrait while she sipped champagne, enjoying the scenery and the overwhelming feeling of happiness that engulfed her.

'I hope you're making me look beautiful.'

'I don't need to make you look beautiful because you are, and your skin is flawless.'

The feeling of confidence his words gave her surprised her and she glanced down at her body, the red bikini complementing the warm tone of her skin.

'Let me have a look?' She attempted to move to take a peek but Nolan stopped her in her tracks. 'Keep still, don't move.'

'Spoilsport!'

Nearly twenty minutes later, Nolan declared he was finished. Excited to see the painting, Bea strode towards him, sliding her arms around his waist while she rested her head against his chest and stared at the canvas. She gave a tiny gasp. The painting was beautiful; he'd captured her completely, even down to the freckles dotted across her nose. At the bottom, he had written 'Castaway

Bay' with the date and his initials, followed by a tiny love heart.

'What do you think?'

'It looks like me!'

'That's good then.' He laughed, swiftly kissing the tip of her nose.

'I love it and will treasure it for ever.'

'A reminder of our time together,' he said, packing up his paints before washing out his brushes in the shallows. Bea was still staring at the painting, wishing this day could go on for ever but knowing it was drawing to a close. She joined him at the water's edge, the water lapping around her ankles. The inlet was extremely calm and Bea was astonished to see hundreds of tiny fish swimming around. She bent down and tried to cup them in her hands. She giggled as they squirmed through her fingers. Then something sparkling under the water caught her eye. She felt about and attempted to pull it out of the sand. 'I've found treasure,' she declared. 'I think it's a bottle but it seems to be stuck.'

Nolan joined her and looked at the water. 'It *is* a bottle, but it's wedged in the sand at the side of that large stone.' He bent down and began to dig around the bottle with his hands. 'Yes, definitely a bottle.'

'Probably a broken one. Be careful you don't cut yourself.'

He reached for a triangular stone that was lying on the sand, then began to dig around the bottle. 'It's getting looser.' He gave it a tug and finally pulled it out. As he held it in his hands, they could see that the bottle wasn't broken. Bea's eyes widened.

'Blooming hell. It's a message in a bottle! And what's that with it?'

Nolan held the bottle up and tipped it to the side. 'It looks like a necklace.'

'Do you think we should open it?' asked Bea, taking the bottle from him. 'How recent do you think it is?' She couldn't contain the excitement in her voice. 'We could have stumbled across another romantic love story.'

'Or a note that says, "I was here",' Nolan replied, laughing.

'I'm opting for romance. I want to know what the letter inside says.'

'There's only one way to find out.'

Taking the bottle back to the blanket, they knelt and Bea watched as Nolan dried it off. After a couple of attempts, he managed to open it and tipped it upside down. The necklace fell straight on to the blanket but the letter was trapped inside. Nolan scanned the area and pointed to a pile of sticks. 'Grab me a couple of those long thin sticks, please.'

Bea was quickly back by his side and, using the sticks like chopsticks, he managed to clutch the letter and carefully pulled it out of the bottle without tearing the paper.

'My heart is beating so fast,' admitted Bea, turning the necklace over in her hand. 'And it's in the shape of a seahorse. It's beautiful,' she breathed.

Nolan had suddenly gone quiet. He clutched the letter in his hand and immediately Bea noticed his face had paled. 'What is it?' she asked. 'Are you okay?'

Wide-eyed, he looked at her. 'This is from my grandfather.'

'Are you sure?' she asked.

'Absolutely. I know my grandfather's writing when I see it – and he's signed it.'

'Let me see. Show me.'

Chapter Eight

His hand trembling slightly, Nolan read the letter out loud.

'To whoever finds this bottle.

'We've had the best summer at Castaway Bay and discovered a love like no other. We will be together forever in our hearts and we hope you find a love like ours.

'Always in love,

'Morgan & Patsy'

'How utterly romantic is that?' added Bea, looking down at the necklace in her hand. 'I wonder what the relevance of a seahorse is?'

'I've no idea.' Nolan turned the letter over and on the other side was a drawing of a love heart with an arrow and their initials.

'This technically belongs to you,' said Bea, handing over

the necklace. 'You're the last living relative of your grandfather.'

Nolan took the necklace and placed it in the palm of his hand. He was flabbergasted by the discovery of the bottle and the fact that it dated from the day when his grandfather had visited the bay.

'This is unbelievable. This bottle must have been wedged for all these years and we were the ones that found it. What were the chances of that?' Nolan knew the emotion in his voice communicated itself to Bea. He looked up towards the sky. He knew this was some sort of amazing coincidence, but he couldn't help wondering if his grandfather was watching over him.

'And we found it. I wonder why they didn't stay together or carry on their romance?' Bea mused.

'Because more than likely they had their own lives to return to.'

'But surely if their love was this strong, they would have done anything to stay together and make it work?'

'Maybe they took it for what it was and agreed that it was only for the summer.' Nolan shrugged. 'Who knows?'

'A bit like us?' added Bea, the words leaving her lips before she could stop them.

'Most probably exactly like us.' Nolan glanced towards her. 'You're still okay about today?' he questioned, suddenly a little unsure whether a line had been crossed.

'Of course. We're adults, aren't we? I've enjoyed every second of today.' She leaned across and placed a swift kiss on his cheek.

'Good,' he replied, looking back down at the necklace in his hand. For a second he couldn't look Bea in the eye. He'd had a fantastic afternoon, he'd let himself go for the first time in a long time and had experienced feelings that he hadn't felt in even longer. He'd felt desired in such a way that he'd known he wanted to kiss Bea the second they arrived at Castaway Bay. Full of mixed emotions, Nolan couldn't shake off the sudden guilt he was feeling. He was a little sad the day was coming to an end.

Taking her hand, Nolan lay the necklace in her palm. 'I want you to have this. Finding this bottle is the perfect end to a perfect day and when we go our separate ways you have something to remind you of our special day together.'

At such a lovely gesture, Bea's eyes widened. 'I couldn't possibly. What if you find Patsy? By rights this should be hers.'

'I've not found her yet and if I find her in the next couple of weeks, we can cross that bridge then.'

'In memory of Morgan and Patsy, I'll look after it until then, and in the meantime, I'll treasure it. But what do *you* have to remind you of today?'

Nolan gave Bea a lopsided grin. 'The thought of you in that red bikini will be imprinted on my brain for ever!'

Bea swiped his arm playfully.

'And I have painted you also.'

They both looked towards the painting balanced on the easel.

'I'm not sure where I'm going to hang that.' She smiled.

'I'm sure you'll find somewhere to put it,' he replied, leaning in and kissing her softly on the lips.

'I actually need to find a house first. The thought of going back to my home town is not enthralling.'

'Don't think about that now. Keep your thoughts on the here and now.' That was exactly what Nolan was trying to do because, thinking about the past few years, he knew he would be sailing The Hemingway out of Heartcross sooner rather than later.

'I'm trying,' Bea replied. 'Life forty-eight hours ago seemed all dark and hard work and yet now it seems colourful and fun.'

Nolan knew exactly what Bea meant. He'd woken up this morning after a good night's sleep and couldn't wait to begin the day, knowing he would be seeing her. Someone like her hadn't crossed his path in a long time.

'Why couldn't I meet someone like you in the real world?' she murmured, taking his hand. 'I could stay here for ever.'

'Mmm, have you seen those clouds?' Nolan pointed to the sky. Even though the air was still warm, there were dark clouds looming above. 'I think there's going to be showers tonight so we should probably head back. I'll leave the cool box in the hut. I can come back for it at another time.'

'Maybe we could come back for it together?' Bea hoped he'd say yes. In the next two weeks she wanted to spend as much time with him as possible.

'I'm sure we can make that happen,' he replied, glancing up at the sky again.

Just at that moment, the sky opened up. Feeling the large droplets of rain against their bare skin, they were up on their feet and running briskly towards the hut. Grabbing her clothes from her rucksack, Bea quickly pulled them on then placed a towel around her shoulders like a cape. Nolan began to pack everything up and moved the painting and easel inside the hut along with the picnic blanket.

'Are you sure we should leave the painting here?' asked Bea.

'Yes, it'll stay dry in the hut.'

'But, what if someone turns up here and they're greeted by a portrait of a semi-naked woman wearing a red bikini?'

'There's not a soul in sight and if they do, they will be disappointed. You're taken for the summer and I'll be the only one admiring your beauty.'

Bea smiled. 'Taken for the summer? I'm only here for the next couple of weeks.'

Nolan leaned forward and kissed her on the tip of her freckled nose. 'My guess is two weeks will fly by and you'll want to stay. What have you got to rush back for anyway?'

'My job,' Bea answered straightaway.

Nolan cocked an eyebrow. 'Really? I thought you were here to make a plan and sort the rest of your life. That, to me, sounds like you're going to fall straight back into the same routine as before. It might be all you've ever known, but even I can see your worth. Be braver.'

Bea was pensive for a second. 'I need a steady income.'

'And? There are loads of jobs out there. Ones that have sociable hours and that would put a smile on your face. The smile on your face disappears as soon as you mention that job.'

'It's not that easy to get a job.'

'Is that the best argument you can come up with? You already have a trial shift lined up at The Little Blue Boathouse tomorrow!'

'You do have a point there.' She mulled over Nolan's words as they stood in the doorway of the hut and looked out over Castaway Bay. It was beautiful and calming and that wasn't the feeling she got back at home.

'I think it won't be quite the same when you've gone.' She nudged his elbow lightly. 'Are we going to make a run for it?' She nodded in the direction of the boat.

After stuffing the bottle and letter inside the rucksack, they took off from the hut. Thankfully, the rain wasn't too heavy at the moment and the breeze was slight. Sitting in the boat, Bea held on to the sides as Nolan pushed it into the water and grabbed the oar before jumping aboard.

As he began to row, he watched Bea closely. This was the first day he'd felt alive again in a very long time and he hoped the next two weeks would be just as happy as today. Maybe things were beginning to change for him.

'What's the plan about the bottle?' asked Bea.

'I think my first stop might be the graveyard.'

She raised an eyebrow. 'I wasn't expecting that answer. Why do you say that?'

'Think about it. How old would Patsy be? There's a good chance she might have passed away.'

Bea knew that Nolan was possibly right.

He hesitated and stared straight at her. 'If she is alive and I track her down, I have something for her.'

'Besides the necklace? Tell me more.' Bea was intrigued.

'When my grandfather passed away, I began to restore The Hemingway and discovered a small box that was full of memorabilia, items I can only assume were memories from the summer they spent together.'

'Like a memory box, how romantic! What sort of things?'

'From what I remember there was a ticket to the bandstand at Primrose Park—'

'Must have been a band playing,' interrupted Bea.

'My thoughts exactly. There were also shiny rocks, shells, a small notepad of sketches, postcards of Heartcross, a pack of cards, a small teddy bear, receipts ... but the thing that stood out the most was an unopened letter addressed to Patsy.'

Bea gave a tiny gasp. 'And what did it say?'

'I don't know. I haven't opened it. It's not addressed to me.'

Bea was impressed; curiosity would most probably have gotten the better of her. 'And do you think your grandfather wrote it after the summer they spent together?'

'Yes, I do.'

'And did the letter have her surname on it?'

Nolan shook his head. 'But we know Patsy's surname begins with a G.'

'Do we?' asked Bea, perplexed. 'How do we know that?'

'Because of the love heart written on the back of the letter in the bottle – MH & PG.'

'You're like Sherlock Holmes! I would never have even thought of that. But what are you going to do if you discover a grave with the name Patsy and a surname that begins with a G? Are you going to open the letter then?'

'I'm not sure, but if I discover the grave, I might be able to track down a living relative. Who knows?'

'Who knows indeed. This is all very exciting.'

'I know there's got to be a churchyard in Heartcross, so that's my first stop tomorrow.'

'Don't go without me! We're in this together now and I want to help to uncover the romantic love story of Morgan and Patsy, and find out what became of her.' She flapped her hand between the two of them. 'We need to come up with a name now we're a brand-new detective duo.'

'How about Nolan and Bea?'

Bea hooted. 'Dead original.'

Nolan grinned. 'Hemingway and…?'

'Fernsby,' Bea supplied.

'Hemingway and Fernsby has a great ring to it,' said Nolan.

'I think Fernsby and Hemingway has a better ring to it.' She cocked an eyebrow, laughing.

'Whichever way round it is, you can be my right-hand woman.'

Bea couldn't stop smiling. She liked the sound of that.

Chapter Nine

B ea woke as soon as the alarm sounded. It was 7.30am and she was already excited about her trial at The Little Blue Boathouse. Her shift was to start at 9am and Julia would be showing her the ropes. Bea knew the Little Blue Boathouse was owned by Julia's partner, Flynn Carter, who was a famous property tycoon and according to the internet was worth millions. Bea wasn't going to admit to anyone that late last night she'd spent a lot of time googling Heartcross and its residents. Never mind a mini St Tropez with all the boats, it was like a mini Los Angeles with its celebrity residents! Wanting another few minutes in bed, she reached for her phone on the bedside cabinet. There was a message from Emmie asking her to call.

'Good morning, Sis!' trilled Bea, sitting up in bed and pulling the duvet around her middle.

'Is that you, Bea?' asked Emmie, sounding a little unsure.

'Of course it's me, why wouldn't it be me? Unless my phone has been stolen and the thief is phoning my sister.'

'Because you don't sound like yourself … you sound quite happy.'

'Erm, so what you're trying to say is that I usually sound like a miserable sod?' teased Bea, knowing that nothing her sister said could bring her down. She was feeling on top of the world.

'No, of course not,' Emmie said, back-pedalling. 'But I expected you to sound a little more broken-hearted, depressed even. I'm just a little…'

'Shocked?' Bea finished her sentence. 'Look, I'm not dwelling on the past. Carl did me a favour. The relationship was boring, mundane and going absolutely nowhere fast.'

For a moment, Emmie was quiet on the other end of the line. 'Are you trying to make out everything is okay but as soon as you put the phone down you're going to burst into tears and stay in bed all day? Because you do know I'm here for you and you can ring me any time, right? I don't like the thought of you being lonely and upset.'

'I'm neither lonely nor upset,' confirmed Bea. 'I had the best day yesterday, which included swimming in a secluded bay with a handsome stranger.' Bea kept the rest of the details to herself, knowing that if she shared the fact she'd got *very* close to the stranger her sister might turn up in Heartcross and attempt to rescue her from 'going off the rails'.

'Have you been taking drugs?' Emmie's voice was deadly serious.

'I've not even had a coffee yet!' replied Bea, with a chuckle. 'Honestly, it's true, I'm okay. In fact, I'm more than okay! I'm the best I've ever been and today I have a trial shift at The Little Blue Boathouse.'

'What the heck do you mean, you have a trial shift? A job?'

'Yes, for a job.'

'But you have a job back home where you belong. What is going on here, Bea? This isn't like you. I'm beginning to worry even more about you.'

'Maybe I'm fed up of the old Bea. Good old dependable Bea who is boring and reliable. It's time for a change, a new direction. I may not be sure what that direction is, but what I do know is that I don't want the life I've had in the past.'

'You're coming home, aren't you?'

Bea turned over the word 'home' in her mind and thought about Martha's prediction. Avoiding the question, she said, 'Emmie, there's no need to worry. I'm okay, really I am. The job is just for two weeks whilst I'm here. I figured, why not work by the water, enjoy the sunshine, chat to the tourists? You never know what opportunities might spring up.'

'As long as you *are* coming home?' Emmie emphasised the words as though they would be enough to ensure Bea's return.

'You will see me very soon. I promise,' was all that Bea could offer and she ended the call, happy to have avoided answering her sister's question.

An hour later, after breakfast, Bea ambled along the lane towards the river path. The sun was shining and there were only a few clouds in the sky. It was going to be another hot day, which probably meant The Little Blue Boathouse would be busy. The village was already alive with dog walkers, hikers heading towards the mountain pass, and children running with fishing nets towards the rocks by the river. Bea felt excited and a little nervous. Initially, the reason she had offered her services for the next two weeks had been to keep herself occupied and stop her thinking about her ex, but since meeting Nolan, Carl had barely crossed her mind and she was actually relieved that her life was changing and going in a completely different direction.

As she turned the last corner before The Little Blue Boathouse, she saw that even more boats had arrived since yesterday and there were now some impressive yachts on the water. Posters had been erected along the path, advertising the annual River Festival and firework display, and Bea wished she was staying a little longer. Quickly, she scanned the area, looking for The Hemingway. There it was. Just knowing that Nolan was still about put a spring in her step. She hoped that he would come and say hello sometime during the day.

The Little Blue Boathouse was already heaving. Numerous people were standing outside wearing wetsuits or holding paddles whilst others were pulling kayaks into the water. There was also a queue of people along the jetty waiting for the river taxi to take them on excursions. Bea watched as the river taxi pressed its horn. 'All aboard for Heartcross Castle,' a voice boomed over the Tannoy, and people began to file onto the boat. Noticing another group of people, huddled around a table near the entrance, Bea realised they were admiring Nolan's paintings. It was like a mini art gallery: a couple of the paintings were displayed on easels whilst others stood on table stands, making them easy to browse through. Further paintings were stacked in a box, ready to be added to the table as space became available.

Stepping inside The Little Blue Boathouse, Bea was greeted by a beaming Julia. 'Good morning! Sorry I missed you at breakfast, I had to nip to the drycleaners. Oh! Before I forget, you've already got post. I'll serve these customers and I'll be right with you.'

Bea looked down at the handwritten letter that Julia had just handed to her and grinned. She hoped this was from her favourite sailor. While Julia took the money for a couple of excursions from a customer, Bea tore open the envelope to find a hand-painted card with a picture of The Little Blue Boathouse. It was beautiful; the colours were vibrant and the river looked lifelike. Inside the card was written:

To Fernsby,
Good luck today!
I'll bring lunch!
Yours, Hemingway x

Bea loved the way Nolan had written their surnames. She knew it felt daft to think they were some sort of partnership but it just felt so natural to be in his company and he'd begun to creep into her thoughts more and more. With a smile on her face, she put the card back in the envelope before slipping it into her bag, then waited for Julia to point the tourists in the right direction for the river excursion.

As soon as they'd stepped outside, Julia blew out a breath. 'With the weather like this it's going to be a busy day. I've not stopped since I arrived.'

'I can't wait to get stuck in,' replied Bea. 'Where shall I put these?' She held up her bag and cardigan.

'I'll show you to the staff room. Actually, the words "staff room" are a little too grand. Basically, it's a cubbyhole with a chair, table and kettle. Come on.'

Bea followed Julia through the door with the 'staff only' sign hanging on it, which was situated behind the pay desk. Julia wasn't exaggerating; it was a very small room, with cream wooden panelling, an old table and a couple of chairs. There was also a small sink along with a fridge and a microwave.

'Mugs and glasses are in there. Washing up liquid and cloths over there. Milk is in the fridge, and Wilbur keeps custard creams in that biscuit tin. I know it's not all mod cons but its workable for what we need.'

'Absolutely,' replied Bea, looking through the small, round window by the sink. 'Look at that view.'

'It is breathtaking, isn't it? I've noticed there's a few

more boats arrived this morning. With the River Festival getting closer we'll be busier than usual and, I have to say, I'm feeling a little guilty throwing you in at the deep end.'

'If you're throwing me in, I hope you have a spare life jacket,' joked Bea, looking at The Hemingway through the window. There was no sign of Nolan on board but then she noticed a familiar rowing boat heading up the river. She watched him for a second before turning back to Julia. 'I'm looking forward to every moment of it, don't worry.'

'A life saver is what you are. You can hang your belongings on that hook.' Julia gestured to the long line of hooks on the wall. 'And here's a key to this room. There's a lot of people milling around and you can never be too careful. Keep it locked at all times.'

'Thanks,' replied Bea, slipping it into her pocket.

'And I have to say, that's a very beautiful necklace you're wearing, very unique,' admired Julia, taking a closer look. 'I noticed it the second you walked in. It looks old too.'

'A present,' replied Bea, beaming. 'And I'm guessing it's several decades old.'

'I love seahorses. They're a symbol of good luck and fortune and also meant to represent strength and power.'

Bea ran the necklace through her fingers. 'I didn't know that.' She immediately thought of Morgan and Patsy. Maybe this represented the strength and power of their love for one another that summer.

Locking the staff room door behind them, Bea followed Julia to the counter. 'Even though this place is going to be busy,' Julia told her, 'it's quite straightforward and you'll have the hang of it in no time. As you can see, wetsuits to hire are along that wall on the rails, and the ones to buy are on the opposite wall alongside the swimming costumes, goggles, fishing nets, et cetera. All the sale items have the new prices attached to the labels. I know the till looks like it's been through the war, it's that prehistoric, but it's so easy to use.'

Julia took an item off the rail and showed Bea how to ring it through the till. Bea was used to more complicated technology, working on the late night checkout at the supermarket, and found this easy to use in comparison.

'There's more cash in the safe if you run out of change but these days most people pay by card. You put the receipts for items sold on this side of the till, including excursions, and at the end of the day I'll take you through cashing up and balancing the books.' Julia bent down and picked the cashing up book from under the pay counter. 'We then put the cash in the safe and Flynn usually pops in and picks it up most evenings.'

'What about the excursions and boat hire?' asked Bea, wondering what to charge for each.

'Very simple. All boats are hired for an hour or half a day. The prices are up there so you can see them and so can the customers. There's a discount for family hire.' Julia tapped the poster. 'The excursion prices and times are here; they leave every hour on the hour and the river taxis run every twenty minutes over to The Lakehouse restaurant. Roman is in charge of the river taxis and no doubt he'll pop in at some point to say hello. Any questions?'

Bea shook her head. 'Not that I can think of.' She looked up at the couple approaching the desk who wanted to hire a couple of kayaks for the next hour. Julia tapped a small book by the till, which logged the kayaks in and out, and Bea checked there were enough available. After taking the money and pointing them in the direction of the life jackets and oars, Bea had officially made her first sale.

'That was fab! You have such a warm way with the customers,' observed Julia. 'And by the way, there's just a little bit of housekeeping – make sure the shop is kept clean and tidy, and the same outside too.'

Bea nodded. She was already thoroughly enjoying herself. The whole place had a lovely relaxed atmosphere about it.

'Oh, and before I forget, there are some beautiful paintings for sale just outside the door, which Flynn has agreed to with a young artist called Nolan Hemingway, as he's around until the River Festival. All his paintings have the prices written on the back in pencil. Cash sales only and here's his tin. Any money for his sales goes in there.'

At the sound of Nolan's name, Bea felt her heart beat a little faster. Julia didn't fail to notice the smile that had crept on to her face.

'You should introduce yourself to him; you must be around the same age. He's very easy on the eye. Get yourself out for a drink with him.' As soon as those words left Julia's mouth, she looked apologetic. 'I'm so sorry, that was very insensitive of me, especially given the reason you're here. I bet you don't feel like looking in the direction of any young man at the minute. I've not even asked you how you are.'

'Don't be daft, there's no need to apologise, and surprisingly I'm really good.' Bea smiled but didn't share the reason why she was feeling on top of the world. 'It's great to make new friends, even if it's just for a couple of weeks. I'll look him up.'

'You do that. He seems very lovely and is obviously talented.' Julia picked up a bag of files from behind the counter and walked towards the staff room.

'Before I forget, you need to sign in, in the logbook, for health and safety reasons. It's just here.' Julia pointed to a book on the shelf by the staff room door. 'And I'm going to do a little work in the staff room so if you need anything just ask.'

'I'll get that done now. Thank you again for the trial. I can't wait to get going. Oh, there's just one thing I don't know … the number for the coastguard or lifeboat station. What if someone gets into trouble in the water?'

Julia spun round. 'Unfortunately, there isn't one.' She pointed to the sign on the wall. 'It's at their own risk.'

Bea stared at the sign and immediately her thoughts turned back to when she was a teenager, her heart suddenly thumping faster for all the wrong reasons. It had been an afternoon of sunshine, the temperature hitting a whopping thirty degrees, and she'd been hanging out with her friends at the local lake. The water looked inviting and, not realising the dangers, some of her friends began to paddle near the edge. There was an island in the middle and soon they were daring each other to swim across. Bea tried to talk her friends out of it but they wouldn't listen. She remembered they'd argued and Bea took off home. It wasn't until a day later that she discovered one of her friends had got into trouble and hadn't made it. The town was in mourning for weeks, the funeral packed. It was a devastating tragedy.

'But why is there no lifeboat or coastguard? Surely with so many people out on the water it's a must?'

'I suppose funds. The cost would be considerable.'

'But what about the cost of someone's life? You can't put a price on that.' Bea's voice was passionate.

'I hear you, I really do, but keeping a lifeboat always ready to go to a rescue is an expensive business. There's also the crew – we would have to rely on volunteers. Not to mention the crew training and actually running the lifeguard service and campaigning for water safety. There's also the kit ... everything would depend on donations. It would take thousands.'

'Has anyone tried?' asked Bea. 'Look at the amount of people out on the water right now.' Bea pointed through the open hatch towards the river.

Julia shook her head. 'Not to my knowledge. The tourist industry in this area rocketed after the village of Heartcross hit the news with the bridge collapse. Then throw in local celebrities, the building of Starcross Manor, The Lakehouse and the reopening of Heartcross Castle, and of course the biggest mountain to climb in the Scottish Highlands, the annual boat race, the River Festival... People flock here. I feel like I'm trying to sell you a holiday.' Julia smiled, obviously attempting to lighten the mood.

Bea understood everything that Julia was saying, but Heartcross was now on the map and surely it should be a huge priority to keep everyone safe. Julia touched her elbow. 'I need to get on. Anything you need, just shout, and don't forget to sign in for your shift in the logbook, otherwise you won't get paid for today. We can have a chat at the end of your shift about what's next.'

Watching Julia disappear into the staff room, Bea grabbed the logbook and placed it on the counter. There were numerous people looking through the wetsuits, and children trying to persuade their parents to buy them fishing nets. Bea smiled and let them know she was there if they needed any help. Then she opened the book. Julia had already signed in on arrival and Bea did the same: name, date and time of arrival. She turned back through some of the pages, discovering that the book went back several years.

The morning had flown by and before Bea had time to catch her breath it was midday. She'd lost count of how many excursions she'd sold and kayaks she'd hired out. Roman, who was in charge of the river taxis, had popped by to introduce himself, and she had even managed to sell a handful of Nolan's paintings. The door to the staff room opened and Julia placed a mug of tea on the counter for her.

'Here you go, take five. You haven't stopped. How's it going so far?' she asked.

'Love it,' replied Bea, meaning every word. 'I mean, look at that view! And everyone is so happy and friendly. When I work in the supermarket it's complaint after complaint from customers and I hardly see anyone smile.'

'The difference here is that they're all on holiday and when the weather is as gorgeous as this it makes the world a whole different place.'

'Agreed,' replied Bea, taking a sip of her tea. 'I've hung the life jackets that have been returned back on those rails there and marked them in the book. I've sold four wetsuits too.'

'You have taken to this job like a duck to water. How would you feel if I offered you the rest of the shifts for the next two weeks? That will give me time to sort out a job advert and interviewing schedule.'

'How would I feel? I'd say, "Yes, please," but I've been thinking…' Bea had a huge smile on her face. 'I don't want to miss out. I would like to stick around for the River Festival and extend my holiday.'

'And you want to work here until then?'

Bea put her hands together as if praying. 'If you'd have me?'

'I'd bite your hand off and Flynn will be chuffed. It gives us extra time to sort out staffing … but what about your job back home?'

Bea had thought about nothing else all morning. In between customers she'd written down on a piece of paper what she liked and didn't like about her employment at the supermarket, and what she didn't like outweighed what she liked by quite a bit.

'It's been on my mind all morning. I think I've fallen out of love with it and I've decided it's the first thing I'm going to change about my life. I'm going to take the bull by the horns and resign.' Bea knew she was maybe being a little impulsive but it felt right, even though there was the slight worry of how she would pay her bills. She did have a small amount put away in her savings account to help her out for a short time. Leaving her job would be the first step on this new adventure of living life for herself.

'It sounds to me like you're making some brave decisions – and I have to say that smile on your face suits you.'

'I honestly feel like a huge weight has been lifted off my shoulders now I've made that decision. I just know there's more to life, and there's something about the fresh air, water and sun … it makes everything seem okay.'

'It does, I love it here.'

With a lull in customers, they took their mugs of tea and sat outside on a bench. The white cliffs towered behind them and the river was a spectacular sight. Bea burst out laughing and pointed to a cheeky seagull that had swooped down and stolen a man's sandwich clean from his hand.

'You have to watch those. I left my lunch on the bench once and came back to five seagulls fighting over it.'

'Yes, I can imagine. Has this place really been up and running for over sixty years?' Bea was looking at one of the posters for the River Festival.

'It originally opened just over sixty years ago but on a much smaller scale. I'm not sure why it then closed down but The Little Blue Boathouse was shut for many years. Flynn bought it around five years ago, refurbished it, bought all new boats, paddleboards, et cetera, and set up the river taxis and excursions. I came across the original signing-in book when I was cleaning the attic room as part of the refurb. It was amongst the books on the shelf. Talking of the attic room, if you want to move in for the time you're here, I'll leave you the keys before I go.'

'I love your B&B, but waking up to the view of the river and the mountains…' Bea placed her hand on her heart. 'It's going to be amazing. This just doesn't feel like work.'

'Those types of jobs are the best jobs,' said Julia, giving her a warm smile.

'Thank you,' added Bea.

They watched the river taxi making its way towards the jetty and Roman waved his cap in the air towards them. Julia saluted. 'At the River Festival all the boats line up and parade on the water. There's music, and the firework display is spectacular.'

'It sounds like it's going to be rock 'n' roll on the river. I'm glad I've made the decision to stay longer.' Bea's eyes were fixed firmly on The Hemingway. Her decision definitely had something to do with Nolan being around, which she knew was daft, given that she barely knew the man, but there was something about him that excited her. She wanted to get to know him better.

'I need to nip back to the B&B for a couple of hours. Are you going to be okay on your own? And would you like me to bring you back some lunch?'

'I'm okay on all counts but thank you.'

Julia took both mugs back to the staff room and returned with a key. 'For the attic room. You can move your stuff in whenever you want. At one o'clock, lock up the Boathouse for an hour and take your lunch. And here's my mobile number in case any sudden emergencies or questions arise.'

It was half an hour until lunch and Bea took another glance towards The Hemingway but there was still no sign of life. She was wondering whether she should have asked Julia to bring her back some lunch or whether Nolan would actually turn up with food. Hearing a loud growl from her stomach she hoped it was the latter.

Bea breezed through the next hour and, right on time, grabbed the CLOSED sign from underneath the counter and walked towards the open door. Hearing footsteps approaching, she was just about to make her apologies when she was met by a grinning Nolan, causing an immediate flurry of goosebumps across her body. He held up a white paper bag. 'Lunch!'

'Right on cue! How did you know this was my lunch hour?'

'Call yourself part of Hemingway and Fernsby?' He rolled his eyes and shook his head in jest.

'Fernsby and Hemingway,' she corrected, watching him tap the wooden sign next to the door.

'It says "closed between 1pm and 2pm", and it doesn't take a detective to know that must be when staff take their lunch hour.'

'You're very clever,' she said, grinning and, after putting the sign on the door, pushed him playfully inside the Boathouse. She waggled the key in front of him.

'What's that, the key to your heart?' Nolan teased.

'You wish. It's the key to my new room for the next month.'

'Month? I thought you were only sticking around for two weeks?' Nolan handed her a paper bag. 'Sandwich and flapjack.'

'Perfect, thank you,' she said, leading him through to the back of the shop. 'Two weeks was my initial plan but Flynn and Julia were feeling the pressure to recruit before the River Festival and it seems daft if I know the ropes to leave them in the lurch.' Bea knew it was better she tell a little white lie and make out that they had asked her to stay on, rather than admit to Nolan that part of the reason she wanted to stay was him. 'I'd already made the decision not to go back to the night shift, and this way I'll have a little more time to work out what I'm doing and get paid in the meantime.'

'It sounds like you have it all worked out.' Nolan was

now looking at the ladder in front of him. 'You have to climb up there?'

'I do, but wait till you see the view. It's going to take your breath away.'

'It already has,' he replied with a mischievous glint in his eye. 'Ladies first.'

After handing him her sandwich Bea began to climb the ladder, then looked back over her shoulder. 'You just wanted to look at my backside!'

Nolan gave her a lopsided grin. 'I'm saying nothing, except the view just got better!'

'Don't be cheeky,' she ordered, pulling herself into the attic room then reaching down she took the food from Nolan who followed and immediately walked over to the chair positioned by the window. 'Wow, you can see for miles!'

'There's everything you could want – the river, the town, the bridge, the castle. I think this is the best view I've ever seen, and it's going to be mine for the next month.'

'You're one lucky girl,' he replied, still taking it all in.

Bea grabbed the wooden chair and its cushion from the little dressing table and placed it next to the armchair in front of the window. They both sat down and tucked into their sandwiches. She took a sideward glance and caught Nolan looking at her.

'What are you looking at?' she queried, trying to control the hundreds of fireflies that were flying around in her stomach.

'You. So how has your morning gone so far?'

She waggled her finger in his direction. 'You'll be pleased to know that I've made you a few quid today. Your paintings garner a lot of attention.'

'That's good to know. I've got another one to finish today. It's of the river running under the bridge and the castle towering in front of the mountain. It's such beautiful scenery to paint, but maybe not as good as yesterday's scenery.'

Bea bit her lip. She felt a twinge of blush to her cheeks, remembering how confident and sexy she felt, posing whilst he painted her. She knew the feelings that were flooding her body were desire but today she felt shy for some reason. Her feelings towards Nolan were moving way too quickly. How could they not? He was drop dead gorgeous! But she knew that she had to keep hold of her emotions. He'd made it crystal clear they were just living for the moment; this wasn't something that was going to grow into a love story. She might have bought herself some more time with him but she already knew it was going to be difficult not to get carried away and let her feelings escalate into the first flush of love.

'And what have you done with your morning?' she asked, thinking about how she'd seen Nolan rowing up the river earlier.

'Just messing about on the river and a quick walk around the village.'

'You haven't been to the graveyard without me?'

'Of course not. I said you were my right-hand woman. I was hoping you might be free after work?'

'I'm moving out of the B&B and into here, but that shouldn't take too long. We could go after?'

'Great stuff,' he replied, finishing his sandwich.

Suddenly, Bea remembered what Julia had said about the original logbook being on the shelf and she got up to take a look. There it was, a book with a red spine and Bea pulled it from the shelf.

'What do you have there?' he asked, looking over his shoulder.

'The original signing-in book for The Little Blue Boathouse. If you think Patsy worked here then this might give us some more information.'

'I'm impressed. You're clearly taking your detective duties seriously.'

Bea laid the book on the small table and opened the cover. They both hunched over and cast their eyes on the first page.

'There she is. Signing in for her first shift in mid-July.' Bea stared at Nolan.

'And it was that August she met my grandfather... There's no surname. There's just what looks like a swirly G,' Nolan said, checking out the entry from different angles.

'That matches the letter inside the bottle. Maybe her surname is just G, like G-e-e!' Bea couldn't contain her excitement, her pulse beginning to race as she gently tapped the book. 'But never mind that, can you see what I can see? There's an address. That's where she must have lived – in Glensheil. You have a starting point!' Bea's eyes widened.

'*We* have a starting point,' corrected Nolan. 'I thought

we were in this together. Hemingway and Fernsby, one summer only.'

'Damn right we are.' Already she was not liking the idea that in four weeks their time together would be over. She gave herself a reality check; why was she allowing this man to consume her thoughts so quickly after such a short time spent together?

'I think our best bet is to check the cemetery first and if there's nothing there, we can investigate further at this address.'

'It's exciting, isn't it? Can you imagine if we find her and deliver the letter? We might make her a very happy woman! I wonder if your grandfather was the one who got away. Or the one who loved her first. I think it's so romantic. I know your grandfather has passed away but I'm hoping his letter brings Patsy some joy.' Bea stared into Nolan's eyes. She had to give herself a little shake because all she could think about was the moment she would have to say goodbye to him. Trying to push that thought from her mind, and realising she didn't have a clue about his personal life, she blurted, 'Have you ever been in love?'

There it was again; Bea was sure she'd seen a flash of sadness in his eyes, but he composed himself quickly. Whatever his story was, it was still painful. He stared at the floor and raked his hand through his hair. Maybe he'd been in a similar situation to her? 'Sorry, it's none of my business. I shouldn't be so nosey.' Even though she was curious, she saved him from having to answer her question because there was a part of her that didn't want to know. She didn't like the thought of him being close to anyone else.

Standing up, Nolan checked his watch. 'I best let you get on.'

Hesitantly, Bea stood up too and wished she'd never asked the question, because it felt like Nolan was running. They walked back towards the ladder and he lingered at the top of the hatch.

'It's a lovely place you've got here for the next few weeks.' He paused and took both of Bea's hands. 'You do know I'll be leaving after the River Festival? I don't want you to get your hopes up and—'

'Of course.' Bea swallowed. 'I know exactly what the score is here, and just for the record, you're definitely punching.' She was trying to make light of the situation but she could feel her heart racing.

'I agree.' He grinned. 'And yesterday was a great day. You made me feel special, thank you.'

Bea wasn't expecting him to say that. 'You don't have to thank me. You're the one who made me feel like me again, alive and free,' she admitted.

They stared into each other's eyes. 'I would love to spend some more time with you,' he said, 'but I appreciate you have come here to sort out your life, and me hanging around may not be—'

Bea stood on tiptoe and kissed him in mid-sentence. 'Shut up,' she murmured. 'You can hang around as much as you want. Anyway, we have a case to solve.'

'That we do, and by the way, the necklace suits you.'

Nolan touched the seahorse and turned it over in his hand. 'This must have been special for a reason.'

'If we find Patsy, we can find out what it was and give it back to her. But in the meantime, I'll enjoy wearing it.'

'Maybe we should do our own message in the bottle when we sail off in our separate directions,' suggested Nolan.

'Maybe we should,' she replied.

Nolan tilted her face towards him. Bea had never been attracted to anyone in this way. She was experiencing feelings that she'd never had before.

He checked his watch. 'Fifteen minutes of your lunch hour left.'

'And I know exactly how to spend that time.' Taking his hands in hers, she lowered herself onto the bed and pulled him on top of her. She had never wanted anyone so much as she wanted him now. Pressing her body against his she gasped with desire, the electricity sparking between them. Her eyes locked with his as she reached for his belt. Never in her life had she ever done anything like this. Bea was always the one who weighed up both sides and worried about the consequences, but not since arriving in Heartcross. No, now she was living life in the moment and enjoying every second of it. Embracing the tingling pleasure that was flooding through her, she sighed as Nolan kissed her again, stealing the breath from her body.

Chapter Ten

'How was your lunch hour?' asked Julia, waltzing back through the door just after 2pm. 'You look flushed. Are you okay?'

Bea knew exactly the reason she looked flushed – she'd just spent the last fifteen minutes wrapped in the arms of a drop dead gorgeous man! 'It must be the weather and the fact I am high on life.'

'I absolutely admire how you've pulled yourself around so quickly. I think I would have locked myself away, feeling sorry for myself.'

'But then I had the perfect opportunity fall at my feet when I walked into the B&B. From now on, I'm definitely going to take every opportunity that crosses my path. A change of scenery and being away from my normal routine have already shown me that there's a whole new world out there.'

'Good for you, girl, and how are you getting on?'

'All of Roman's excursions are sold out for today. The kayaks are hired for the majority of the afternoon and there's only a couple of rowing boats still free,' replied Bea, looking in the book. 'And I've even sold several paintings.'

'You're Superwoman! Flynn will be pleased his profits are soaring! I'm going to get some paperwork finished and then I'll show you how to cash up at the end of the day.'

Julia disappeared inside the staff room and Bea leaned on the open hatch, looking out at the river. She breathed in the fresh air and watched the hustle and bustle all around her. Over at The Hemingway she could see Nolan standing on the deck chatting with a man on the boat next to his. She wondered what they were talking about. On the one hand she wanted to know everything about him but on the other she didn't want to get too emotionally attached.

'Put on your big girl's knickers,' she reminded herself. Nolan had been honest that after the River Festival he would be sailing to his next destination and whatever was going on between them was temporary. This was a here-and-now thing with no future. Just a bit of fun.

Hearing her phone beep, she checked and saw it was Emmie, asking how her morning had gone.

'*All good, really enjoying my shift.*' She took a quick photo of the spectacular scenery in front of her and pinged it across to her sister. '*No filter needed,*' she quickly added.

'*Carl has been to see me*' came the instant reply.

Reading that text, Bea rolled her eyes. She didn't want thoughts of him flooding her perfect day. She was surprised by how quickly she was getting over him and moving on with her life.

Her phone pinged again. *'He's sorry for what he's done and wants you back. If you just come home, you could talk and put this sorry mess behind you.'*

Bea was frustrated. Why didn't her sister want better for her? She didn't want to appear rude by telling her to mind her own business but she had to say something.

'I deserve to find somebody who makes me feel like I'm the only girl in the world.' Bea typed back her reply, knowing that was exactly how Nolan made her feel. *'I'm at work, can't talk now.'*

Bea knew that wasn't strictly true but it was a subject she didn't want to think about or have a deep conversation about and she wished her sister would take her side for once. Why wasn't she turning around to Carl and telling him he didn't deserve her sister? After throwing her phone in the drawer and serving a few more customers she locked up the till and took a walk to the water's edge to check that everything was okay out on the river. A teenager was pulling himself up on one of the paddleboards. As much as the water looked calm and everywhere everyone was enjoying themselves, Bea understood what a dangerous place the water could be. It still made her feel unsettled that there wasn't any life rescue in operation. As soon as the teenager was safely back on the paddleboard, Bea wandered back inside, and for the next ten minutes tidied up the wetsuit rail, swept the floor and then took a look through Nolan's paintings.

Without a doubt he had talent, and she could visualise them hanging on a gallery wall in his very own exhibition. There were more paintings stacked in boxes on the ground, and Bea began to take a look through them. They were mainly of landscapes and landmarks, each one telling a story of somewhere Nolan had visited. But one took her a little by surprise. She held it in her hands and felt a stab of jealousy.

The woman was young and beautiful. She was much the same age as Bea, who suddenly felt a slump in the pit of her stomach. Was this girl like her? Was she someone whom Nolan had met on his travels, and had they too had an affair? Bea gave herself a shake and reminded herself that she'd quite willingly got into the situation with Nolan, knowing that he wasn't going to stick around. So why was she feeling jealous of the woman in this painting? She stared at it a little longer and breathed a sigh of relief. This girl couldn't have been just a fling, because she was holding up her hand and there on her finger was a wedding ring. Maybe she was a friend, an old work colleague or even a relative. Placing the painting back in the box, Bea reminded herself to stop overthinking things. Nolan was a free spirit and could do exactly what he wanted … even if Bea didn't like the thought of him being with anyone else.

Suddenly there was an influx of customers and a long line of tourists had formed, wanting to book excursions for tomorrow. As a mother of three children handed over her credit card to pay for a trip, she said, 'What a lovely place to work. I would love a job like this overlooking the water.

Even though that view will change throughout the seasons, I bet each time it is equally stunning.'

'It is a lovely job but I'll let you into a little secret. It's my first day! I can imagine how stunning the view is in winter but I'm afraid I'm only here for the summer.'

'Here for the summer? I'd be here for ever. This village is beautiful.'

Bea smiled and handed over her receipt and tickets for tomorrow's trip. Once she'd cleared the rest of the queue, she fired up the computer behind the counter at the back of the shop. It wasn't password protected and Bea went online to search for jobs back home. She was soon disappointed as there was nothing that jumped out at her or caught her interest. They were all like the mundane job she already had.

Feeling dispirited, she next searched amongst the available rental flats in the area. On her wage, all she could afford were small flats in far from salubrious areas of town. She sighed. There wasn't even the possibility of moving in with her sister, as her small town house was already packed with a husband, children and two dogs.

'That was a loud sigh. I was just going to make a drink. Would you like one?'

'Yes, please,' replied Bea.

'Is everything okay?' asked Julia, hovering in the staff room doorway.

'Yes and no. I hope it's okay but whilst it was quiet, I thought I'd start to look for places to rent back home.'

'Isn't there much available?'

Bea leaned to the side so Julia could take a look at the screen. 'They're all in areas that I don't particularly want to live in and I certainly wouldn't feel safe in. I don't want views of backyards, overflowing bins and people frequenting the nearby flats for drugs.'

'That wouldn't enthral me either. Do you have to stay in that area?'

'It's about the only town in that area I can afford – if I kept my job at the supermarket, and I may have to. I've already looked at available jobs and they aren't much better than what I already have.'

'There's just an easy answer to that then,' Julia said, smiling. 'There's only one thing for it – you'll have to stay here!'

'If only.' Bea thought Julia must be daydreaming.

'You wait there, let me make a drink and I'll be back to have a chat.'

Bea shut down the computer and, while she waited for Julia to return, checked in the kayaks that had been brought back and hung up the life jackets ready for the next tourists who'd hired them out.

'I know I don't know you well,' Julia continued when she returned, 'but even from this morning I can see you're a hard worker and extremely charismatic with the customers.'

'You're going to make me blush,' interrupted Bea.

'What is keeping you in the town where you've just come from? Because when you talk about home you don't seem to be filled with enthusiasm.'

'What's keeping me there is … it's all I've ever known and my sister lives there.'

'And how often do you see your sister?'

Bea didn't have to think about that answer. 'Barely ever, because I've been working nights for as long as I can remember, and at the weekends, if I happen to have a day off, she's busy with her own family.'

'To me, it sounds like there's no quality time spent seeing each other.'

Bea agreed.

'What about friends in that area, hobbies? What do you like to do in your spare time?'

'With working through the night, I didn't really have a social life. I kind of fitted things in around my ex, which I'm now beginning to realise wasn't healthy. He didn't like my friends much so I left them behind.'

'Us girls always need good girlfriends to lift us up. I have such a great group of friends in the village. What we need to do is introduce you to a few more villagers. There's always something going on so leave it with me, I'll check what free nights I have and maybe we could go for a drink in the pub.'

'That would be good, thank you.'

'And I do know there will be a few secret meetings coming up regarding Martha's surprise birthday party, so as an honorary villager for the summer, let's get you involved too.'

'I can help organise anything you need,' offered Bea.

'Have a chat with Isla and offer your services. Over the

next few weeks, you'll have the opportunity to live like a villager and my guess is you're going to love it. This community is exactly that, a community that looks out for one another, supports each other and lifts each other up when it's needed, and it sounds to me that's a little different from what you're used to.'

It was indeed very different from what Bea was used to. She mulled over everything that Julia had said. 'Yes, that sounds like a plan. I'll have a chat with Isla.'

'A change does us good but I'll share with you now that that room up there can't be rented out on its own. It comes with the job because there's no separate entrance – the only way to access it is through the Boathouse. We also don't charge for the room because anyone who is up there is doing us a favour; we have someone on the premises and that type of security gives us piece of mind. We would only charge for the bills but as you've gotten us out of a hole for the next few weeks, we'll take care of those for now. Maybe,' Julia pointed towards the attic room, 'it's something to think about as a long-term option?' She touched Bea's arm and gave her a knowing look.

'Are you saying you wouldn't mind if I stayed longer?' Perched on the stool behind the counter, Bea sipped her tea.

'I'm saying I've got a good vibe about you and my gut feelings have never let me down in the past. If needs be, use this place as a stop-gap. I know you're capable of a lot more than working here, but it may help you get back on your feet and give you some breathing space.'

Bea listened carefully to every word that Julia was saying.

'Heartcross is a thriving tourist destination – and Flynn also owns Starcross Manor and The Lakehouse. If you work hard – and I've seen it happen before – he could possibly give you the chance to transfer to a more challenging role in one of those establishments. I know for a fact he's trying to bring in in-house wedding planners and dress designers to Starcross Manor as the wedding side of the hotel is beginning to grow. There's always something going on. Anyway, it's food for thought, and I'm always here if you want a chat.'

'Thank you. This certainly is food for thought. Is everyone this kind in Heartcross?'

'You'd better believe it.' Julia gave her a warm smile and pointed to the queue that was forming in front of her.

Bea placed her mug down and greeted the next customer, her mind turning over the information that Julia had just shared. Once all the customers were served, she stood outside The Little Blue Boathouse and stared out over the water. Bea knew there was only one thing possibly stopping her from moving here: Emmie.

In theory, it was great to be by family, but Julia had been right. How much quality time did she actually spend with her sister? If Bea stayed, maybe Emmie would make the effort and bring the children to visit.

Could she really move away from everything she knew and the town where she grew up? This seemed like the ideal opportunity to give it a go. What was the worst that could happen if it didn't work out in Heartcross? It was simple: she would rethink her plans and move back home if necessary.

Coming to a decision, she logged on to the computer and accessed her email account. Sitting in her inbox was her shift rota for when she returned to work. She sighed, the sight of it confirming she had no enthusiasm whatsoever for returning to the same routine. She decided the only mature way to make a decision was to flip a coin, and took one from the till. 'Tails, I resign. Heads, I stay at the supermarket.'

Squeezing her eyes shut, she threw up the coin and heard it bounce back on the counter. Slowly taking a peep, she saw tails staring back at her.

Before she could question her decision, Bea began to type her resignation, along with a lovely message to her boss explaining that her personal life had taken a nosedive. She was laying it on thick, hoping her boss would be sympathetic towards her situation and relieve her of working out her notice, because the last thing she wanted to do was live in a house with Carl and work any more shifts in the supermarket.

After she'd read over the letter, Bea's finger hovered over *send*. Before she could change her mind, she pressed the key. Hearing the whoosh of the email disappearing, she knew there was no going back. All she needed to do now was pluck up the courage to tell Emmie she wasn't returning home as soon as everyone thought.

Hearing the door open behind her, Bea turned and

beamed at Julia. 'I've only gone and done it! I've resigned. It's not like me to be so impulsive...'

'Wow! How do you feel?'

'Mixed emotions. Relieved and confused. Glad to be leaving that place behind. A fresh start is what I need ... but am I running away? Everyone will think I've lost the plot but I'm excited about what will happen from here.'

'Sometimes we worry way too much about what others think. We have to look after ourselves and put our own well-being first. I know for a fact that so long as you stay in Heartcross everyone will welcome you with open arms. My gut feeling is telling me you've made the right decision.'

'And mine is too. Thank you for giving me the chance to take some time and get myself sorted.'

'You're very welcome. Now, I think there's only one thing for it. We have to pinch one of Wilbur's biscuits to celebrate. I'll fetch the tin!'

Even though Bea was feeling apprehensive about how her sister would react, deep down she knew she'd made the right decision. This was the push she needed to make changes in her life.

'Are there any chocolate ones?' she shouted after Julia.

With the decision made and the resignation sent, this day was already a success. And in a few hours' time, things could only get better, because Hemingway and Fernsby were investigating their first case and she would be spending the evening with Nolan. Looking out of the doorway, she noticed a woman admiring the painting of the girl with the wedding ring. Instantly, that twinge of anxiousness was back in the pit of her stomach. The woman popped her head through the door.

'Isn't she beautiful!' she said, holding the painting up towards Bea.

'Very,' replied Bea, watching the woman place the painting back in the box. As soon as the woman walked away, Bea went and picked it up. If the right moment came up tonight, she was going to ask Nolan who she was.

Chapter Eleven

B ea could not believe how swimmingly her day had gone. She had enjoyed every second of working at The Little Blue Boathouse. The afternoon had been as busy as the morning and after Julia had shown her how to cash up and to clean down the boats, life jackets and hired wetsuits, they locked up and walked back along the river path towards the B&B.

'The takings are up and excursions are booking up in advance. Flynn and Roman will be chuffed.'

'That's good to hear,' replied Bea, taking a swift glance over towards The Hemingway as they turned the corner, but there was no sign of Nolan.

She knew that it wouldn't take long to pack up her belongings at the B&B. There was a parking space for her car at the back of the Boathouse, and Julia had given her directions to a dirt track that would provide access past The Old Bakehouse and the Clover Cottage Estate. There was something appealing about the thought of waking up to the sound of the river and the gulls circling above. Within the next hour, Bea was setting up home in the attic room.

Julia had kindly given her some plates, cutlery, mugs, a couple of pans, towels and the most beautiful shabby-chic floral cushions that Bea had ever seen, which were now propped up in the middle of the bed. Bea had kicked off her shoes, hung up her clothes and pushed her suitcase under the bed. Also included with Julia's kindness was a box of essentials packed with tea, coffee, milk and cereal for breakfast.

Now lying on her bed and contemplating whether to give Emmie a quick ring, Bea felt her eyes closing and soon dozed off. She was only asleep a matter of minutes, though, as a loud bell sounded and she bolted upright. There it was again. She looked all around her room and couldn't work out what the hell it was. Poking her head down through the hatch she listened again and prayed it wasn't some sort of intruder alarm. She shouted, 'Is there anyone there?' but thankfully was met with silence.

Then she heard a short burst of tapping on the window. What the heck was that? Maybe a gull had flown into it. Then she heard a voice she recognised.

'Bea, Bea, wherefore art thou, Bea?'

Smiling, she threw open the window and took in the sight of Nolan grinning up at her.

'I didn't know you were a fan of Shakespeare.'

'Huge fan,' he replied, holding up a white carrier bag. 'I've brought you chips from the fish and chip van. But don't worry, if you don't want them, I'm sure the gulls will be happy for another meal.' He looked over to the flock of gulls scavenging in the nearby bin.

'Do not feed my chips to the gulls!'

'You'd better come and get them then. I already rang the bell but there was no answer.'

'You wait there, I'm coming down!'

Quickly slipping on her trainers and grabbing a jacket, Bea slid down the ladder as fast as a fireman down his pole and locked up The Little Blue Boathouse behind her.

Nolan had pulled his rowing boat right up to the entrance and chained it to the rack and was now sitting on a huge rock, balancing a tray of chips smothered in curry sauce. 'Here you go. I wasn't sure what you liked, so I got you the same as me – chips with extra salt and vinegar.'

'Exactly the way I like it. Thank you.'

'Shall we head to the cemetery?'

'Ooo, chips and graveyards, you do know how to give a girl a good time.'

'You better believe it. Everyone's dying to go there, you know.'

Bea groaned and rolled her eyes, taking the tray of chips off Nolan. 'I actually feel like I'm on holiday. Chips, the water, fantastic scenery … and the company isn't bad too.'

'I was just thinking the same, but I'll warn you now, where we're going, the people aren't that talkative.' He gave her a lopsided grin as he jumped down from the rock and began to take the path towards the bridge that would lead them to the bottom of Love Heart Lane.

Bea shook her head and pointed in the opposite direction. 'That dirt track leads to the far end of the village and Primrose Park. The church isn't far from there.'

'Perfect, let's walk that way then.'

Stabbing a hot chip with the small wooden fork provided, Bea blew on it and began to eat as she followed Nolan.

'It'll be your turn to wine and dine me tomorrow.'

'I don't see any wine,' replied Bea.

'Two bottles of beer in my rucksack.'

Turning left on to the dirt track, Nolan stopped and pointed over to Bea's car where it was parked at the back of The Little Blue Boathouse. 'You drive a battered old turquoise Fiesta with psychedelic flowers painted all over it?'

'Been with me since I was seventeen, and I'm not giving her up any day soon.'

'I'm finding out more about you every second we spend together. It does look like it's seen better days though.'

'She's never let me down though, unlike some I know.'

Nolan grinned across at her. 'You do make me smile. Try not to dwell on the past. It's the here and now that's the most important – and here and now we have chips. I have to say these are the best I've tasted in a while.'

Bea couldn't agree more. The wind in her hair, the best chips and curry sauce, and walking at the side of a handsome man … could life get any better than this?

'Guess what I did today?' she said excitedly as they headed up the steep path.

'Are we talking about any particular time of the day?' He gave her a mischievous grin.

'After lunchtime, which I have to say was one of my most memorable lunchtimes in a very long time—'

'Glad to hear it,' Nolan interrupted.

'I resigned.'

Nolan stopped in his tracks. 'You've resigned on day one?'

'Not from the Boathouse. In fact, I successfully passed my trial. No, I resigned from my job at the supermarket. All I need to do now is pluck up the courage to tell my sister that I've done so and will be extending my holiday here in Heartcross.'

'I'm impressed. It's a powerful moment when you become brave enough to change the life you're leading. You've taken the first step of moving away from the past. I admire you for that. It's not easy.'

His words took Bea by surprise, and she noticed that Nolan's voice had faltered a little. Glancing at him, she suddenly wondered whether he was running from his own past. That would certainly make sense, given the way he never settled in one place.

'Some of your carefree attitude must have rubbed off on me,' she said, still watching him closely.

'It's the best way to be.'

'Do you ever make plans for the future?' She was intrigued to discover more about the real Nolan.

'Not anymore.'

'But you did once?' probed Bea.

'You think your future is one thing and then the next thing you know, it's something else entirely. The only day I think about is the one I'm in.'

Nolan didn't elaborate and Bea was conscious that his gaze was fixed on the path ahead, and he was refusing to look in her direction.

'Maybe you could stay longer too?' she said hopefully, stabbing another chip.

'Nah, there's a whole world out there to explore. But in the meantime, Hemingway and Fernsby need to crack the case of "Who is Patsy G?" I do think you did the right thing, deciding to stay. This place will suit you.'

'And why wouldn't it suit you?'

'It will for a few weeks but then it will be time for me to sail on to the next wonderful place.'

Any romantic notion Bea might have had that he would stay if she did was quickly starting to fizzle. The second she'd set eyes on him she'd been captivated by his smile and sparkling eyes. The immediate connection had taken her completely by surprise, but judging by the way he spoke about moving on to the next destination he must not feel the same.

Had she actually made the right decision, or had she been carried away on day one of a working holiday simply because it was a change from the norm?

Bea forced a brightness into her voice that she wasn't feeling. 'Well, until you sail off into the sunset you're stuck with me.' She nudged his elbow.

'I think I can put up with that,' he replied, tossing their

empty chip trays in a bin as they passed it. There were numerous people out enjoying the summer evening – kids on bikes and families walking dogs – and Heartcross Mountain stood in the distance, with the fells rising each side. It was a stunning scene to witness.

They climbed over a stile and the mossy rocks underfoot gave way to a meandering trail passing through purple heather and bracken. The slight breeze feathering through the wild grass carried the sound of crickets and grasshoppers whirring.

Bea took in the view as they walked over a small wooden bridge and made their way up the crest of the hill towards the church. The weathered wrought iron gates were an impressive entrance to the graveyard, and the gardens within were well maintained, with paths weaving between the graves.

'What's the plan?' she asked, spreading her arms wide. 'It's a big area to cover.'

'We split up and meet in the middle. I'll go to the back and you start here. If we walk up and down horizontally, we should cover each grave.'

'And we are looking for a Patsy, preferably with her surname beginning with G.'

'See, you're showing signs of being a good detective,' he teased, before following the path towards the back of the churchyard.

Bea began to walk up and down and immediately noticed that some graves were immaculately looked after whilst others were overgrown, making it difficult to read the names. It took a little under an hour to meet in the middle. Neither of them had spotted a grave with the name Patsy.

'Maybe it's worth asking the vicar. Surely there will be records?' suggested Bea.

'Yes, but all we have is a first name, an initial for the surname and no date of birth. He might not be able to find her.' Nolan's tone was wreathed with disappointment.

'Why are you sounding so defeatist? Surely this is a good thing?'

'How do you make that out?'

'She's not dead, you wally!'

Nolan laughed. 'I hadn't actually thought of that.'

'Call yourself a detective?' She rolled her eyes.

'But how do we know she even stayed in this area? It could be that she's buried somewhere else.'

'We don't know for sure, but I've got a gut feeling she's here in the Heartcross area. And on average, women live longer than men so there is a good chance she is still alive – and don't forget we have the address from the logbook.'

'I've forgotten to bring that with me.'

'It's a good job I haven't then.' Bea took out a crumpled piece of paper from her pocket, on which she'd jotted down the address. 'If we walk that way, past The Old Bakehouse, and turn left onto the main high street, it's going to take us about forty minutes to get there. Alternatively, we can jump on the river taxi? They run all the way until midnight and I might even be able to get us a discount.'

'Now you're talking.'

Within twenty minutes they were walking down towards the jetty and joining the queue for the river taxi. Roman welcomed everyone on board and when he got to Bea and Nolan, he pulled the rope across behind them. 'Made it by the skin of your teeth. The boat is full. You're the last two.'

'Roman, can I introduce you to Nolan?'

'You can.' Roman extended his hand. 'I'm Roman. Are you—'

Bea sensed that he was going to say 'together' and she quickly interjected, 'Nolan owns The Hemingway.'

'I was wondering who that wonderful boat belonged to. It's a beauty!' Roman shook Nolan's hand. 'If you're ever doing tours, I'd love to have a look.'

'Pop over and take a look anytime.'

'I'll do just that. I've admired it from afar since you arrived. Are you sticking around for the River Festival?'

Nolan nodded. 'That's the plan, leaving the morning after.'

'By my reckoning, it's going to be very busy this year with the glorious weather – it brings everyone out in their droves. I mean, look at this boat … every time, full to the brim. Most are off to The Lake House restaurant hoping for a spot on the roof terrace. Make sure you don't leave Heartcross without giving it a visit. People travel from far and wide to eat there.'

'And it's usually full of celebrities too.' Bea had been reading up on it. It had been very famous decades ago and was frequented not only by the rich and famous but also by royalty. 'How long has Flynn owned the restaurant?' asked Bea, wondering whether he would be a good person to chat to about Patsy.

'Only for the last five years. There's a couple of seats next to me, do you fancy a ride up front?'

'Yes please!' accepted Bea, full of enthusiasm.

'This way.'

They both followed Roman to the front of the boat and Bea asked, 'Do you know who the most knowledgeable person in the village is?'

'Is that code for the nosiest?'

'Possibly,' admitted Bea, laughing.

'There's Hamish, who owns the village shop, which is opposite the pub. His mum Dolores lives above the shop in the flat – she must be near a century old and would certainly know a thing or two.'

'Dolores Henderson, the world-famous singer?' asked Bea.

'The very one. Or there's Rona at the teashop; her mum Bonnie owned the shop before her and they've been in the village all their lives. Bonnie has passed away now but I'm sure Rona is full of information. There's also Aggie, Fergus's mum, he works up at Foxglove Farm with Drew… Oh, but the best person has got to be Martha. What Martha doesn't know isn't worth knowing.'

Why hadn't Bea thought of that?

'Why do you ask?'

Bea looked towards Nolan. It wasn't her story to tell and maybe Nolan didn't want everyone knowing his business.

'You both look very cloak-and-dagger,' observed Roman.

'I'm trying to track down my grandfather's...' Nolan thought for a second. 'I'm not even sure what to call her. My grandfather's girlfriend for the summer, many moons ago.'

'This sounds intriguing,' said Roman, repositioning his cap on his head. 'Was it his childhood sweetheart?'

'I think it was someone my grandfather never got over. After he passed, I found a letter addressed to her – it just says "Patsy", no surname, but possibly begins with the letter G. I'm trying to trace whether she's still alive. I'm hoping so as I'd really like the letter to be delivered.'

'And wouldn't that be truly romantic. I would check with Martha, Rona and Aggie. I'm sure if anyone knows anything about anyone, they will be the best ones to ask. And where are you off to now?'

'We've discovered an old address for her so we're headed to Glensheil to see if that leads us anywhere.'

'Do let me know!' Roman gestured to the seats just behind the wheel. 'Thankfully the waters aren't choppy today but the weather is going to change at the end of the week for a couple of days. You'll find that business will slow right down at The Little Blue Boathouse,' he said to Bea as she and Nolan took their seats. 'Shall I drop you over at the lighthouse round the corner? Are you wanting the centre of town?'

'I've already Google Mapped it. It's not far from a

market area, looks like quite near the centre,' confirmed Bea, leaning in towards Nolan. 'Who's making the better detective now? Thinking ahead I was.' She gave him a knowing look, leaving Nolan looking bemused.

Roman started the engine and Bea and Nolan sat back and watched the view sail past. No wonder Nolan liked living on The Hemingway; everything looked picture perfect from the water. With sweeping bays and sand dunes, gulls hovering over the white cliffs, there was something therapeutic about watching the waves as the boat glided through the water.

'This part sometimes gets a little choppy,' confided Roman, just as Bea was jolted to the right, her hand landing directly on Nolan's thigh.

'Are you okay? You've gone a little pale,' he observed.

'Absolutely fine,' she replied, not daring to admit she suddenly felt queasy. As her stomach churned some more, she tried to concentrate on the breeze whipping through her hair.

'Take deep breaths and focus on the horizon line,' whispered Nolan. 'It always helps.'

Bea stared at the sterling blue river lapping against the rocky shoreline of colourful stones.

'Here we go, the first stop, the lighthouse.' Roman pulled on a lever that slowed the boat and guided it towards the wooden jetty, where it bobbed in the water until he turned off the engine. He jumped onto the dock and tied up the boat securely before pulling the gangplank forward. 'Good luck with your quest,' he said as Bea and Nolan stepped off the boat.

'We'll let you know how it goes!' replied Bea.

As soon as she was back on solid ground, Bea began to feel better. She snagged a glance at Nolan, who grinned straight at her.

'Why are you looking at me like that?'

'Because I've never seen anyone turn green so quickly before. Thank God you're selling boat trips because I don't think you would last long sailing the boats.'

'Okay, busted. I honestly thought there was a possibility that I would see chips and curry sauce for the second time in less than an hour.'

'Ew! Too much information.'

The short walk into the town of Glensheil was busy and they had to weave their way through pedestrians as they headed towards the high street. Bea checked Google Maps and pointed straight in front of them. 'This way.'

The side streets were full of fancy bistros and cocktail bars and the shops were still open, which Bea assumed was because it was a tourist town and they opened all hours. The tree-lined pavements looked picturesque in the evening sunshine and the hanging baskets burst with colour where they swayed from the lampposts in the light breeze.

'We're looking for Clyde Square, which, according to

this...' Bea looked up at the street sign then back towards her phone '... is past Claret Row, which is this way.'

They navigated the streets and turned down an alley, stepping over beer cans and crumpled litter strewn all over the ground. They walked past graffitied brick walls, grimy barred windows and doorways, and heard the clink of bottles slamming in bins. Bea was very grateful Nolan was by her side.

'This doesn't have a good vibe to me.' As she looked at the windows above, she realised they were being watched. 'I feel like I'm trespassing.'

'I have to say, I quite agree.' Nolan's voice was low and they stopped walking as a voice shouted down to them.

'Oi, you two. Want do you want?' The voice was far from friendly.

Bea could feel herself slightly trembling and was relieved when Nolan slipped his hand into hers.

'We're looking for Clyde Square.' Thankfully, Nolan's voice was steady.

'Next street along,' the voice shouted back.

'Thank you,' replied Nolan, taking the lead and guiding Bea through the alley, keeping her closely by his side.

They could feel eyes watching them everywhere. Curtains twitched and people began to open their doors and stand on their steps with their arms crossed. Bea felt like she was in the middle of a scary movie.

'This doesn't look as bad,' reassured Nolan as they turned the next corner, but Bea continued to grip his hand tightly. 'What number are we looking for?'

'Flat 4A,' replied Bea, double-checking the crumpled bit of paper. 'It must be that one up there. What's the plan? Are we going to knock? I'm not sure it's the right thing to do. I kind of get the feeling the only people who knock on these doors are bailiffs.'

'I think that may be a little overdramatic.' He gave her a comforting smile but they both jerked when they heard a dog thud against an iron gate and burst into aggressive barks.

'I'm really not liking this.'

The wooden screech of an old window being forced open above made them both look upwards. An old woman leaned out of the window and flicked ash from her cigarette.

'Are you lost? Not seen you around these parts before.'

Feeling brave, Bea shouted up, 'We're looking for flat 4A.'

'Wait there.'

They heard the sound of a heavy metal lock being unbolted and then the door opened and the old woman was standing in front of them.

'What do you want? Are you police? Because if you are—'

'No, we aren't police or anyone bad.' Bea noticed the woman was gaunt, with a few teeth missing, and those that weren't were rotten.

She dragged on her fag. 'Then what do you want?' She narrowed her eyes, watching them closely.

'It's a long shot but we're looking for a woman who lived in flat 4A over sixty years ago, Patsy G?'

'Never heard of her. And you expected her to be here after all this time? It's bad enough living here for six months, never mind sixty years.' The woman cackled. 'Whoever Patsy G is, she had a lucky escape … unless she was pimped out or possibly shot. And now I suggest you with your posh class get out of here as soon as possible.'

Bea didn't need to be told twice. She tugged at Nolan's hand. 'Thank you for your time,' she said walking away as fast as she could.

Five streets away, life was a different story. People were suited and booted, standing outside a wine bar drinking champagne. Posh cars lined the streets and the smell of expensive perfume had replaced the rancid odour of urine.

Bea blew out a long, shuddering breath. 'I'm not judging the people that live in that part of town, and I'm aware sometimes circumstances put you in situations that make your life spiral out of control, but I've not felt that scared for quite some time.'

'I know exactly what you mean, but seeing the place where Patsy once lived has made me think of a reason why she and my grandfather couldn't be together. Let's head back down to the river and I can tell you my theory.'

'So why do you think they couldn't be together?' Bea asked as they walked, liking the fact that Nolan was still holding her hand as they walked along the street.

'Back then there were different social rules and different classes couldn't mix. In an ideal world, we wouldn't have ever had any class distinctions and everyone would have the same access to education and jobs, but that's never been the case.' Nolan stopped in the middle of the payment and gestured to the wine bar behind them. 'Do you think people in Clyde Square mix in the same social circles as the suited and booted?'

Bea looked at the long line of posh cars parked up the street and the people frequenting the tables outside the wine bar, all of whom were wearing designer clothes and drinking what looked like champagne. 'No, I don't suppose they do.'

'Exactly. People unconsciously seek a similar dynamic to what they're used to. It's natural to want a partner that fits in with your social circle or family because otherwise there may be a clash over lifestyles. There's also always the fear of being judged or even rejected.'

'Interesting. Why do you think they were of different classes?' asked Bea, intrigued by the theory.

'Because I can't see Clyde Square ever having been an affluent area, can you?'

Bea shook her head. 'Maybe not.'

'And my grandfather didn't have to worry about money. Even though you may look at The Hemingway and think it's not worth much, that was my grandfather's decoy.'

'What do you mean by decoy?' asked Bea.

'My grandfather owned all kinds of planes, trains and automobiles. I'm not exaggerating. He was a multi-millionaire.'

'Woah! I wasn't expecting that. Do you think Patsy knew?'

'From what I know, that wasn't information he bandied about. He kept his cards very close to his chest because he felt he had to be wary of anyone suddenly wanting to become his friend. If they knew about his money, he thought they'd want him for what they might get, not for who he was.'

'It must be awful living like that, even if you have the benefits that come with having money.'

'That's why he chose to travel the waterways in The Hemingway. He discovered that people accepted him for himself if it appeared he didn't have anything. He was never a show-off. He made his fortune by accident but still worked hard all his life. He didn't take anything for granted and donated a lot of money to charity.'

'Sounds like a very kind man, but surely if he was keen on Patsy he would have told her. They could have worked it out...'

'They were both really young – my grandfather was in his very early twenties – and from what he told me, I believe Patsy was in her late teens.'

'Why can't life be simple?'

'Because then it would be boring,' replied Nolan, crossing over the road towards the jetty and leading her towards the river taxi.

Roman tilted his cap as they headed towards them. 'And? Did you discover anything?' he asked, as they climbed on board.

Nolan shook his head. 'Unfortunately not.'

This time they enjoyed the views from the back of the boat and it wasn't long before they arrived back at The Little Blue Boathouse.

'It's a lovely night. I've got a bottle of wine chilling in the fridge if you fancy a drink. Unless you've got other plans?' asked Bea.

'No plans whatsoever.'

Standing at the end of the jetty, Bea smiled. That was what she'd hoped he would say. 'What's the plan now regarding Patsy?'

'I think I'll ask around and then after that … I'm not really sure. If I can't trace her, the letter will never be read.'

Bea nodded and pointed to a wrought iron table and chairs by the edge of the riverbank. 'Shall we sit there? I'll nip in and get the wine and two glasses.'

'Yes, we can watch the boats. Before you go, I've brought you this.' Nolan walked over to his rowing boat where it was chained up outside The Little Blue Boathouse. He brought out the canvas that he'd painted of Bea at Castaway Bay, along with the painting of the Boathouse. 'A memento of our time together. Something to remember me by.'

As soon as she heard those words, she felt a tiny pang in her heart. She didn't want Nolan disappearing anytime soon. He'd made such an impact on her life in such a small space of time. She hadn't ever been one for believing in love at first sight but there was something about this man that she couldn't shake off, and she wanted to spend as much time with him as possible.

She felt panic. 'You wouldn't ever sail off without saying good bye, would you?' She didn't want to open her curtains one morning to find The Hemingway and Nolan gone.

'Of course I'll say goodbye.' He smiled, handing over the paintings.

'You'll be pleased to know you made over two hundred pounds today. Your paintings sparked a lot of interest.' Bea looked down at the painting of herself and immediately thought of the girl in the other painting. Who exactly was she, and what was she to Nolan?

'That's brilliant news. I've already researched where I'm off to next and I'll get some paintings done from the Google images before I arrive so they're ready to sell.'

'Is that what you did for Heartcross?'

Nolan nodded.

'And do you make memories with lots of girls in different bays and paint them too?'

Nolan looked puzzled by the question. 'Not usually. Why do you ask that?'

'Because for a tiny moment when we were at Castaway Bay, I thought I was special and that's why you chose to paint me.'

By the look on Nolan's face, he had no idea where this conversation was heading and Bea was already kicking herself for showing her insecurities. She had no reason to feel jealous – she knew the score between them – but she couldn't help the way she was feeling.

'It was a day I'll never forget.' Nolan looked directly at her. 'That day will always be special to me.'

Bea now wished she hadn't let her thoughts run away with themselves. But she knew the more time she spent in Nolan's company, the more she wouldn't want to say goodbye to him.

'Is something wrong? I'm sensing you may be upset but I'm not sure why,' he said tentatively.

'That painting of a girl that was amongst your other paintings on display today. Was it someone you met here before me?' Bea knew there was a possibility she wasn't going to like the answer.

'I've not met anyone here.'

Bea's head was full of muddled thoughts. All she wanted to know was who it was.

'Then who is she, that beautiful girl wearing a wedding ring?'

Suddenly, Nolan looked stricken. 'Where is the painting?'

'Inside the Boathouse, if it hasn't been sold.'

'Can I get it back, please? It shouldn't be in there.' His voice was earnest. 'It's not for sale and will never be for sale.'

The atmosphere had suddenly dropped to freezing and Bea was beginning to wish she hadn't said anything.

'Of course, is everything okay?' she asked, already knowing the answer.

'Just … the painting, please, Bea.'

She looked over her shoulder as she led him towards the Boathouse door. 'Was she someone like me?'

'And what does that mean?'

'Someone you had a bit of fun with on your travels?'

'Why would you even ask such a question?' Nolan's tone had suddenly changed.

'I suppose because my gut is telling me there's something not quite right here.'

Nolan didn't answer.

Bea unlocked the door to The Little Blue Boathouse and pointed Nolan in the direction of the stored paintings.

'Do you know what I think?'

'Enlighten me,' Nolan said as he began to search through the paintings.

'I think you're running away from something, that's why you travel around so much. It's not normal not to want to put down roots.'

Nolan turned and faced her. There was a glimmer of anger in his eyes. 'And who dictates what normal is? Who says it's normal to put down roots? Society makes you believe the only way you can be happy is by meeting someone, being in a couple, getting married, buying a house, having children… It doesn't mean you're an outcast if you don't follow everyone else that picks that path. My life is *my* life and my time is precious and it's up to me how I choose to spend it. You have no clue about who I am or my life so who are you to judge me? Do you know what I think?'

'Enlighten me,' replied Bea, mirroring his words.

'I think you probably shouldn't think.'

Bea raised an eyebrow and pointed towards the painting. 'Does she have a name?'

Nolan didn't answer.

'Oh my God. You are married, aren't you? Is this your wife?' Bea felt herself trembling as her thoughts tumbled over each other. 'You've painted her, she's wearing a ring and she's not on this trip with you because...' Bea wound her hand in a circle, encouraging Nolan to explain but he remained silent.

Bea continued. 'She's probably stayed at home due to work commitments, and you've travelled back to look for Patsy and bumped into me and thought you'd take your chance and have a little fun for a few weeks and when you sail back home, no one will ever be the wiser. Is that it? I thought you were different but you're just the same as all the others.'

Nolan shook his head and began to walk towards the door.

'Have you not got anything to say?'

The silence hung heavy in the air.

Bea threw up her hands. 'You can't even tell me I'm wrong.'

'I owe no one any explanations – and I get the impression it doesn't matter what I say because you've already lumped me in the same box as your ex.'

Bea exhaled and squeezed her eyes shut as her heart

sank to a new depth. 'And here was me thinking you were different.'

He walked through the door and out of her life. He didn't look back.

The second she'd set eyes on Nolan, Bea knew the chemistry between them was off the scale. Now she was mad with herself for letting her emotions get the better of her. He'd made her feel like she'd been kicked to the kerb and the day at Castaway Bay meant nothing.

Watching him leave, she gave a slow, disbelieving shake of the head. She felt humiliated and betrayed ... which was daft really, as Nolan had never promised anything. No, the way she was reacting was down to her own insecurities, which hadn't been helped by Carl's deceit.

The lust and excitement of the time they had spent together had now turned into shame and embarrassment. Feeling stupid, she shut the door behind him and blinked back the tears. She'd come here to sort out her life and now she felt like she was in a bigger mess than when she arrived.

Taking a deep breath, she climbed the ladder to the attic room. She'd never intended the night to turn out this way and now she was beginning to question her judgement. Emotion poured through her body, and frustrated tears ran down her cheeks.

'Urghh,' she gasped, slumping in the armchair. Her own pangs of self-doubt had just sabotaged their time together, and she'd made a mountain out of a molehill. Nolan had every right to walk away and not give an explanation.

Whoever it was in that painting was his business and he didn't have to explain himself to her.

Wanting to put this right, she opened the window. Nolan was rowing across the river towards The Hemingway, so she cupped her hands around her mouth and shouted at him with all her might to come back. But her words were lost in the wind and the sounds of the gulls circling above.

He didn't look back.

Her mood plummeted to an all-time low.

Chapter Twelve

B ea was exhausted the next morning after tossing and turning all night thinking of Nolan. Slipping out of bed and pulling on her faithful baggy sweatshirt, she made herself a mug of tea before pulling back the curtains, hoping to watch the beautiful sunrise across the River Heart from the attic window. With her hands cupped around a mug, she felt glum about how things had panned out last night and wished she could turn back time. The more she thought about how she'd reacted, the more she was embarrassed by her behaviour. The look on Nolan's face as he'd walked away was one of despair and sadness.

Yes, Carl had betrayed her trust, but she needed to remember that there were good men out there, and, though she might be battling her own demons, she shouldn't lose her ability to conduct herself with dignity. What had happened last night was the result of her trying to bypass the grieving process and the emotions that had brought her here in the first place. Attempting to be upbeat and pretending that life was hunky-dory clearly wasn't working. Pulling her knees up to her chest, Bea hugged them tight and rested her head on top of them. For a moment she let the tears fall, before finishing her tea and placing the empty mug in the sink.

As she turned back around, she looked at the two paintings propped up at the side of the desk. She picked up the painting of The Little Blue Boathouse and looked at the inscription on the back. Nolan had added some more words, which made the tears fall again.

Hemingway & Fernsby. The only way to solve the case is together.

Bea felt at rock bottom and, wiping the tears away with the sleeve of her jumper, she sat back down in the armchair and looked out across the water. It was going to be the last sunny day for a couple of days, as according to the weather forecast the rain was on its way. There was a storm brewing and Bea knew that meant it would be a quiet time for the Boathouse because the river wasn't an enjoyable place to be in torrential rain.

A couple of new boats had arrived and were anchored near the riverbank. Her eyes skimmed over the water but didn't find the one boat she was looking for. Feeling panicky, Bea sat up straight and moved to the edge of her seat. Bringing her hands up to the seahorse necklace around her neck, she clutched it tightly.

'No, please no.'

The Hemingway was gone. And there it was again, that

horrible feeling in the pit of her stomach that she'd never wanted to feel again. He hadn't even said goodbye like he'd promised. She slumped back in the chair and realised that last night was the last time she would see Nolan. She was devastated. He'd disappeared out of her life as quickly as he'd appeared and now there was nothing she could do about it.

Hearing her phone ping, she quickly looked at the screen. It was a text from Emmie.

If you wake up before 7 give me a ring, it would be lovely to hear your voice.

'Hi, it's me.' The second she spoke, Bea was tearful.

'There she is! How are you?' Emmie was overly chirpy for this time in the morning.

Bea swallowed. It took Emmie a second to realise that Bea was upset.

'Are you okay? Talk to me. I knew you were putting on a brave face.'

Bea was upset, but for reasons that Emmie could never have imagined.

'Look, he wants you back, if that helps.'

It didn't help. Carl had hardly crossed her mind. 'I'm not upset about him in the slightest.'

There was a short silence at the end of the phone. 'Then why are you upset?'

'I think I've done something stupid.'

'Then you'd better tell me all.'

Bea shared the story of her whirlwind romance and their

day at Castaway Bay. She wasn't entirely sure whether she felt better for getting it off her chest or not.

She was met by silence on the other end of the phone.

'Say something,' urged Bea.

'I'm completely lost for words. This isn't like you. He's not the man for you. It's a rebound thing and this won't make you feel any better. You aren't thinking straight. I think what's best for you—'

Bea felt a little defensive and cut in. 'Maybe it is like me.' She didn't want to hear what was best for her, she just wanted someone to listen with no judgement. 'And there's something else.'

'Go on,' said Emmie.

'I've resigned from the supermarket and am staying on at The Little Blue Boathouse for a while longer.'

'And how long is a while longer?'

'I'm not sure – and please don't go telling me what you think is best for me because coming back home right at this moment is not what is best for me.'

Emmie blew out a breath and, much to Bea's relief, didn't challenge her. 'I don't know what to say.'

'That's a first,' joked Bea, trying to lighten the mood.

Thankfully, Emmie didn't take offence but kept the mood light. 'I know you find me infuriating at times but I am still your sister and I do want what's best for you. Please don't be lonely or upset all by yourself. You can ring me any time. Promise me that.'

'I will.'

Feeling a little better, Bea hung up the call. Maybe it was

the best thing that Nolan had gone. He was going to go at some point anyway and this meant that she wouldn't get more attached to him than she already was. The only things she regretted were not apologising and missing the chance to say goodbye. She was surprised he hadn't stayed to solve the mystery of Patsy but he must have had his reasons for deciding to give up on his search.

After pulling a brush through her hair and cleaning her teeth, she got changed and slipped her feet into her trainers before looking at her reflection in the mirror. The seahorse necklace kept catching the light of the sun through the window. She turned it over in her hand.

'Strength and courage,' she murmured. She knew the only thing she could do was pick herself up and keep moving forward. 'Don't dwell on Nolan, just enjoy the fact that it was nice while it lasted,' she said to herself as she fastened the clasp of the necklace around her neck. She smiled at her reflection in the mirror as she thought back to the afternoon at Castaway Bay. She'd not felt so carefree in a long time. It was a day of happiness. The most beautiful things in life were memories, feelings in the moment and smiles and laughter, and that day had had all of those. She wanted more of those moments in her life. The thing that Nolan had taught her in so short a time was: if you're not happy then make a change – and that's exactly what she was doing.

Climbing down the ladder, she stepped into The Little Blue Boathouse and opened the hatch before unlocking the door. Julia breezed in with a smile on her face and placed a sausage sandwich in Bea's hand. 'Leftover from breakfast at the B&B. I thought you might like it.'

'Just the ticket, thank you.'

'Did you have a good night last night?'

For a moment, Bea wondered if Julia knew that she'd spent the evening with Nolan.

'I know sometimes it's hard to sleep in a new place and those gulls can be noisy,' continued Julia.

'Out like a light and up with the gulls,' replied Bea, knowing that was a little white lie. Unwrapping the sandwich and taking a bite, she sighed in appreciation. 'This is good.'

'There's nothing better than waking up to the sound of the water rushing.' Julia looked out towards the river. 'It's going to be busy today, but with the couple of days of rain we're due for, our takings will be down, so try and encourage people to book trips towards the end of the week.'

'Will do,' Bea said, observing the tourists that were already walking down the river path towards the Boathouse. She wouldn't mind being run off her feet today; it would help her not to dwell too much on Nolan.

'I can't stay today – lots of changeover guests at the B&B – so I just wanted to check if you're okay to manage this place by yourself?'

'Of course, and I have your number if anything crops up.'

'I knew I could rely on you.' Julia gave her a warm smile. 'Make sure you shut up shop for an hour at lunchtime.'

'Is Bonnie's Teashop the best place to grab something to eat?'

'Either there or The Old Bakehouse with the chocolate shop next door.'

'That sounds like a Friday treat to me,' replied Bea.

With Julia gone, Bea was in charge of the shop and she quite liked it. After serving the first influx of customers, who were now messing about on the river on paddleboards and in rowing boats, Bea was dragging the 'open for business' sign outside when she spotted Nolan's paintings that he'd left behind. Wondering what to do with them, she decided to display them outside, just like the day before. It wasn't as though she'd been told any different, and she had a tiny hope that he would return to collect his money. The terrible thought of never seeing him again was playing on her mind.

The morning passed quickly and it was soon lunchtime. After locking up The Little Blue Boathouse, Bea slung her bag over her shoulder and ambled towards Bonnie's Teashop.

Everyone she walked past was friendly, happy to pass the time of day. Bea couldn't believe the difference between the town she'd come from and village life. She was used to people not even making eye contact as they walked past. Here, people were standing around having actual conversations and she didn't see one person with a mobile phone in their hand or to their ear. Soon she was passing the whitewashed terraces of Love Heart Lane. Heartcross Mountain towered directly in front of her and she took in the stunning view before swinging open the gate to the teashop and heading towards the door.

As soon as she stepped inside, an old-fashioned bell alerted Felicity to her arrival and she gave a welcoming smile.

'Bea, how's it going at The Little Blue Boathouse?'

'Loving every minute of it. I can't believe how busy the place is. I've even decided to stay on until the River Festival.'

'That's brilliant! And how are you in general?'

'Honestly, I'm good.' Bea was focusing on the positives. 'And I'll be even better with a slice of that Victoria sponge for my lunch, with one of those pork and apple baps oozing with stuffing. They look delicious.'

'Selling like hot cakes,' replied Felicity, reaching for a paper bag. 'And did you go and have your fortune read?'

'I did. There's going to be danger, compromise is the key, a chance meeting is going to change my life and I'll find my forever home.'

'Woah, that's a lot to be getting on with. Maybe some

wealthy yachtsman is going to arrive for the River Festival and sail you off into the sunset.'

'You never know.' Bea grinned but automatically thought of Nolan. 'I think I need to take some time to work on me. Put me first and do what makes me happy. Even though I'm not liking the sound of the danger Martha's predicted.' She passed over a handful of coins from her purse.

Felicity pointed to Bea's necklace. 'That's beautiful and unusual. It keeps catching the light and it's full of sparkle. It looks old.'

Bea twisted the seahorse around in her hand. 'I'm just minding it for a friend but couldn't help showing it off in the meantime.'

'It's very pretty. Have you been introduced to Aggie?' Felicity was smiling at the woman approaching the counter. 'This is Fergus's mum, aka my future mother-in-law, if we ever get around to tying the knot.'

'Pleased to meet you. I'm Bea. I'm working at the Boathouse.'

'And I'm pleased to meet you too,' Aggie replied, smiling at Bea before looking over her shoulder and then back at Felicity.

'Are you avoiding someone?' asked Felicity, looking towards the door. 'You're acting very suspicious.'

'Martha. She has eyes and ears everywhere! Do you know how difficult it is trying to sneak Gwen into the country without anyone knowing?'

'It's like a military operation.' Felicity turned towards Bea. 'Gwen is Isla's mum.'

'The original plan was for her to stay at my cottage but we've had to swap her to the B&B because Martha keeps just turning up. We really need to make sure that Martha doesn't get wind of it, even though I'm worried about how it will all pan out.'

Overhearing the conversation from the kitchen, Rona joined them. 'Hopefully after all these years bygones will be bygones and they can put the past behind them.' She wiped her hands on her pinny and looked at the three of them.

'Gwen moved to New Zealand after an argument with Martha and hasn't been back since,' Rona explained.

Aggie raised her eyebrows. 'It must have been one hell of an argument to be gone all this time! I imagine Gwen is a little nervous returning to Heartcross but hopefully seeing her grandchildren and Isla will outweigh any difficulties from the past.'

'You'd hope so, wouldn't you?' added Felicity. 'Now, we must stop gossiping.'

Rona disappeared back into the kitchen and Bea turned towards Aggie. 'You don't happen to know of anyone called Patsy that may have frequented these parts at any time in the past, do you?' Even though Nolan had left the village, Bea was still wondering about Morgan and Patsy's love story.

Rona thought for a moment. 'That name doesn't ring any bells at all, but then, I'm useless at names. Now Martha, on the other hand, never forgets a face. If anyone will know, she will. Is it someone important?'

'Just someone that possibly worked at the Boathouse when it first opened. I love history and would love to learn how it's changed over the years,' said Bea, twisting the truth slightly.

'Martha loves a little bit of history. I'd try her. Now as I'm watching my waistline ... expand,' she said with a laugh, 'I'll take a piece of that lemon drizzle, please.'

Felicity handed over a slice inside a paper bag. 'Obviously on the house,' she said with a smile.

'And that's why I love my future daughter-in-law owning a teashop.' Aggie squeezed Felicity's hand over the counter. 'Whilst I remember, Flynn has closed The Lakehouse for a few hours for Martha's birthday. The menu looks scrumptious... Oh! The very reason I came in...' Aggie held up a carrier bag. 'Old photographs of Martha that Isla found up in the attic. She suggested we could pick the best ones and project them on a screen at her birthday dinner. What do think?'

'I think that's a great idea. I'll take these from you for now,' said Felicity, taking the bag. Aggie waved goodbye and walked towards the door.

'Before you go, Bea, have you seen the weather is changing over the next few days? Sometimes by the river it can get a little wild. In the past the river has even burst its banks. If that happens again, there are sandbags in the small outhouse at the back of the Boathouse. Stack them up by the door but don't be stranded – you can always come and join us here at the cottage, or I'm sure Julia will find you room at the B&B.'

'Thanks for the heads-up. I'm sure I'll be okay.'

Bea thanked Felicity for the paper bag of goodies and headed out of the teashop to enjoy a walk in the sunshine along the banks of the river. As soon as she arrived back at the Boathouse, she headed up to her room, locking the main door behind her. Before sitting in the chair, she opened the window wide and enjoyed the blast of fresh air. Whilst eating her lunch, she watched the boats bobbing on the water, but there was still no sight of The Hemingway. Deep down, a small part of her had hoped it would be there.

As soon as she'd finished her lunch, and with Nolan still very much on her mind, she picked up her phone and googled 'Nolan Hemingway'. Immediately, his social media accounts appeared and Bea was drawn to his profile picture. There was no denying he sailed a fine line between handsome and downright sexy. There was nothing Bea could really find out about his personal life. His privacy settings were tight, his friends hidden.

She hovered over the message button and thought about sending him a message but stopped herself. What was the point? One thing Bea had learned about herself in the last few days was that a casual relationship wasn't for her. She couldn't cope with the emotional turmoil it brought. She wiped away an escaped tear with the back of her hand. She'd felt a connection with Nolan but, judging by the way he'd upped and left, he hadn't felt the same.

Being careful not to click on anything she shouldn't, the

only images that were viewable were his profile pictures. She smiled at the first one; it must have been taken years ago, because it showed Nolan as a young boy sitting on the deck of The Hemingway, dangling his legs over the side and holding a fishing rod, with his grandfather sitting next to him. He looked so young and cheeky. The next photo was of an older Nolan sitting next to a campfire, leaning on a guitar with a bottle of beer in his hand. After scrolling through a couple more photos, Bea stopped in her tracks. The next image was of four people standing around a BBQ, Nolan with his arm around the waist of a girl. Her heart racing, Bea zoomed in and recognised the girl from the painting. There was no mistaking the wedding ring on her left hand, but Nolan's hand was hidden.

Bea exhaled. She didn't want to believe that he was married but all the evidence was pointing in that direction. Feeling a fool, she stood up, took Nolan's painting of her and slid it under the bed out of sight. Not knowing if Nolan had really liked her or if she was just another conquest on his trip around the world, Bea knew it was best if she forgot that he'd ever crossed her path. It was time to move on.

Chapter Thirteen

The next day, after work, Bea was finishing chaining the last of the kayaks together and pulling them into the lockup along with the paddles. As she paused to take in the view of the river she could feel there was a change in the air. The storm was looming. In the last twenty-four hours weather warnings had been all over the news but it hadn't seemed to dampen anyone's spirits. Everyone had soaked up river life as much as possible and enjoyed every bit of sunshine.

Bea watched a fork of lightning light up the sky in the distance and then heard the thunder roll, tumbling through the darkened clouds that were heading her way. Turning around, she nearly jumped out of her skin. 'You frightened the life out of me.'

Martha was standing behind her, lowering a pair of binoculars from her eyes. 'I'm sorry, I didn't mean to. I was just stretching my legs before the rain sets in.'

'And here it comes.' Just at that moment huge dollops of rain began to fall over Heartcross and Bea was thankful that all she needed to do was lock up the Boathouse, cook her tea and put up her feet. There was also a good book with her name on it. 'Let's hope it moves on quickly. You're going to get caught in the rain if you don't make a move. I hope you don't get too drenched on your way home.' Bea went to walk past Martha, who hesitated. She looked like she wanted to say something.

'Are you okay?' Bea stood in the doorway of the Boathouse to shield herself from the rain. 'Do you want to come inside?' she asked. 'I'm sure there's an umbrella knocking about somewhere that you can borrow.' She began to unzip her coat and immediately noticed Martha's eyes widen. She was staring at Bea's neck.

'That's a beautiful necklace.'

Bea brought her hand up to the pendant. 'It is, isn't it? Seahorses represent strength and courage.'

'They do indeed,' replied Martha, her eyes still locked on the chain around Bea's neck. 'Where did you get it?'

Bea told Martha exactly the same as she'd told Aggie. 'I'm just looking after it for a friend.'

Another boom of thunder rolled out across the sky, causing both Bea and Martha to jump.

'I best get back to the farm, I don't want to be caught in this.'

'Yes, it's only going to get worse. By the way, I didn't know you were into bird watching,' added Bea

'Huh?' replied Martha, looking confused.

Bea pointed to the pair of binoculars hanging around Martha's neck.

'Oh, I'm not. I discovered them in the back of the cupboard this morning and thought I'd try them out, but with the weather like this it's impossible to see much.'

'Fair enough. You take care along that path home.' Bea shut the door of The Little Blue Boathouse and locked it behind her. Taking the key out of the door, she threw it in the drawer of the desk and climbed up the ladder to the attic room. Peeling the coat from her back, she hung it up and kicked off her shoes. After turning on the lamp, she moved towards the window and watched Martha walking along the riverbank. When she stopped and turned, Bea took a small step back from the window. Martha brought the binoculars up to her eyes and fixed them on the boats on the river. How very odd.

An hour later, Bea was dressed in her PJs, with a book resting on her lap. She checked through her emails but there was only the usual junk mail, which she disregarded, and a text from Emmie, checking in. She was momentarily distracted by the rain, now thrashing against the windows as the wind had picked up. Bea didn't envy anyone anchored on the river. Despite the bad weather the scenery was still spectacular, reminding her of one of Nolan's paintings. The next boom of thunder caused Bea to jump. The eye of the storm was getting closer. With only a few passengers onboard, the last water taxi of the day was sailing into the jetty. Everyone quickly dispersed, pulling their hoods over their heads against the drenching rain. Bea watched Roman secure the boat then pull on his waterproofs before wheeling his bike from the deck. She didn't envy him cycling over the bridge back to Glensheil in the wind and the rain. As he reached the end of the jetty, Roman noticed her in the window and waved before he threw his leg over the saddle and cycled up the river path.

With a warm cup of tea in her hands she curled up in the chair again, pulling a blanket over her knees. Her thoughts turned back to Martha as she scanned the river path and looked up at the clifftop. It was a little strange that Martha had picked that moment to try out a pair of binoculars, knowing a storm was looming. Sitting upright, Bea thought back to what Martha had said. It struck her that Martha hadn't been quite truthful. She couldn't have found the binoculars in the cupboard this morning because Bea remembered that when she was rowing to Castaway Bay with Nolan she'd spotted Martha standing on the clifftop looking through a pair of binoculars. Bea had the feeling that Martha was hiding something, but exactly what, she wasn't sure.

Chapter Fourteen

The weather warning had been correct. Three days of blustery, stormy weather had engulfed the village of Heartcross. The weather in the Scottish Highlands was unpredictable and, just as Felicity had warned, the river was ferocious and the water rising.

The Little Blue Boathouse was closed as the weather was too risky for anyone to be out on the river, but during that time Bea had been productive. She'd cleaned the Boathouse within an inch of its life and had refreshed the paint on the inside walls, something that Julia had told her Flynn had been meaning to do for the last six months. She'd snapped some photos and pinged them over to Flynn and Julia, who couldn't praise her enough.

Bea had spent the early part of the afternoon lugging sandbags from the outhouse and piling them up against the door, which was certainly taking a battering in the high winds. With the storm raging on, she decided there was only one thing for it: she would climb under her duvet and get comfy. She was about to lower the window blind when a sudden movement on the jetty caught her eye. A flashlight was being waved frantically around and she could just hear the sound of a woman screaming at the top of her voice. Instantly, Bea knew there was something wrong. As she grabbed her coat and forced her feet into shoes there was a banging on the door of the Boathouse.

'Help! Please help!'

Bea fumbled in the drawer for the key and quickly opened the door. She was greeted by a woman she'd recognised from the start of the week, when she'd come in to buy excursion tickets. She was drenched, her body shaking, raindrops dripping off the end of her nose. Bea ushered her inside. Grabbing Bea with both hands, the woman stumbled over her words: 'My little boy has gone missing.'

Time stood still for a moment.

'Don't panic, he couldn't have gone far,' Bea said in a calm voice, sounding in control but feeling a rapid increase in her heart rate. The weather out there couldn't be any worse and all she could picture was a frightened little boy they needed to find fast.

'I can't get a signal. Please ring the coastguard. I think he must have fallen overboard into the water. I'm anchored right next to the riverbank but he's gone.'

Bea met the woman's worried stare. Her face was pallid and her legs buckled underneath her. Bea caught her and guided her to a chair. 'Take some deep breaths.

Unfortunately, there isn't a coastguard or a lifeboat station on this part of the river. What's your name?'

'Amy. It's Amy.'

'And your son's name?'

'Lucas.'

'Okay, Amy. Here's what I'm going to do. I'm going to ring the emergency services and get as many people as possible out here searching as quickly as possible. What I need you to do is try to stay calm.'

As Bea reached for the telephone, Amy stumbled to her feet and headed back outside into the torrential rain shouting Lucas's name at the top of her lungs. Dialling the emergency services, Bea was met with a barrage of questions she didn't know the answers to.

'How old is Lucas?' the voice on the other end asked.

'I don't know.' Bea took an educated guess. 'Maybe around five.'

'What is he wearing?'

'I'm so sorry, I have no idea.'

'How long has he been missing?

'I don't know. Please can you get a search team to The Little Blue Boathouse as quickly as possible?'

As soon as she hung up the call, Bea opened the contact book at the side of the till and dialled the number for the B&B. Within three rings Julia picked up the phone.

'Julia, it's Bea.'

'Are you okay? You sound—'

'Far from okay. There's an incident on the river, just outside the Boathouse. The emergency services are on their way but there's a possibility a small boy has fallen off one of the boats into the water. We need as many people up here as possible to help with the search.'

'Flynn is still away on business but Isla is here with me. We'll send Drew and Fergus up right away and alert the rest of the villagers. We'll all be with you in five.'

Relieved that help was on the way, Bea hung up and rushed outside. The wind was pushing her hard, attempting to lift her off her feet. The only thing in their favour was that it wasn't dark yet, though the terrible weather was causing a few problems with visibility. Panic was written all over Amy's face. She was shivering and her teeth were chattering. Bea wondered if she was going into shock.

'Help is on the way,' reassured Bea, looking out over the turbulent water. The river had an eerie feeling about it today and Bea was praying with all she had that Lucas hadn't been swept away. She and Amy began to run up and down the riverbank scanning the water, but they couldn't spot him anywhere.

'How long do you think he's been gone?' asked Bea.

'Fifteen minutes at most.'

Bea knew that was a long time for a small boy to be in these waters. They checked up and down the jetty and searched the outhouses at the back of the Boathouse but still there was no sign of him. Amy was sobbing. 'He's only just got his first swimming badge. He will never survive in that water.'

'What was the last conversation you had with him? Can you remember?' asked Bea.

The tears were streaming down Amy's face, her cheeks streaked with black mascara. 'Yes, we were watching the storm through the window of the boat and he saw something sparkle on the rocks and thought it was treasure. I told him to go and get his PJs on whilst I nipped to the loo, but then, when I went to check on him, he was gone and the door to the deck was open.'

Bea looked towards the boat. Was it possible for a small boy to jump the distance from the side of the boat to the bank? She wasn't sure, but anything was possible.

'What if someone has taken him?'

'I'm sure he can't be far,' Bea replied, thankful her voice sounded calm. 'Which rocks did Lucas think he saw treasure on?' Call it a hunch, but Bea was convinced that the little boy had somehow attempted to get to the rocks.

Amy pointed.

'I'm going take a look up there, but I want you stay here. Help is on its way.'

With the rain stinging her cheeks she rushed back to the Boathouse and grabbed a life jacket in case she needed it. Battling against the wind, she ran up the path, praying the little boy would be okay. She continued to shout his name, but there was still no answer. Her heart was aching with worry. Lucas could have easily slipped on the bank but that wasn't a thought Bea wanted to consider, with the water flowing so fast.

Adrenalin had taken over her whole body as she pushed towards the rocks. She took a quick glance over her shoulder and could make out a Land Rover heading up the river path, which she assumed was Drew. In this weather, she knew there was no time to waste.

'Lucas, are you there?' yelled Bea, finally approaching the rocks.

A glimpse of something yellow caught her eye and moving closer she saw that a wellington boot was wedged between the ragged grey rocks. Bea's heart began to pound even harder. She remembered seeing Lucas in a pair of bright yellow wellingtons when he came into The Little Blue Boathouse with his mother.

She bellowed back to Amy but she was too far away to hear. For a second, Bea considered going back to tell the others, but she was here now. Already drenched to the core, she decided to climb over the rocks. Pushing her wet hair from her face and without stopping to consider the consequences, she sat on a rock and, not daring to look down at the ferocious water, carefully lowered herself. She felt herself slipping, and though it was a long way down to the next rock, she had no choice but to launch herself over the edge. There was a possibility Lucas was down there.

'Lucas, are you there? Its's Bea from The Little Blue Boathouse. If you are there, please make a sign, shout to me.'

She looked down but couldn't see anything or anyone, the rocks and rain blocking her view.

'I'm here! Help!'

Bea sat still. Had she just heard a small voice or was it her mind playing tricks on her?

'Lucas, is that you?'

Again, a small voice came from somewhere underneath her, but she couldn't see him.

'Stay where you are, I'm coming for you!' Bea sounded braver than she felt. She guessed it was a few feet or so down to the rock below. Slowly turning herself over on her tummy, with her legs dangling in mid-air, she attempted to lower herself, but as her feet touched the wet rock below, she slipped. Her chin scraping the rock as she fell, she landed with a thud, turned her ankle and cried out in pain. The life jacket she was carrying slipped into the river.

Managing to crouch on her bum gave Bea a little relief from the throbbing pain in her ankle. Looking over at the next rock, she saw a wide-eyed, cold-looking Lucas staring back at her.

'I'm okay, don't worry. I've just twisted my ankle and my chin is hurting a little. Are you okay?'

Lucas nodded.

'Do you remember me? I'm Bea. We met the other day when it was sunny. I prefer the sunshine. How about you?'

Lucas gave her a small smile and continued nodding.

'Help is on its way. How did you get down here?'

'I was looking for treasure but my wellie got stuck and I fell to here.'

'Are you hurt?'

This time Lucas shook his head.

'I'm going to try and crawl to you and then we have to sit tight until help comes.'

Dragging her throbbing ankle Bea managed to slowly crawl towards Lucas. Her chin was smarting too, the sharp pain coming and going. From the blood splattered on her coat, Bea thought it possible she might need stitches.

'Bea!'

Her name was being shouted.

'Bea! Where are you?'

There it was again.

'Do you hear that? We're going to be rescued very soon.' Relieved, she smiled at Lucas and rested her arm around his shoulder as he snuggled in close to her.

'We're down here!' she shouted back with all her might.

Hearing voices above her, Bea shouted again, as loud as she could. 'Help! We're stuck on the rocks. HELP! Lucas is here. Safe and well but I've hurt my ankle.'

'Stay where you are. Do not move. We're coming down to get you.'

Instantly, Bea's pulse began to race faster. She recognised that voice.

It was Nolan.

Chapter Fifteen

Her lips trembling, Bea saw a rope being lowered. Her ankle was in excruciating pain but thankfully it wouldn't be long before it was strapped up and she could numb the pain with medication. Trying to hold it together for Lucas's sake, she blinked back the tears.

'And who have we here?' Drew asked, appearing on the rock kitted out in a helmet, waterproofs and sturdy climbing boots.

'This is Lucas. He's been on an adventure but lost a wellie in the process,' reported Bea, still with her arm wrapped around him.

'Would that be this one?' Drew held up a yellow wellington boot and passed it to a now smiling Lucas.

'And why are we hiding out in rocks in such torrential weather?' asked Drew.

'I was looking for pirates' treasure,' replied Lucas.

'And did you find any? Because if you did, it's only right you share.'

Lucas shook his head.

'I'd say better luck next time, but if we could stick to looking for treasure in the glorious sunshine and not at night in the rain, I think we would have more of a chance of finding some.' Drew high-fived Lucas before looking up at the rocks and shouting, 'They're both here, safe and sound. Are you okay Bea?'

'My ankle is hurting, possibly a bad sprain. I'm hoping it's not broken.'

Drew took a quick look at Bea's ankle and shouted towards the top of the rocks again, 'But we need medical attention for Bea; possible broken ankle and a deep cut to her chin. Can someone call an ambulance?' Drew turned back to Bea. 'I'm going to get Lucas to the top and then Nolan is going to come down and guide you back up. It won't be long before we can get you some pain relief and back in the warmth.'

Bea hadn't realised she was shivering and her teeth were beginning to chatter.

'Right, buddy, let's get you out of here. Your mum is waiting for you at the top so let's get you up safely. I want you to climb on my back and hold tight around my neck. Do you think you can do that?'

'Yes,' replied Lucas.

'Good man,' said Drew, crouching down. 'And don't you move,' he reminded Bea. 'Nolan will be down for you in just a sec.'

'I'm going nowhere,' she said, wondering when and why Nolan had arrived back. This wasn't quite the reunion she was expecting and she felt a little apprehensive about seeing him. Then, hearing a commotion at the top of the rocks, followed by a cheer, she knew Lucas had been reunited with his mum.

She watched as a pair of feet were lowered onto the rock and Nolan's body came into sight. He turned towards her and grinned cheekily, putting her instantly at ease. 'I can't leave you alone for a minute!'

The second she set eyes on him, a shiver ran up her spine and she felt a blush to her cheeks. Even though Nolan had disappeared without saying goodbye her attraction to him hadn't wavered.

'You came back.'

His eyes skimmed hers. 'Come here. You look like you could do with a hug.' He crouched down beside her and opened his arms wide. Taking a deep breath, she slipped into Nolan's arms. He held her tight, kissing the top of her wet hair. In shock, Bea began to sob. 'It really hurts and I'm feeling a little sick.' She closed her eyes for a second and put a hand to her chin, feeling the stickiness of the blood.

'It's a nasty cut, and you'll probably need stiches. For now, you need to work with me to get up to the top. The rocks are slippery so go slowly and try not to put any direct weight on your ankle.'

Nolan slipped his arms underneath hers and gently pulled her to her feet. Lifting her ankle off the rock, she balanced on one leg as she clung to him for support. 'Hold on to the rope. There's a ledge up above you, try and put your right foot on there. I'll push you but also Drew and Fergus are going to pull the rope from the top and hopefully we'll be up in no time at all. Drew, Fergus,' he called up. 'We're ready when you are.'

Bea gripped the rope with all her might, struggling to balance on one leg as the river splashed against the rocks. The sharp pain in her ankle took her breath away. As Nolan gently pushed from behind, she began to move, and very soon she felt two strapping arms pulling her up and placing her gently in a chair. She jumped as two wet arms engulfed her in a hug. Amy looked hysterically happy. 'Thank you, I can't thank you enough.'

'It's okay,' replied Bea. 'I'm just glad he's safe.'

'Oh my God, you're hurt. Your face.'

'I'm not sure which is hurting more, my ankle or my chin.' She looked up at a man standing beside her.

'Pleased to meet you, Bea. I'm Dr Ben Sanders, based at the doctor's practice in Heartcross. We're going to get you inside the Boathouse and out of the rain so we can have a look at you. The ambulance is on its way ... in fact... Great timing! It's here now. If you can lean on Fergus and myself, we'll try and lift you inside the Boathouse.'

'We really do need some type of water rescue out here,' Bea managed to say as the men lifted her up and carried her the short distance to the Boathouse, where Julia, Isla and Felicity were waiting.

Julia was pouring hot water from the kettle and handing out polystyrene cups of tea. After passing a couple to Drew and Fergus she handed another to Nolan, before wrapping a blanket around Bea's shoulders. 'Now, I'm not sure this is in your job description,' she teased.

'Me neither.' Bea attempted a smile but her face was smarting.

'The paramedics are here and they're going to give you a quick check over before they take you off to hospital.'

Bea knew that she should go to hospital but all she really wanted to do was go upstairs, get warm and change her clothes. Then it hit her. 'How the heck am I going to climb a ladder to my room if I've got a broken ankle?'

Julia patted her lightly on her shoulder. 'Let's worry about getting you dry and pain-free first. Shall I quickly pack you an overnight bag to take with you?'

'Would you? That would be a great help. PJs, clean clothes, underwear, toothbrush and the book I'm reading is by the bed.'

'Of course.'

With Dr Sanders by their side the paramedics introduced themselves and, after checking Bea over, administered some pain-killers. They confirmed she needed stitches in her chin, and said the sooner they got an X-ray of her ankle the better.

Amy and Lucas, who had been chatting to the local policeman, came over to Bea. 'I'm sorry you're hurting because of me,' Lucas mumbled, looking sad.

'It's okay. I'm just glad you're safe. But please promise me one thing in the future – don't go anywhere without telling your mum first.'

'Promise,' replied Lucas, taking Amy's hand.

'We're going back to the boat to get dry. Is there anything we can do for you?' Amy asked.

Bea shook her head. 'No, but thank you.'

As Bea watched them walk out of The Little Blue Boathouse, she thought back to that summer's day by the lake when her friend had lost her life. Even though Lucas's story had a happy ending it could have been so different.

'Are you okay?' Nolan bent down beside her.

'I think so but the more I think about tonight the more I know this stretch of the water needs a life rescue.'

'I agree,' replied Nolan.

'And where have you been?' she asked Nolan as the paramedics pushed a wheelchair towards her.

'We need to talk, but obviously not now.'

She wasn't sure what Nolan wanted to say but he was right, this wasn't the time or the place. After helping Bea into the wheelchair, one of the paramedics pushed her towards the back of the waiting ambulance.

'Is everyone okay, have they found the little boy?'

Everyone looked up as Martha breezed through the door, lowering her hood from her head.

'It's brutal out there.'

'Yes, Bea found him. But hang on, Granny, who has my children?' asked Isla.

'Don't worry, I haven't abandoned them. I'm not that senile yet. Rona stayed with them so I could come down here and help with the search.' Martha noticed Bea in the wheelchair. 'And what happened to you?'

'This is the hero of the hour,' chipped in Nolan, giving Bea a warm smile.

'I wouldn't go as far as "hero". I slipped on the rocks, scraped my chin and busted my ankle looking for Lucas.'

'Whom she found,' Nolan added proudly.

Martha waggled her finger at Bea and gave her a knowing look. 'I told you there would be danger! You've done well, my girl.'

'I would prefer no more danger from here on out,' replied Bea.

'Martha?' Nolan extended his hand. 'I've heard all about your psychic readings. The best in the business, I believe.'

'Flattering will get you everywhere.' She shook his hand. 'And you are?'

'Nolan Hemingway.'

'Hemingway…' Martha repeated. Looking like she'd seen a ghost, she paled, which didn't go unnoticed by Bea, as the paramedic began to push the wheelchair up the ramp of the ambulance.

The moment was interrupted by Julia, who handed Nolan Bea's overnight bag. 'Can you pass that to the paramedics whilst I just grab a cup of tea? Do you want one, Martha?' she asked.

'Any sherry to go in that?' asked Martha. 'I think I need one.'

'Don't be silly, you're not in shock. Unlike Bea. I bet *she* could do with a strong drink.'

'I beg to differ,' murmured Martha, but her words were

lost in the commotion of making Bea comfortable in the back of the ambulance.

The siren had stopped but the blue light was still whirling. Dr Sanders stepped into the back of the ambulance and asked Bea a series of questions before one of the paramedics took her blood pressure. After wrapping her in a blanket, he strapped her to the bed.

'The road is going to be quite bumpy once we're through the village, as we have the track before we reach the bridge, and we need to try and keep your ankle as still as possible. The sooner we get to hospital, the sooner we can get that chin stitched and that ankle strapped up.'

Nolan watched the proceedings from the door of the ambulance. 'Would you like me to come with you?'

Bea nodded. 'Yes, I'd like that.'

Sitting on a chair at the bottom of the bed, Nolan strapped himself in.

'Are you okay?' asked Bea, noticing that his eyes looked bleary.

'Don't you worry about me.' He reached across and held her hand.

Julia, who had been bringing tea to the paramedics, appeared at the door of the ambulance. 'And it's okay if you're late for work tomorrow,' she teased.

Bea's eyes widened. 'I'm so sorry, I'm going to be leaving you in the lurch.'

'Far from it. Flynn is going to be here in the morning, and Nolan has already offered to take over the afternoon shift until we know what's going on with you. We have everything covered. Just get better soon.'

Bea felt a twinge of guilt at letting Julia down but then the throb in her ankle reminded her she had no choice. She caught Martha's eye just as the ambulance door slammed shut. Just then, an image suddenly flashed through her mind.

'Castaway Bay,' she murmured.

'What's up?' asked Nolan. 'Do you need something?'

Bea shook her head. 'No, I'm okay. Just feeling a little tired.'

'Close your eyes,' suggested Nolan.

Resting her head on the pillow, Bea did exactly that but there was only one thing on her mind – the painting on the wall inside Martha's caravan. She was suddenly sure it was of Castaway Bay.

Doors closed, the ambulance sped off towards Glensheil Hospital, sirens blaring.

Chapter Sixteen

As soon as they arrived at the hospital, Bea was whisked off up a corridor towards the X-ray department while Nolan took a seat in the waiting room. It wasn't long before Bea's ankle was strapped up and her chin stitched.

'I can't believe they're keeping me overnight.'

'At least your ankle isn't broken. It could have been a lot worse,' Nolan said from where he was sitting at the side of Bea's bed.

'You're right, and I've been thinking...'

'That's dangerous,' Nolan teased.

'Don't be cheeky! The first thing that Amy said to me when Lucas went missing was "Call the coast guard". It was also one of the first things I asked Julia about when I arrived at the Boathouse. But there isn't one. Heartcross has become so popular since the bridge collapsed and it hit the news all those years ago. What with Starcross Manor and

The Lakehouse, and celebrity chef Andrew Glossop living and filming his cookery show from Heartcross Castle, this place has become a huge tourist attraction. The river is packed with tourists and we need to make sure the waterways are safe for everyone.'

'It would cost a hell of a lot of money to get a search and rescue operation up and running,' Nolan said.

'But worth every penny if it saves lives.'

'Yes, you're right there. But they would need premises and staff. I'm not sure The Little Blue Boathouse is capable of housing rescue boats and a crew of people.'

'I've been thinking about that too. What if I can raise enough money for at least one lifeboat to start with and set up a charity? A kind of ... Heartcross Rescue. It could be run by the community – driven by our own values of selflessness, courage, dependability and trustworthiness. We could educate, influence, supervise and rescue those at risk from drowning. Surely a building to house a boat, with a living area and kitchen, couldn't cost *that* much money.'

'It would take hundreds of thousands.'

'There's the old lighthouse.'

'That's a possibility.'

'We have enough influential people in the village who could use their contacts to help raise funds. Felicity managed to raise thousands to build the new bridge by getting the whole community on board so surely this is worth a try. I'm going to call a meeting at The Little Blue Boathouse. This is important.' Bea could hear the passion in her voice. 'I'm going to make this happen. Please could you pass me my bag?'

Nolan looked at her with admiration. 'You have fire in your belly and this is a worthy cause … but you're meant to be resting.' Still, he passed her the bag without hesitation.

'I was reading some old newspaper articles during the storm and I saw that Felicity managed to get the local paper on board, and that brought it to the attention of TV news, at which point the story was picked up nationally. I think I can do this.' Bea took out her mobile phone. She had a few missed calls including several from Emmie.

Quickly, she scanned the texts. Eyes wide, she looked up at Nolan. 'My sister is on her way to Heartcross. I wasn't picking up my phone, so she called the Boathouse and of course Julia was still there and she told her I was on my way to hospital.'

'It will be nice to see her, surely?'

'The first thing she'll do is try and convince me to go back home.' Bea sighed. 'I love it here. There's something about this place that is endearing and charming – and calming, apart from the past few days. My sister's arrival will shatter that tranquillity.'

'You're right about the weather. I've felt sick on The Hemingway, the waters have been so choppy.'

'And where have you been?'

Nolan paused. 'I needed some time out after…'

'Our row. I know I must have sounded like a jealous loon and I'm sorry.' She paused. 'Actually, I'm not entirely sorry about that.'

Nolan raised an eyebrow.

'Because it shows you I care. I just didn't deal with it in the best way. For *that* I am sorry.' Bea took a sip of water from the cup on her bedside cabinet. 'You've made it pretty clear where you've stood from the start and so I'm going to be truly honest with you. I never expected to feel a real connection with anyone so soon after my break-up. It took me completely by surprise.' She was putting her heart on her sleeve but why not? She didn't have anything to lose.

'I want to be honest with you, too – it might explain a few things, such as the reason I prefer to live on the boat and just want to keep moving – but it's a conversation I'm going to find very difficult to have.'

Bea noticed that Nolan looked anxious. 'A problem shared and all that.' She followed his gaze to his hands and noticed for the first time that he was wearing a wedding ring. 'You're married.' She'd had a hunch but seeing the evidence was a shock. 'You really didn't tell me the whole truth, did you?'

After everything that Bea had been through, how could he do this? However much of a connection there was between them, she would have never crossed that line if she'd known he was married. A small part of her now wished he'd never come back.

'Do you mind…' He pointed to the jug of water and a spare cup.

'Be my guest.'

Nolan sipped some water, then took out his wallet and opened it. Inside was a photograph in a clear plastic sleeve.

Bea swallowed a lump as Nolan passed it to her. It showed a younger-looking Nolan with his arms around the girl from the painting.

She risked the question. 'Is this your wife?'

'I promise you I have not made a fool of you, but yes, this is my wife … *was* my wife.'

Bea noted the past tense.

'Hannah passed away four years ago.' There was a calm to Nolan's voice that she wasn't expecting. 'It was our wedding anniversary two days ago and even now I still don't know what to do with myself on that day, except hide away.' His eyes were brimming with tears and he closed them for a moment.

Bea hadn't been expecting this and was completely at a loss. 'I'm so sorry, Nolan. I don't know what to say, except I'm really sorry.' She could kick herself for the idiotic way she'd acted over the painting.

'That's okay.' He took a breath. 'I suppose it was partly my continued grief that led me to throw myself into renovating my grandfather's boat. It was a way to keep my mind off things. A much-needed distraction.'

Bea could relate to that. She could see his hand slightly shaking as he took another sip.

'And that's why I prefer to be out on the water. Everyone I have ever got close to leaves me in one way or another, so maybe I thought if I kept moving, I could be the one who leaves, rather than the one who is left alone.'

Bea reached across and took his hand.

'How did she die?' she asked tentatively.

'Hannah had just started a new job and had begun to complain of headaches. I just brushed it off as a side-effect of working in a new, stuffy office, with the heating ramped up because it was winter, or the strain of staring at a screen all day. I didn't even encourage her to go to the doctor.' Nolan blinked back the tears. 'Then, a couple of days later, I was in the garden when an ambulance turned up out of the blue at the front gate. I thought they'd got the wrong address ... Hannah had collapsed and somehow managed to alert the emergency services from the upstairs phone. At the hospital, the worst was confirmed. Hannah had an advanced brain tumour and was given six months to live. She only made it to four.'

There was a sadness bleeding through the room and Bea felt herself well up. There was nothing she could say to make this awful situation any better.

'That was the last time I was in an ambulance before today.' He paused. 'I'm not all those things you think I am.'

'It's okay, you don't owe me any explanation.'

They stared at each other. Nolan broke the silence. 'Like I said, it's the reason I took to The Hemingway. I decided to embrace being alone and thought that if I kept sailing, no one could hurt me. Not that I'm saying Hannah hurt me... It's difficult to explain. I was devastated to lose her and it frightens me to put myself in that situation again.

'Bea, you took me by surprise. You were so easy to be around and I was surprised at how happy I felt just to be in your presence. I hadn't felt that since Hannah. Not with anyone ... because despite your assumption that I have a girl in every port, there hasn't been anyone else besides you since Hannah passed away.'

Bea knew how difficult it must have been for Nolan to share all that information, and the fact that he'd told her gave her a warm and fuzzy feeling inside. She was also relieved to hear that she hadn't been one of many, and that Nolan had felt the incredible connection that she had, too.

Just at that moment, the curtain around her bed was pulled aside and a nurse gave Bea a warm smile. 'How are you doing? Is the pain manageable in your ankle?'

Bea was feeling as comfortable as she could be. 'I'm doing okay,' she replied.

'If you need anything, just press your buzzer,' said the nurse to Bea before turning to Nolan. 'It's getting late now, so I'm going to have to ask you to leave.'

Whilst the nurse checked Bea's pulse and noted the information down on the chart at the end of the bed, Nolan pulled on his jacket. As soon as the nurse left the room, he moved closer to the side of the bed. 'They should let you out in the morning. I'll come back to get you then.'

'You don't have to.'

'I want to.'

'Can I ask, did you come back to Heartcross because of me?' Bea knew it was a risk asking the question but she wanted to know the answer.

'I can neither confirm nor deny.' He gave her a cheeky wink. 'There's no Hemingway and Fernsby without Fernsby.'

'Or without Hemingway.'

Both of them smiled smiles that got bigger and bigger.

'Try to stay out of trouble until the morning,' said Nolan.

'Don't you go sailing off into the sunset without a word.'

'I don't know if it's escaped your notice but there is a storm out there that would make that impossible, But even if the sun was shining, I wouldn't be going anywhere.'

'That's good, because if you leave, you'll be missed.' Bea tilted her head and gave him a lopsided grin.

Nolan disappeared through the curtain with a wave and Bea lay her head back on the pillow. She knew it must have been hard for him to open up to her and she couldn't imagine what it must have been like for him to lose his wife so young in such a tragic way. But despite the sadness of it all, there was one thing that gave her hope – he'd trusted her with all that information when he didn't have to. Honesty meant the world to Bea. After everything that had happened in the last ten minutes, she felt their connection was growing stronger.

Chapter Seventeen

B ea woke the next morning to the sight of a doctor at the side of her bed. The blinds were open at the far end of the ward, showing her that the wind and rain had stopped and the sun was once again trying to break through the clouds.

'You'll be pleased to know you can go home today, but I need you to keep your weight off that ankle for a couple of days, and you will need to make an appointment with your doctor to take those stitches out of your chin.'

'I will,' she replied.

The doctor propped a pair of crutches against the side of the bed. 'For you.'

Bea watched as he scrawled something on the chart and turned to the nurse. 'Bea is ready to be discharged.'

'Is there anyone you'd like me to call to come and pick you up?' the nurse asked.

'It's okay, I have my phone, but thank you.'

Pushing herself up in the bed, Bea phoned Julia. 'Good news! I'm allowed home but I need a lift.'

'That's good timing, we were just talking about you.'

'We?'

'Myself and Nolan. Nolan was telling me your idea about setting up Heartcross Rescue. It's going to take some doing.'

'It is, but I think this really needs to be done.'

'I think it's a great idea. Last night was a wake-up call and things could have been a lot worse.'

'Agreed. How about Monday night?' Bea was taking control. She was passionate about this. Her heart had been in her mouth when Lucas had gone missing. Knowing there could be possible back-up help in future situations would give everyone a little more peace of mind.

'Yes, Monday night would be great. I'll share the details in the community WhatsApp group and the rest I'll leave in your capable hands.'

Suddenly Bea felt nervous. She was a temporary newcomer to the village and here she was organising a meeting for the wider community.

'And in other news, Nolan's taxi has just left! He's on his way to pick you up. Is there something going on between you both that I need to know about?'

Bea smiled as she twizzled the seahorse necklace up and down its chain. 'We're just very good friends,' she replied. 'Nolan will be sailing away on his travels after the River Festival.'

'Mmm, if you say so,' replied Julia. 'I'll see you when you get back.'

Bea hung up. Even though Julia had been teasing, Bea knew being out on the water, sailing from place to place, was what Nolan needed right now to heal. She understood that, because it was the very reason she'd come to Heartcross.

———

Within thirty minutes Nolan appeared in the doorway. 'Are you ready to hop along?'

Bea was ready and waiting, sitting on the edge of the bed. 'Born ready,' she replied.

With a grin on his face, he helped her to her feet and passed her the crutches. 'Here you go.'

'These are so difficult to manoeuvre on.' Bea attempted to walk forward on her good leg, with her swollen ankle bent behind her, but as she put the crutches forward, she wobbled and collapsed on to Nolan. Fortunately, he caught her.

'I've been here less than five minutes and you're falling for me already.'

'You wish,' she teased, standing up straight and attempting another go.

Once again, she wobbled and fell straight into Nolan's arms. 'This is a lot harder than it looks.'

'Begin your step as though you're going to use the

injured foot, but instead bear all your weight on the crutch,' Nolan advised.

With a few more attempts, Bea had the swing of things and was racing up the corridor towards the main entrance. 'Come on, slow coach,' she joked, leaving Nolan behind.

Within twenty minutes the taxi was driving the back way towards the river. The second she set eyes on The Little Blue Boathouse, Bea felt uplifted.

'Home sweet home,' she murmured.

Everywhere looked positively gleaming, thoroughly cleaned by the storms of the last few days. Hordes of people were back out on the water taking advantage of the clear blue sky. 'Heartcross Rescue... I can see it as an extension of this place.'

Julia and Flynn appeared in the doorway, Bea recognising him from social media.

'Here she is, the hero! It's great to meet you at last.' Flynn thrust his hand forward then realised Bea would find it difficult to shake hands. 'Sorry,' he immediately apologised. 'We don't want you falling over.'

'Pleased to meet you. I'm sorry about this. I take the job and now for a couple of days I'm fit for nothing.'

'You have nothing to apologise for,' said Julia. 'If it wasn't for you, Lucas could have been washed away. That river was rising fast.'

'Anyone would have done the same,' replied Bea,

hobbling inside, where she was greeted by an enormous bouquet of beautiful blooms.

'For you,' said Julia. 'They arrived this morning.'

'They are utterly gorgeous.' Taking in the aroma, Bea sat down in the chair and passed her crutches to Nolan.

'Julia has been filling me in about your ideas surrounding Heartcross Rescue,' said Flynn. 'We've put it out there for a meeting this Monday and already the majority of the community have confirmed they're going to be here.'

'That's brilliant! Thank you for doing that,' enthused Bea. 'I've been thinking more and more about this. Is there a local carpenter or builder that could help?'

'Eleni, my right-hand woman at the B&B, goes out with Jack, who's part of a family building business, and he will be coming on Monday.'

'Perfect. Whilst I'm laid up, I'm going to look into potential costs so I can have some figures ready for the meeting.'

Nolan looked at her proudly. 'She's got it all sorted.'

'I love it when a plan comes together.' Bea crossed her fingers. 'But I know it's not going to be easy.'

'I'll be here on Monday but I have to disappear now as I've got a meeting and Julia needs to get back to the B&B,' said Flynn. 'But what are you going to do about the attic room? That ladder might prove a little difficult to climb up for a couple of days.'

All Bea wanted to do was get upstairs, sit back and watch the boats on the river from her armchair, but Flynn was right: for a couple of days it might be a little difficult.

'There's a room at the B&B available on the ground floor. It's yours if you want it,' Julia offered.

'I think that sounds like a plan. Thank you.'

'Are you okay to take over, Nolan?' asked Julia. 'With Bea watching over you, I'm sure you'll get the hang of it, and I'll be back in a couple of hours.'

'I'm sure I'll manage.'

They watched Flynn and Julia walk up the river path before Nolan took his place behind the counter. 'These are beautiful flowers,' he said, moving the bouquet to one side. 'I'll have a look for a vase.'

'The staff room is that way. The key is in the drawer of the desk.'

Nolan opened the drawer. 'This one?' he asked and Bea nodded.

'And these flowers are gorgeous. Do I have you to thank for them?'

'I wish I could say they were from me, but afraid not. There's a card though.' He took the white envelope and passed it to Bea before opening the door to the staff room. 'Do you fancy a cup of tea?'

'That'll be good.' She smiled. 'Milk, one sugar.'

Opening up the small white envelope, Bea stared at the words on the card. Her heart began to pound.

I want you back, please come home. All my love, Carl xx

The flowers were addressed to The Little Blue Boathouse, which meant Carl knew exactly where she was staying. There was only one person who could have shared that information with him – Emmie.

As Nolan walked back through the door with two mugs, he was chatting away. 'Last night when I arrived back in the storm, I realised something was going on. I could see Drew's Land Rover and all the villagers were out on the banks of the river and as I anchored The Hemingway, I heard them saying you had gone after Lucas and they didn't know where you were. I didn't like the thought of that. I can't even describe the feeling in the pit of my stomach. I felt physically sick.'

'It's good to know you care,' she said, smiling.

'You're a good person, Bea. You have good qualities.'

'Don't stop there, do feel free to list them all,' she teased, winding her hand round in circles to encourage him.

'We don't want your head swelling as big as your ankle,' he said cheekily, 'But you're kind, considerate, not to mention beautiful and funny, even if that chin of yours is stitched up in a funny zig-zaggy sort of way.'

Bea liked what she was hearing, but it didn't take away the fact that soon after the River Festival Nolan would be back on the water. In the meantime, though, she was going to enjoy every bit of his company.

'Aww, it sounds like you care just a little,' Bea teased.

'Don't go overboard.' Nolan grinned. 'And I think it's brilliant that you want to get Heartcross Rescue up and running on the river. I quite agree that it's in everyone's interest to make the water a safer place.'

'I'll do everything in my power to rally the community

around on Monday night,' she said, taking a sip of her tea. 'And I was going to ask, are Hemingway and Fernsby back on the case? Because I think I may have a development...' Bea was just about to tell him about the painting on Martha's caravan wall when she heard the crunch of tyres outside on the gravel followed by a slam of a car door, then the sound of voices that Bea immediately recognised. She froze.

'This is it, The Little Blue Boathouse. That's the name of the place from her email.'

'You had no right to go snooping in her emails.'

'I have every right. Her name is on the rental agreement for our flat, just like mine, and if she's quit her job how is she going to pay rent?'

Nolan looked through the open hatch and saw a man striding towards the door with a woman struggling to keep up. 'It sounds like we have customers.'

'They are not customers. Brace yourself.'

'We're looking for Bea,' Carl announced as he strode inside the Boathouse.

As soon as Emmie saw Bea, she raced towards her. 'There you are. We didn't know if you would still be in hospital.' She flung her arms around Bea's neck. Bea said nothing as she stared over her sister's shoulder at her ex. The day had been going so well up until now.

As Emmie pulled away, Bea glanced towards Nolan, who'd probably guessed this was her sister, as there was no mistaking the striking resemblance, but it was possible he'd think the man standing behind her wafting a piece of paper in the air was Emmie's husband.

'Nolan, let me introduce you to my sister, Emmie.'

Emmie's eyes widened as she shook his hand. Bea was regretting telling her sister about Nolan and she prayed that conversation had stayed private. Nolan shook her hand then held out his hand towards Carl.

'And this is my ex, Carl.'

Nolan didn't flinch as they shook hands. 'Pleased to meet you.'

There was nothing pleasing about this situation at all. In fact, Bea hoped she was fast asleep and would soon wake up from this nightmare. Unfortunately, the pain creeping back into her ankle because the painkillers were wearing off told her this was very much real.

'What are you both doing here?' asked Bea. 'It's a long way to come just to hire a kayak for the weekend.'

'Always the joker,' Emmie said, evidently trying to make light of the situation by rolling her eyes in Nolan's direction. 'You've been caught in a storm, trapped on some rocks and ended up in hospital. Why wouldn't we be here? We're family.'

'This came for you.' Carl pushed an envelope into her hand.

Bea looked down at the opened envelope then turned it over. It was addressed to her. 'You've opened my mail. Isn't that against the law?'

'What was I supposed to do? You went missing.'

'I didn't go missing. I *left* you. Or did you forget that part?'

Carl briefly looked over his shoulder at Nolan then lowered his voice. 'It's not as simple as that.'

Bea wondered whether he really wanted to do this in public but it seemed so. 'Because your father passed away?' Her voice softened. She'd always been fond of his father, a successful businessman but more importantly a genuine, kind man who was completely devoted to his family and would never have dreamed of committing any kind of infidelity.

'It's been difficult for me.'

Bea couldn't believe what she was hearing. There were no words that she could muster up so she looked down at the envelope. It contained a letter from her previous employer, accepting her resignation.

'You've resigned.'

Bea noticed how he'd swiftly changed the conversation so that she was the one on the hot seat. He had a habit of doing that.

'I have, and feel so much better for it.'

'I should leave you all to it,' Nolan said, edging towards the door. 'I'll go and take a walk on the jetty.'

Once Nolan was outside, Emmie was the first to speak. 'We've been worried about you. I let Carl know where you were when I heard about your accident last night. He's really sorry for what he's done. He's been a part of the family for such a long time. Surely you two can work it out so you can come home?'

Bea's jaw dropped wide open. Speechless didn't come close. She couldn't believe what she was hearing. These two were standing in front of her assuming she had no self-worth and was a weak woman who couldn't live without a two-timing rat in her life.

'I've made a mistake, I'm only human.' He couldn't even look her in the eye. He was shuffling from side to side.

If this was his pitch to win her back it had already gone down like a lead balloon.

'I will never take you back, Carl.'

'But we have a good life together. We've known each other since school. It was me and you, for ever. Against all odds. Come on, Bea. Come home. I'm sure the supermarket will give you your job back.'

'I don't want my job back. I have a job and a place to live here.'

'But it's only for a few weeks. I know you've extended your holiday but you're coming back, right?' Emmie stared at Bea.

Carl put his hand out towards her. 'Look, I know it's been tough and that's all my doing. Please just come home and we can sort this out. You belong with us. You like routine and being surrounded by what you know. You don't really want all this, do you?'

There were those words again. The words he always used to try and manipulate her into doing what he wanted her to do.

Just at that moment some customers walked through the

door, followed by Nolan, who took his place behind the counter. He mouthed 'sorry' towards her.

'We're staying at Starcross Manor for a couple of nights, if you want to talk.' Carl walked towards the door and waited outside for Emmie.

Carl had a confidence about him that suggested he thought Bea would go and see him, but she knew that in the last week she'd come to see that the only person you can rely on is yourself. Everything is figureoutable. It's like a super power … figureoutable. Bea didn't even know if that was a word, but she liked it.

Emmie hadn't moved.

'What were you thinking, bringing him here?' Bea's voice was low as she looked at her sister.

'We're allowed to be worried about you. He still cares for you and wants to care for you. This isn't where you belong.'

Bea felt exasperated. Once again, Emmie was telling her what was best for her. 'Do you know what I've learned since arriving here?' She didn't give Emmie a chance to answer. 'That nothing in life is that complicated. Things change, people change and nothing is ever set in stone. I may not know what my career path is but on a personal front I know how I want to be treated, the main quality being honesty from the person who is meant to be my partner.' Bea pushed herself up on her crutches. 'I do appreciate you were worried about me, but I'm okay. I really am.' Bea pointed her crutch towards the door. 'It's a nice walk along the river path, through the village and back towards Starcross Manor.'

'Please let me say this,' said Emmie, as they walked towards the door. 'All this is just a holiday. You aren't thinking straight. Don't go throwing everything away on a romantic notion that life is hunky-dory here and you're going to fall madly in love and live happily ever after, because it's too soon. You're on the rebound.'

'I'm just living in the moment,' replied Bea. 'I'll drop you a text later.'

Watching Emmie and Carl walk away up the path, Bea heaved a sigh of relief, but Emmie's words were still whirling around in her head. Was this just a holiday and was she still hoping that Nolan would stick around? For the few days that Nolan was gone she'd thought about him non-stop, checking the river every morning as soon as she woke up to see if The Hemingway had returned. Whether she liked it or not, Emmie had planted a tiny nugget of doubt in Bea's mind.

What if she was right?

Carl had been Bea's whole world and she didn't really know life without him. With Carl she knew exactly what she was getting, but the life she could potentially create for herself in Heartcross now would be a magical mystery tour. Bea had to work out whether she was brave enough to buy a ticket for the unknown.

Chapter Eighteen

As soon as there was a lull in customers Nolan blew out a breath. 'You okay? That all seemed a bit heavy.'

Bea was sitting outside on the bench, her crutches leaning against the picnic table. 'I expected Emmie to turn up but didn't realise she would have him in tow.'

'How are you feeling about that?' asked Nolan, perching on the end of the bench.

'Braver than I expected. Hopefully, I'll get to see Emmie on her own before she goes, but I won't be rushing over to Starcross Manor for a reunion with Carl any time soon.'

'You can't,' Nolan said cheerfully, pointing to her ankle. 'We need to work out how to get you back to the B&B, but I think I've got the solution.' He grinned and disappeared around the back of the Boathouse, reappearing a moment later holding a bike that had seen better days.

Bea burst out laughing. 'I can't ride a bike, in case it's

escaped your notice.' She gestured towards her ankle. 'And that contraption doesn't look very safe.'

Nolan pretended to be hurt. 'This bike is as safe as houses.' He patted the seat. 'We can balance your crutches across the handlebars, you can sit on the seat and I'll pedal.'

'Are you insane?' Bea threw back her head and laughed. 'That chain is as rusty as hell and that seat has seen better days. It's an antique. I think a penny-farthing would be safer.'

'That's nothing a bit of oil won't fix and the seat isn't too bad.'

'You don't have to sit on it! Life with you isn't boring, is it?'

'Who wants boring? More customers, wait there.'

'Funnily enough, I'm not going anywhere.' He leaned the bike against the wall and greeted the customers. Bea took the opportunity to watch him. He was very charismatic. Just then he looked up from under his fringe and caught her looking at him. He gave her a cheeky wink and her heart gave a little flip. He was everything she imagined the perfect partner to be. Charming, talkative, fun... She also admired his courage. It must have taken a lot to pick himself up and carry on after Hannah's passing. Bea's thoughts turned to Carl. What did she admire about him? Nothing sprang to mind. Bea couldn't even remember the last time they had laughed.

'Penny for them,' Nolan asked, once the customers disappeared.

'Nothing worth mentioning,' she replied, tilting her

head towards a couple who were looking through Nolan's paintings. 'I think you're about to get a sale,' she mouthed.

'These are really good,' said a woman, bringing the painting inside. 'Is this artist local?'

Bea pointed to Nolan. 'You're looking right at him.'

'I would love to take this one. Can I ask, is this a real place?' The woman placed the painting down on the counter, her partner standing next to her.

Bea took a look at the painting and recognised the place straightaway. Castaway Bay.

Nolan nodded. 'It is a real place but a secret place. Only a few have had the pleasure of stumbling across it.' He smiled across towards Bea.

'Wherever it is, it's beautiful.' The woman handed over the money and Nolan signed the back of the painting for her.

As soon as they walked out of The Little Blue Boathouse, Bea was flapping her hand in front of her face. 'That reminds me! I forgot to tell you. I was just about to share this when Carl and Emmie showed up. I think this snippet of information promotes Fernsby to the front of the partnership.'

'Because…' Now Nolan was waving his hand to hurry her up.

'I think Mystic Martha has been to Castaway Bay.'

Nolan took in the information. 'I'm sure a lot of locals know about the secret secluded bay.'

'I'm sure they do, but when I went to have my fortune told there was a painting hanging on the wall. It didn't mean anything to me at the time but I admired it and now I recognise it was of the bay. And there's something else.'

Nolan had her full attention. 'Go on…'

'I may be wrong but during my meeting she mentioned a boat, a different type of boat, and then I mentioned The Hemingway.' Bea narrowed her eyes as she remembered. 'Martha looked at me in a way that was a little unnerving and brought my reading to an abrupt end.'

'Describe "unnerving",' encouraged Nolan.

'She stopped looking into the ball and stared at me. She asked me to say it again. As soon I did, she stood up and gestured towards the door. The reading was over.'

'That does sound a little strange. Why didn't you tell me this earlier?'

'Duh! You weren't around and it's only now I think it's of some significance. What are you going to do about it?'

'I think I should go and see Martha and ask her about the painting and Patsy. See what she knows. But in the meantime, it's nearly lunchtime so I'm going to straighten up the kayaks, hang up the life jackets from this morning so they dry out, and take you to lunch.'

Bea pointed to the bike. 'I'm not getting on that thing twice in one day.'

Nolan laughed. 'You don't have to. Lunch is on The Hemingway. It's anchored right by the riverbank and I'll carry you on board.'

Fifteen minutes later Bea was giggling like a schoolgirl. Nolan had squatted down as low as he could and she'd climbed on to his back.

'Stop squirming,' he protested, 'otherwise I'll drop you and that will be two busted ankles.'

'Do not drop me,' she ordered.

'Wait until you see The Hemingway. I've done a little rearranging.'

With her arms wrapped tightly around his neck, Bea briefly closed her eyes as she took in the gorgeous aroma of his aftershave. Nolan took a big stride onto the deck of The Hemingway and lowered Bea into a soft padded chair before jumping back onto land and grabbing her crutches.

Bea couldn't believe her eyes when they went through the doorway. The inside of The Hemingway looked very different from the last time she was on board. The space had been cleared and – with the exception of a small living area in the corner – had been turned into a floating art gallery. All of Nolan's paintings were hanging on the wall, with some displayed even more prominently on easels.

'What do you think?'

Bea pushed herself up on her crutches and scanned the paintings. 'I think you have a wonderful talent. It's like a mini art gallery on the water, which was your dream.'

'That's exactly what I was trying to achieve.' He picked up a wooden board that was propped up against a small table. 'I'm going to leave The Hemingway anchored by the bank. I've spoken to Flynn and Roman about all this. If I stand this sign at the bottom of the jetty it will hopefully encourage tourists to come on board. Fingers crossed, I'll make a few more sales than usual, and while I keep an eye on the gallery I can get more painting done.'

'This is a wonderful idea.' Bea was impressed. Nolan had set the area up beautifully and she loved each and every painting. Right in the middle of the exhibition was the painting of Patsy and his grandfather Morgan. 'Surely you aren't going to sell that painting?' She looked at him.

'No, but there's a method to my madness. If it's on display you never know who might walk on to the boat and recognise Patsy. It might spark something in someone.'

'Good idea. She really is captivating, such a natural beauty … and look at that hair. It's right down her back … I'm planning to invite the local press to the River Rescue meeting – maybe you could have a word with one of the reporters about Patsy? You never know, their archives may just throw up something, especially from when The Little Blue Boathouse opened up all those years ago.'

'Why didn't I think of that? You're not just a pretty face, are you?' said Nolan, catching her eye and grinning.

'Nope, I have a bust ankle too!' Bea laughed as she pointed to the empty easel. 'What's going on that one?'

'That's something I wanted to talk to you about.' There was a painting in the far corner, covered by a cloth. Nolan picked it up and gestured for Bea to sit down. She hobbled back to the chair and rested her crutches against the side of it. She didn't know what to expect as he slowly uncovered the painting.

She gave a tiny gasp. 'Is that me?'

'Yes, I did it from memory.'

The painting was impressionist but it was clearly a girl, her face not visible but the red bikini clear. She was paddling at the edge of the water and in front of her was the view from Castaway Bay. The main feature in the painting was the seahorse necklace. 'Nolan, it's beautiful.'

'I'm glad you like it and that you're still wearing the necklace.'

Bea touched it then pointed to Patsy's painting, where she was also wearing it.

'Yes, I know. Would you mind if I put this painting in the show?'

'I would be honoured,' she replied, meaning every word.

He placed it on the easel, and it completed the exhibition. 'I know it's not in a proper gallery but I feel quite emotional seeing all my paintings displayed like this.'

'And so you should. It looks fantastic. What a way to earn money, by doing the job you love from a floating home you renovated. When are you thinking of letting the customers through the door?'

'As soon as you're back at work.'

Bea looked down at her ankle. 'I'm sure I'm going to be all right in the next forty-eight hours or so, but how about in the meantime we do a job swap? I'll sit here and try and sell your paintings whilst you man The Little Blue Boathouse. It's a win-win situation.'

Nolan thought about it for a second then thrust out his hand and shook Bea's. There it was again, that electrifying feeling that sent shock waves through her body. How did he do that to her every time? 'Deal. Now let me get you a sandwich. I made some earlier in case you were hungry when you got back from the hospital.'

'You're a keeper, aren't you?' she joked, as he disappeared into the galley and returned with two cheese and ham sandwiches on delicious chunky granary bread, along with a custard tart and a glass of lemonade each.

'This is just what I needed,' said Bea, tucking into her food. 'What's the plan with Martha?' she asked.

'After I've dropped you off at the B&B tonight, I think I'm going to cycle over to Foxglove Farm and pay her a visit. See if I can get myself a reading and have a look at the painting on the wall.' Nolan was thoughtful for a second whilst he took a bite of his sandwich. 'I know I'll recognise my grandfather's style. I'm so curious to know if he could have painted that picture of Castaway Bay.'

'Ooo, I never thought of that. What if it is his painting?'

'Then I can be quite honest and say the artist was my grandfather and ask if she knew him or Patsy. You never know, I might even get my future predicted.'

'I can predict your future,' she replied, looking at the paintings displayed. 'You're going to become famous as the artist on the floating boat and travel all over the world selling your paintings.' She smiled, but a tiny part of her hoped the last part wasn't true. Even though this was Nolan's dream and he was already putting his plan into action, Bea wasn't looking forward to saying goodbye.

When they finished their lunch, Nolan checked his

watch. 'I best get back over to the Boathouse. All of Roman's excursions are full this afternoon and I don't think there's a paddleboard or kayak free until gone three-thirty.'

'Why don't I start here this afternoon? With the sign standing on the jetty, you might get people on board. Tourists like a good mooch. Then everyone's a winner.'

'Are you sure?'

'Absolutely. I may as well be sat here trying to make you money whilst you're working my shift.'

A huge smile hitched on Nolan's face. 'That would be great. What really excites me is the thought of my paintings hanging in people's homes and them taking pleasure from looking at them. It sounds daft really.'

'It doesn't. You have such a talent and it's cool to think of them hanging in people's homes.'

'If you sell out there are more stacked up in the corner.'

Nolan had been busy; there were paintings of Heartcross Castle, Heartcross Mountain, Primrose Park, The Old Bakehouse and even one of the pub, The Grouse and Haggis.

'I'll do my best to sell them all,' enthused Bea.

'I'll get you a jug of water, and there's books and magazines too, in case it's quiet.'

'Honestly, I'll be okay, I'm going to sit here and watch the world go by.'

'That sounds like a perfect afternoon.'

Tucking the sign under his arm, Nolan jumped back onto dry land and Bea watched as he placed it at the bottom of the jetty. It read *Hemingway's Floating Art Galley* with an arrow pointing towards the boat. He turned and gave her a thumbs-up before strolling over and opening up The Little Blue Boathouse.

As soon as Nolan was out of sight, Bea made herself comfy. She was glad the calmer, warmer weather was back again. With her perfect view of the river, she watched Roman sail the water taxi back towards the jetty, ready to take the next load of diners to The Lakehouse restaurant. Flynn also had other boats out on the water with their own captains ready to take the tourists out on their excursions. The rest of the river was full of boats, and further upstream were the kayaks and paddleboards. Walking along the river path eating ice-creams were hordes of tourists, and Bea hoped they would step on board and take a look at the paintings.

Her phoned pinged, Emmie's name staring back at her from the screen. For the last hour she'd managed not to think about their visit this morning and she hesitated to read the message now. All Bea wanted was an afternoon of calm. She was going to take the opportunity to plan her speech for the Heartcross Rescue meeting. Julia had added her to the community WhatsApp group and, judging by the response, it was possible that over a hundred residents might attend the meeting. Rona and Felicity had said they were going to bring big aluminium urns to serve tea and coffee and bake a selection of refreshments too. Bea was feeling nervous but she reflected that all the villagers who had crossed her path so far were friendly and welcoming and everyone was going to benefit from the cause. Still, the volunteers she would need would have to come from the community. Would they have the time to spare from their busy lives?

'Bea!'

She looked over towards the bank and saw Lucas and Amy waving madly at her. She waved back.

'We're off to visit Heartcross Castle,' shouted Amy.

Bea could see by the look on Lucas's face that he was excited as he skipped along the riverbank. Knowing that yesterday could have had fatal consequences just increased Bea's conviction that the community needed a rescue team, a lifeboat and equipment, along with a small headquarters. Noticing a pen and pad on the table, Bea hobbled across and grabbed them before sitting down again. She was going to research the villagers and their businesses and see what she could do to persuade them to get involved. Then she was going to work out numbers, like how many volunteers they would need on a rota at any time. Bea knew it was a huge ask as the rota would be twenty-four hours a day, three hundred and sixty-five days a year, but it would be worth it if they could save even one life.

Her phone pinged and once again Emmie's name was on the screen. She read the message and sighed. Carl was on his way back down to speak with her. Just when she thought she was in for a pleasant, quiet afternoon.

Five minutes later, Bea couldn't quite believe it. An excursion boat had sailed into the jetty and the majority of the tourists were wandering in her direction. She felt a twinge of excitement at the possibility of making her first sale. Then she saw him – following the crowd was Carl, who'd spotted her sitting on the boat. The timing couldn't be worse.

Plastering a smile on her face, Bea welcomed the tourists onto The Hemingway. They breezed between the pictures, giving them lots of praise, and before she knew it, Bea had sold three on the bounce. On the table next to where she sat, Nolan had left tissue paper, paper bags and a card reader. He'd thought of everything. She chatted away to the customers and was trying to enjoy herself, but knowing that Carl was looming at the back of the group was putting her on edge. As soon as she was free, she looked in his direction.

'Are you buying a painting?' she asked, knowing full well that wasn't the reason he was here.

'May I?' He pointed to the chair next to her.

Bea nodded. He looked upset but this wasn't something that was new to her. Last time he'd also turned on the tears, promising her the world, but things clearly never changed. She didn't like to see anyone upset, but he should have thought about how his actions would affect her.

'Please come home. I promise you things will change. I want the same as you, marriage, children, a proper home.'

'When was the last time you asked me what I wanted?'

'I know you don't want all this…' He waved his arm around the boat. 'You don't really want to be here, do you?'

Bea felt her heart begin to race for all the wrong reasons. 'Why wouldn't I want to be here?'

'Because it's not home. I know what you like. You like getting in from work and having a brew in the garden no matter how cold it is. You like watching box sets curled up with a box of chocolates with your fluffy throw. You like being a home bird surrounded by what you know. I know I've made a mistake and I'm sorry but please let me put this right. Our song is Rick Astley, "Never Going to Give You up", and that's my motto. It's me and you.'

Bea had to admit that he did look genuinely sorry. He reached across and put his hand on her knee. His eyes were brimming with tears as he pleaded with her.

She thought about everything he'd said.

'And you're genuinely sorry?'

'I am,' he replied.

'I'll accept your apology.'

Carl exhaled. 'I knew you'd come round.'

Bea wasn't smiling. 'Like I've just said, I accept your apology but there is no us. That ended when you made a fool out of me for a second time. Yes, I may like all those things you've just listed, but I can do them wherever I am,' she said calmly.

'You don't belong here. You know you don't.' Carl stood up and took a couple of steps forward. He raked his hand through his hair, something he did when he was frustrated. 'All this is a holiday and you're turning it into a deluded dream.' He walked off towards the paintings and Bea hoped he was taking a moment to calm down. He hovered in front of the painting of Patsy and Morgan before moving slowly on to the next then spinning back around towards her. His eyes were wide, and he now looked angry. Bea wasn't quite sure what was going on but noticed his eyes were fixed on the seahorse necklace hanging around her neck.

'Who's the artist?' Carl asked, not taking his eyes off her.

'Nolan Hemingway.'

Carl pointed at the painting of Bea enjoying her day on Castaway Bay. 'Is this you?'

'Yes,' she replied.

'And are you and him…?'

The question hung in the air.

Carl exhaled again. 'We've been through so much together and this is just a blip. There's always going to be good and bad times and we can get through anything. As a team. Please, can we put everything behind us? I just want you back at home where you belong.'

Bea didn't answer.

'Just think about it. Like I said, I'm staying at Starcross Manor. I'll wait around for you until 8pm tomorrow night. If you don't turn up, I'll know you aren't coming home and I won't ever contact you again.' His ultimatum issued, he walked off the boat and made his way up the riverbank.

Bea was nonplussed. Could they put it all behind them and start again? But then her eyes flicked towards The Little Blue Boathouse, where Nolan was leaning against the door, drinking from a mug. He looked devilishly handsome. He smiled over at her and just his smile raised Bea's spirits. He waved before disappearing inside.

Bea glanced towards the little attic room above The Little Blue Boathouse. She was conflicted. Was this just a holiday, a blip in her life, as Carl said? How would she feel about this place once Nolan had left? So many questions were whirling in her mind.

Chapter Nineteen

Bea let out a squeal, her arms gripped tightly around Nolan's waist. She was laughing hard as Nolan pedalled the bike over the bumpy ground. With the wind in her hair, she closed her eyes and prayed she didn't fall off. 'Slow down, you're going too fast,' she bellowed.

'I can't slow down! If I do, we'll stop and you'll fall off. I've got some momentum going. Just hold on.'

With a racing heart, Bea held on for dear life. Although she was protesting, she was enjoying every second of it.

'What I want to know is: how do you not know how to ride a bike?'

Ten minutes earlier Bea had confessed just that. It wasn't something that she'd learned as a child and she'd never had reason to think about it since.

'There's no point when you can have a seat and let someone else do all the hard work.'

'Cheeky!' Nolan began to swerve in a zig-zag pattern,

causing Bea to scream some more and squeeze her eyes shut.

'Stop it!'

As they raced along the river path Bea reflected that the scenery and company were just perfect. People were out walking and she shouted good evening to all of them as she and Nolan rode past. She always felt so happy and safe in Nolan's company.

Turning up the lane towards the B&B, Nolan applied the brakes and brought the bike to a gentle stop outside. Lowering her legs to the ground, Bea steadied herself with Nolan's help. They both wore wide smiles.

'I have to say, I loved every second of that – even though my bum is a little sore.'

'Not as sore as my ears with you screaming,' replied Nolan, handing her the crutches. 'Right, I'm going to carry on with our investigations, and if there is anything to report shall I call back in on my way home?'

'Er, yes! You can't keep valuable information from your partner. Good luck.' Without thinking, Bea leaned towards Nolan and placed a swift kiss on his cheek.

'Hemingway and Fernsby are about to crack the case!' Nolan swung his leg over the bike, pushed off and rang the bell as his legs turned the pedals. She watched him all the way to the end of the lane, where he waved above his head before disappearing around the corner.

Bea turned around to find Julia watching her through the open window of the reception area.

'Isn't the first flush of love a wonderful thing?' She made

a heart shape with her hands and placed it against her chest.

Bea grinned as she rolled her eyes and pointed to the door with her crutch. 'Would you be kind enough to open the door for me?'

Julia was immediately up on her feet. 'Of course, but silence speaks a thousand words, or so the saying goes ... or something like that.'

Bea hadn't denied it, because she agreed with Julia, but she knew she was going to have to keep hold of those feelings, otherwise in a few weeks' time her heart was going to be smashed into smithereens when Nolan left Heartcross.

Chapter Twenty

N olan cycled up the long drive of Foxglove Farm. The magnificent farmhouse stood in front of him and he could see the appeal of living here. Checking the signpost, he followed the path to the right and immediately saw the vintage caravan, which was just as Bea had described. There was no sign of life. As Nolan propped his bike up at the side of the van, he suddenly felt nervous.

'Who goes there?'

He nearly jumped out of his skin.

Martha had opened the door without him noticing and was peering through the beaded curtain.

'Hi, it's Nolan. We met briefly the night of the storm.'

'We did. And what can I do for you?'

Nolan wasn't sure but thought it seemed as though Martha was a little on edge. 'Have you got time to do me a reading?' he asked, unsure whether he actually wanted her to look into his future. But he needed to engage Martha in conversation if he wanted to see the painting inside the caravan, and this seemed the only way.

Martha parted the curtains and Nolan made his way past the potted cherry-red geraniums.

'Money in the bowl. Five pounds.'

Rummaging in his pocket, Nolan pulled out a five pound note and stepped inside the caravan. It was exactly how Bea had described it. Immediately his eyes were drawn to the paintings on the wall.

'Take a seat. It's very unusual I get a man wanting to know their fortune.' Martha was watching him closely. 'Usually, they think it's a pile of claptrap.'

'I'm willing to give it a go,' replied Nolan. 'It's a very lovely van you have here. I love your paintings. I'm an artist.'

'I know. I've seen your paintings for sale outside The Little Blue Boathouse. You're very talented.'

'Thank you. I think I get that from my grandfather.' Nolan pointed to the painting on the wall. Taking his chance, he said, 'I've been there. It was one of my grandfather's favourite spots. He wrote about it in his logbook.'

'Logbook?' queried Martha.

'My grandfather sailed the seas and the rivers. He logged every trip. Even one to Heartcross many moons ago.' Nolan looked towards the painting. 'He had fond memories of that bay.'

An odd silence descended for a moment, but Nolan

decided to press on. 'I've just renovated his old boat – The Hemingway. It was his pride and joy. But I shouldn't be giving anything away, should I?' He gave a little chuckle. Martha seemed preoccupied and avoided eye contact with him as she stared into the crystal ball.

'Have you been in this area long?' he asked, taking the seat opposite her.

'All my life,' replied Martha. 'Shall we start?'

Realising she wasn't going to answer his questions, he nodded.

'You need to remember my reading isn't set in stone. Your destiny is in your own hands.' Still concentrating on the crystal ball in front of her, Martha began to run her hands frantically over it. Suddenly, she paused. Pulling her veil over her head, she said, 'I'm sorry to see your grandfather has passed away.'

Nolan noticed that Martha's voice had softened and her hands were shaking slightly. He watched her closely.

'Thank you,' he replied.

'He was a good man, a kind man, a generous man and a handsome man.' This time she glanced in Nolan's direction.

'He was all of those things.'

'I see you have had other sadness in your life and I commend you. You have taken time out for you. You're working on being happy within yourself and living your life as you want to instead of how society expects you to. It takes some guts not to have a permanent place to call home.'

'I do have a permanent place to call home.'

'You do,' replied Martha, this time with a smile. 'It just keeps moving about.'

'The Hemingway.'

She nodded. 'You're at your happiest when you're on the boat. It's going to be your lifeline. You have the ability to make money and you will be a success in what you want to do.' Martha's hands kept moving. 'But you're swathed with guilt.' Martha gave him a sideward glance. 'Hannah would have wanted you to get on with your life. She wants you to be happy.'

Nolan's mouth dropped open. 'How do you know Hannah's name?'

'It's in here. Everything is in here. Be true to who you are and there's no need to feel guilty.'

Nolan knew that since he'd set eyes on Bea, he'd felt guilty. When he was married to Hannah, he could never have imagined himself with anyone else. He'd thought they'd grow old together and have a wonderful life. He had never expected things to change as they did. But as the saying goes, time heals all things, and there was something about Bea that gave him that good feeling again, one he hadn't felt in a long time. She was humorous, kind, beautiful and he'd found himself thinking about her even when he wasn't with her. But even though he knew he had feelings for her, he was struggling. Of course Hannah would want him to get on with his life but he didn't know if he was strong enough to do that. He'd never experienced heartache like he had when Hannah passed away, and even though something as tragic was unlikely to happen to him again, the only way he could be sure of that was to not get too close to anyone again.

'You deserve happiness,' added Martha.

Nolan swallowed a lump in his throat. He could feel himself tearing up, the emotion still raw, but he managed to compose himself. Bea had relit a tiny flame inside him but it terrified him to think of letting that flame flare up into a full fire.

Martha stopped moving her hands and stared into the ball. She was silent for a second. 'Your family is going to help you make the decision about what is next for you.' She sat back in her chair and lifted the veil from her head.

'I haven't got any family,' replied Nolan. 'It's just me now.'

Martha stood up and gestured for Nolan to do the same. 'Your grandfather would be very proud of you.'

'Thank you,' he replied, taking another glance towards the painting of Castaway Bay on the wall. He wanted to take a closer look. He knew that his grandfather always signed the back of his paintings. He took the plunge. 'Martha, can I ask you, do you know of anyone called Patsy that lives – or lived – around here?'

'Why do you ask?'

'I would like to talk to her about my grandfather. I know she was based in Glensheil and worked at The Little Blue Boathouse.'

Martha walked Nolan to the door.

'When my grandfather passed away, I discovered some items he'd kept from around the time he visited Heartcross, and a painting he did of them both. In fact, it's displayed on The Hemingway. It's the centre of my new exhibition, but the only painting that's not for sale.'

'Displayed on The Hemingway, you say?'

'Yes. I've opened an art gallery on the water.'

'I'm really sorry, but I can't help you with any of this.'

'I knew it was a long shot, but I would have liked to meet Patsy and reminisce a little about Grandfather. I don't even know if she would still be alive. I checked the cemetery.'

Martha raised an eyebrow. 'What you might think is a romantic love story might not be how it actually was. People run away with nostalgia. Sometimes, things are better left in the past.'

Nolan had never thought about it like that, but Martha had a fair point, one he hadn't considered. Patsy would now be elderly and, if she was still alive, she might be happily married, have children, maybe even grandchildren and great-grandchildren. There was a possibility she wouldn't want a conversation about the past. She might not even remember his grandfather.

He stepped outside and collected his bike, while Martha stood in the doorway and watched him ride out of sight. The conversation he'd just had very much on his mind, his thoughts turned to Hannah, the life they'd had, the laughter and good times they'd shared. After losing her he'd built protective walls around himself, but he could feel that Bea had started to chip away at them, and he was beginning to wonder if the promise that he'd made to himself would soon become impossible to keep.

Chapter Twenty-One

Hearing the sound of gravel crunching, Bea looked up and saw Nolan wheeling his bike up the path towards her. He had a beaming smile on his face as he propped the bike up against a tree.

'I see you're taking it easy,' he teased.

Bea was lying in a hammock that was tied up between two trees at the bottom of the garden. She'd spent the last thirty minutes enjoying the early evening sun whilst reading a book.

'Absolutely! This is the life,' she replied, thinking the norm for her at this time would usually be fighting her way through town to start the night shift. Lying in a hammock was definitely the better option.

Nolan stood admiring the view of the mountainous terrain. 'This place is spectacular. It's really something else. You can see why people don't want to leave Heartcross once they've arrived.'

'That'll be everyone, except you,' remarked Bea, noticing Nolan lost in thought for a moment. 'You okay? I didn't mean anything by that.'

'It's okay, it's not you,' he replied.

'What is it then? For a second there, you looked like you had the weight of the world on your shoulders.'

'It's nothing. Honestly, I think the day is catching up with me.'

Bea wasn't convinced and could see that Nolan had something on his mind but she didn't want to push him. If there was something he wanted to talk about he would come to her in his own time. 'How did it go with Martha? Anything to report?'

'I couldn't get close enough to the painting to see if it was my grandfather's but it's exactly the same style as his.' Nolan didn't elaborate on what Martha had revealed about Hannah. 'But I did get a chance to ask her if she knew anyone called Patsy. She told me I should consider whether Patsy would even want to be found.'

'Interesting. Did she give a reason for that?' Bea sat up slightly in the hammock, being careful not to over-rock it.

'It felt as though she was warning me off.'

'What do you mean?' asked Bea, closing her book.

'I might be overthinking things, but I realised when I was cycling over here that she never specifically answered whether she knew of anyone called Patsy. She might have a fair point though – Patsy might not remember that summer in Heartcross the way my grandfather did. And the more I think about it, what's it going to achieve, finding Patsy? It's not as though my grandfather is still alive to be reunited with her.'

'But there's the letter in your grandfather's box,' said Bea.

'Maybe it's best left unread. They may have fallen in love that summer but maybe a summer love was all it was ever meant to be. Maybe it just wasn't their time.'

'Do you believe in timing?' asked Bea, curiously.

'I do,' replied Nolan, holding her gaze. 'Timing is everything.'

Bea didn't question him further. Maybe if she stumbled across Nolan in a few more years, they would have a chance. A loss like his would shape his life in different ways and she couldn't imagine the pain he was still suffering.

'But,' continued Nolan, 'I do feel Martha might know more than she's letting on. It wasn't anything in particular, it was just more of a vibe she was giving off. When she was looking into the ball she hesitated at one point and pulled her veil over her head. She mentioned my grandfather passing away and if I wasn't mistaken, she looked upset.'

'Maybe she doesn't like speaking of people that have passed because she knows it upsets people to think about those they've lost.'

'Possibly. But apart from taking a closer look at that painting I'm not sure what else I could do now. She did say one thing that confused me though.'

'Which was?'

'That my family was going to help me make a decision.'

Nolan shrugged. 'As I told her, I haven't got a family. It's just me and my boat.'

'The case runs cold for Hemingway and Fernsby then. Maybe it's best just leaving it as the perfect memory it is right now – an ideal summer of love that two people shared once upon a time long ago. Whatever is written in the letter isn't for us to know. Unless, of course, curiosity gets the better of you at some point,' Bea added, trying to lighten the mood.

'It won't,' he said, smiling. 'Even though, I have to confess, I did hold it up to the light once to try and see if I could read anything, but I couldn't,' he admitted. 'And I felt very guilty afterwards.'

'And so you should,' agreed Bea with a grin. 'And did Martha give you any idea what your future held?'

Immediately, Nolan's thoughts turned to Hannah and Martha saying she would have wanted him to be happy. From time to time, Nolan had felt Hannah's presence. On a couple of occasions, it had even stopped him in his tracks when he'd thought he'd smelled her perfume. There was just something about completely letting go and moving on with another person that he was struggling with.

'No, not really,' he said. It was a little white lie. He didn't know why, but as soon as the words left his mouth, he felt restless about it.

'There was nothing at all?' probed Bea.

Nolan was quiet. There was something about Bea that he liked. She'd been the first person he'd ever opened up to about Hannah and the more time he spent with her, the more time he wanted to spend with her ... but was that just going to make it more difficult when it was time to say goodbye?

He swerved the conversation in a totally different direction. 'I saw you had a visitor to the boat this afternoon.'

'I did. He wants me to go home and make yet another fresh start.'

'And how do you feel about that?'

Bea shrugged. 'It's a difficult one. He's all I've ever known. I know what I'm going to get and—'

Nolan interrupted her. 'Do you not think you deserve more?'

Bea exhaled. 'He's part of the family.'

'Is he though? As an outsider looking in, I'd say he was a man you dated and decided to live with. If that relationship breaks down, surely your family would stick by you, their blood. They would have loyalty.'

'You'd think so, wouldn't you?'

'You put your trust in him and your loyalty. Did he give you the same back?'

Bea heard Nolan's point loud and clear.

'Sorry, I shouldn't be saying any of this,' he added. 'It isn't any of my business.'

'It's okay. I agree with you, but going back to my "real life" is what people expect me to do.'

'People?'

'Emmie and Carl. They think I'm out of my mind to just up sticks and move here. They think I'm deluded and that

I'd never cope with the change of routine or living away from the town I grew up in.'

'You deserve to be treated like you're the only girl in the world.' Nolan looked at her with such warmth that her stomach gave a tiny flip.

'But it won't be you that treats me that way, will it? You're going to sail into the sunset and leave me broken-hearted.' She brought her hands up to her chest and pulled a sad face. Even though she was saying it in jest, there was a tiny part of her that hoped Nolan would change his mind. But deep down she knew he wouldn't.

Hearing a woof behind them, Bea turned and saw that Woody, Julia's blue roan cocker spaniel, had spotted a newbie in the garden and was racing towards the hammock. He stopped metres from Nolan and playfully stretched out his front paws, barking at him.

'Woody, it's okay,' said Bea, laughing. 'He's not sure about you!'

Hearing Bea's voice, Woody began to wag his tail frantically and jumped up at the hammock.

'Woody!' The hammock began to sway. 'Oh my!' squealed Bea. She dropped her book and clung on to the sides but she wobbled so much that the hammock swung her right over into the strapping arms of Nolan, who caught her from landing on the grass – and, taking her weight, landed on his backside with a bump, Bea falling right on top of him. Thankfully, her ankle never hit the ground. For a second, they stared into each other's eyes, their faces just centimetres apart. With her heart pounding and the chemistry fizzing between them, Bea mentally ordered herself to calm down.

Woody thought it was all a game. He began to jump all over them, attempting to lick them, which made them both burst into hysterical laughter.

'Is accident-prone your middle name? You shouldn't be allowed out on your own. You're going to end up breaking every bone in your body.'

'That wasn't my fault, it was Woody's. I was quite happily minding my own business in the hammock.'

'You can get off me now, before we both get licked to death by an over-enthusiastic cocker spaniel.'

Bea laughed then realised she couldn't get up. She was sitting on top of Nolan and would have to put her weight on her ankle to move. She looked towards the hammock. If she could grab that, she might be able to pull herself up. The only other option was to roll on to her hands and knees and let Nolan help her up, but that wasn't very ladylike. On the count of three she reached up, grabbed onto the hammock and managed to pull herself upright. With her sore ankle raised behind her, she balanced on one leg before extending her hand to Nolan to help him up. Woody had now lost interest and was off up the garden, sniffing frantically after the scent of foxes.

'I thought you were going to leave me down there for a moment,' he said, grinning as he brushed himself down.

'Death by dog licks is not what I'd want written on my gravestone.'

As soon as the words left her mouth, she noticed that

Nolan's smile had slipped and realised that his thoughts might have turned to Hannah.

'I best be going,' he said, handing Bea her crutches.

Her words had obviously triggered something inside Nolan and she could kick herself.

'I'm sorry, I didn't mean anything by it.'

He touched her arm. 'I know. It's not you.' He exhaled and looked at Bea. 'Every time I'm having fun I feel guilty, knowing I'm alive and Hannah isn't.' He swallowed a lump. 'I am healing, and getting stronger every day… It's taking time but I'll get there.'

'You will. Do you want me to come back with you?'

'I'm going to lose myself in some painting and there's a book I want to finish reading but thank you. I'll come over and pick you up for work in the morning.'

'Okay, but I'm putting a cushion on that bike seat. My backside is so sore from earlier.'

He laughed and began to wheel the bike towards the path that led around to the front of the B&B, Bea walking next to him.

'You've got the hang of those crutches now,' he said.

'It's easy when you know how. My ankle actually feels a lot better tonight.'

'That's good.'

As they reached the gate Nolan hovered for a moment. 'I do like spending time with you.'

Bea could sense there was a 'but' coming, but she cut in before Nolan could say any more. 'I know and you don't need to explain. I'm not sure life is meant to be easy.'

'It's not.' He leaned in towards her and placed a soft kiss on her cheek. 'But I am glad you're here. 8.30am – be ready.'

He swung his leg over the bike, pushed off and began to cycle up the lane. Bea stood and watched him go. Her heart went out to him. She knew he was trying to come to terms with the fact that life goes on, even after a devastating loss, but she hoped that their time together could help him heal a little more.

Nolan was soon out of sight and Bea headed back to the garden on her crutches to finish reading her book. She was thankful that her ankle was feeling better. Hopefully in the next day or so she could return to the attic at The Little Blue Boathouse, because she loved waking up to that view.

Hearing the sound of an engine behind her, Bea turned and saw a taxi pull up at the entrance of the B&B. The door swung open and a slim woman stepped out with hair that bounced above her shoulders – hair that wouldn't look out of place in a TV hair commercial – and a sun tan that gave her a healthy glow and complemented her colourful dress. There was something familiar about her that Bea couldn't quite put her finger on. She knew she'd seen this woman before but couldn't recollect where. Bea never forgot a face so she racked her brains. No doubt it would come back to her soon.

Chapter Twenty-Two

Nolan greeted Bea with a smile as he bounced the tyres over the uneven ground and attempted to pull a wheelie. She'd been waiting for him at the gate for the last five minutes and tapped her watch as he screeched to a halt.

'You're late!' she trilled. 'And that was a poor attempt at showing off.'

'It wasn't that bad,' he protested. 'Jump on board, your carriage awaits.'

Bea handed her crutches to Nolan who balanced them on the handlebars. 'And how is the injured patient this morning?'

'Very good. My ankle feels a lot better. I think I'll take some baby steps on deck today, unaided, and see how I get on,' she replied. Pointing to the seat, she asked, 'What is that?'

'A homemade cushion,' replied Nolan proudly. 'It's a

carrier bag with one of my shirts inside and I've tied it securely around the seat. It's to give you extra comfort.'

'I am impressed,' replied Bea, a smile touching her lips. Easing herself onto the seat, she bent her legs back so that Nolan could easily get his foot on the pedal. With a huge push, he began to move, leaving Bea giving a tiny squeal as she grabbed on to his waist.

'Hold on!'

'I'm holding.'

'How was the rest of your night? asked Nolan, giving her a quick glance over his shoulder as they whizzed along the river path towards The Little Blue Boathouse.

'I had a phone call with Emmie.'

'And how did that go?'

'I told her that I was staying here for an extended holiday and I hadn't made a decision about the rest of my life but when I did, she would be the first to know.'

'That's fair enough.'

'Apparently Carl is heading home this morning. He gave me an ultimatum but I don't think it quite went how he'd planned it.' Last night Bea had watched 8pm come and go and she'd felt nothing except relief. There'd been a time when Carl had consumed her mind twenty-four hours a day – but not now. Bea knew her feelings for him were dead and buried. Even though he was all she'd ever known, it was time for a change.

'But Emmie is coming to the meeting tonight?'

'Yes, and I'm hoping it's going to be packed.'

'I think it will be. I nipped to the village shop earlier and there were posters everywhere advertising it.'

Applying the brakes, Nolan slowed the bike and put both feet on the ground. He kept the whole thing steady as Bea carefully climbed off.

'And how's your backside doing?' asked Nolan.

'Just fine,' she replied, smiling.

'Yep, it looks just mighty fine to me.' With a glint in his eyes, he handed her the crutches then pointed to The Hemingway. 'There's a ramp so that you can walk straight on to the boat.'

Bea looked across at the wooden ramp. 'You've been busy.'

'Roman noticed the sign for the gallery and called in. We got to chatting and he told me there was a spare ramp on one of the water taxis I could use. He secured it to the side of the boat and it works wonderfully.'

There was already a queue of tourists heading towards The Little Blue Boathouse, and with the sun shining it was clear it was going to be another busy day ahead. 'I'd best get this place opened up … and you need to go and make me some money,' he said with a smile.

Bea saluted. 'Such a hard taskmaster.'

Making her way towards The Hemingway, she was soon on board and, after making a cup of tea, she walked round inspecting Nolan's paintings without the aid of her crutches, before opening the door to the deck, revealing the floating art gallery at its finest.

The sun was already shining down and according to the

weather app this was going to be one of the hottest days on record. She positioned her chair under the roof of the boat but where she could still enjoy the warmth of the sun, and, taking her notebook and pen out of her bag, began to prepare her speech for tonight.

More and more boats were arriving for the River Festival. Bea had been added to the WhatsApp Community group and preparations were underway for an evening of spectacular fireworks as well as Martha's special secret afternoon lunch cooked by Gianni, the chef at The Lakehouse. According to Isla, who'd posted in the group this morning, everyone needed to be vigilant because Martha was sensing something was going on and had begun to ask questions.

'Good morning!' Bea looked up to see Felicity walking onto the boat with a huge smile. 'What a beautiful day. How are you doing? How's the ankle?'

'It's getting better. I've just put some pressure on it and it's feeling okay at the moment.' Bea crossed her fingers. 'Have you got time for a drink?'

Felicity checked her watch and nodded. 'A quick one. I've just dropped the aluminium urns off for tonight's meeting. It'll be easier to serve up tea and coffee with those. We also have a selection of refreshments to bring along later.'

Bea stood and walked towards the kitchen. 'Would you like tea or coffee?'

'Just a glass of water will be great.'

Whilst Bea poured her a glass of water, Felicity admired

the paintings and the decor of The Hemingway. 'Just look at this boat. It's magnificent. I can see the appeal of living on the water.' She sat down in a chair next to Bea. 'Especially on days like this, with these doors folded back.'

Bea handed her the water.

'Thank you. And this gallery is such a good idea. These paintings are magnificent. Do you think if I asked Nolan to paint one of the teashop, he would? We could hang it inside.'

'There's no harm in asking.'

Felicity took a sip of water. 'And apart from your ankle, how are you doing? I think there's a possibility I may have met your sister and your ex this morning. They ate breakfast, then he left in a taxi that sounded like it was en route to the train station.'

Bea let out a breath. 'He's gone? That is music to my ears.'

'Julia was telling me you've extended your holiday?'

'I have, even though some people seem to think that I'm not capable of knowing what I want.'

'And these people are?' questioned Felicity, her tone warm and caring. 'Sorry, you might not want to talk about it and here's me firing questions at you.'

Bea smiled. 'It's okay, it's nice to have someone to talk to.'

Felicity rummaged inside her bag and brought out a white paper bag. 'A chocolate flapjack, made by Mother, is always good in a crisis.'

'And you carry it in your bag, expecting a crisis?' asked

Bea, taking a piece from Felicity and devouring it in seconds. 'This is so good!'

'It is, isn't it? It was one of those mornings when I thought, I'm taking some of that before it sells out,' she replied, smiling. 'It's no good for the waistline, owning half a teashop, and most days I find myself walking in the direction of the chocolate shop next to The Old Bakehouse. Have you been in either of those yet?'

'I daren't. I would buy the entire shop. But I must go and take a look.'

'So, who are these people who think you aren't capable of knowing what you want?'

Bea found herself suddenly emotional. 'Everything is a little bit of a mess and I'm torn between what I think I want to do and what people expect me to do.'

'Can you talk to your sister about it?' asked Felicity tentatively.

'It's a tricky one.' Bea didn't want to be disloyal to her sister by bad-mouthing her but she did need to talk to someone. She was a good judge of character, and she could see that Felicity was a kind and caring individual. She also needed a friend right now.

'We don't see eye to eye on most things. Sometimes I think she forgets she's my sister. She talks *at* me instead of to me, if that makes sense? Her way is always the right way and my opinion really doesn't count for much even when it's about me. I think she thinks I'm having a mid-life crisis, turning up here, despite my not being middle-aged. She also thinks that once I've calmed down, I'll return home and go back to the same routine.'

'And will you? Is the ex still an ex? He travelled a long way, I'm assuming to put your relationship right.'

'You assume right. He cheated and it's not the first time but my sister still thinks I should give him another chance.'

'But it's what you want that counts.'

Bea was quiet for a moment. 'I think I want to stay here permanently. It's a very different way of living from what I'm used to but there's something about this place that makes me feel good.' She shrugged. 'I don't know where I'll end up but I do know I don't want my ex back. It's just … every time I speak to my sister, I doubt myself.'

'There's a simple solution to that. Don't speak to her about this situation. You need to come to your own conclusions about what you're going to do. You don't have to make a decision now. Just take each day as it comes. And you don't ever need to feel alone. What you'll find out about Heartcross is that we all rally together in anyone's time of need. We're your friends now and we'll be here for you no matter what. You'll see that for yourself when you meet everyone tonight.'

'I have to admit I'm feeling nervous about the meeting.'

'Don't be. It's good that someone has spotted what we need here in the village. It's a serious subject and it needs to be addressed.'

'I was reading online about your fundraising for the bridge. It was remarkable.'

'Again, it's just about recognising what the community

needs and pulling together. When the bridge collapsed, we were stranded. We couldn't leave the village, but with the power of social media we could get the attention of the rest of the country, and the more people that heard about it, the more who jumped on board.'

Bea liked Felicity. She was warm and honest and very easy to talk to.

'I hope you're planning to stay and see this project through to the end. After all, it was your brilliant idea to get a river rescue up and running.'

'You're right. I do want to do everything in my power to bring awareness and make this happen.'

'And judging by the passion in your voice, you will. As I said, don't make any rash decisions about your life, don't let anyone pressurise you, and take each day as it comes. I'm always around if you fancy a chat, a walk or eating flapjacks on a magnificent boat. Whatever is meant to be will happen.'

'Thank you. It feels good to talk about this with someone who is impartial,' said Bea. She still didn't know if this was just an extended holiday and if she could really move away from home permanently, and her growing feelings for Nolan complicated things, but talking to Felicity had shown her she didn't need to rush into any decisions.

'It is good to talk, but we are all on a mission *not* to talk tonight.' Felicity cocked an eyebrow.

'Huh?' replied Bea, taking a last sip of her drink.

'We can talk about the river rescue but we all need to keep Martha's birthday at The Lakehouse under wraps.

She thinks something is going on and of course she's right. She doesn't miss a trick. It's been difficult keeping Gwen's arrival under wraps and I'm not sure it's going to stay a surprise. But we've not long to go. So, fingers crossed.'

'Isla must be very excited to see her mum.'

'Oh, she is. It's going to be an emotional reunion all around. Anyway, I need to get back to the teashop before my mum sends out a search party. I'll see you tonight and if you ever need to talk...' She scribbled her mobile number on a piece of paper. 'Just call or text me. You don't need to feel lonely in this village.'

'Thank you,' replied Bea. This really was a community like no other.

'Looks like you're about to get busy!' Felicity pointed to the tourists who had just returned from an excursion and were now walking up the jetty and noticing the sign for the little floating gallery. They were heading Bea's way. 'I'll see you tonight.'

She walked across the ramp, stepped back onto the river path and climbed into her car, which was parked at the back of The Little Blue Boathouse. Bea welcomed the tourists onboard and they immediately passed compliments about the floating gallery.

With a couple of sales already under her belt by mid-morning, Bea was happily chatting away to tourists, nearly all of whom said that if they could live in Heartcross, they would.

'But why can't you just up and move here?' Bea asked a woman who'd just purchased Nolan's painting of the bridge with the castle and mountains in the background.

'Roots. You get settled into a routine and only really dream about living in places like this,' the woman replied.

'Dreams can come true though,' replied Bea, handing the woman her receipt.

'If only,' she said with a smile before walking down the ramp, swinging her bag as she went.

'But they can,' murmured Bea. The woman had hit the nail on the head. 'I'm young and carefree and what is stopping me from doing what I want? Absolutely nothing!' Felicity was right, there was no pressure to make a decision about anything today or even tomorrow. All she needed to do was go with the flow and live for the moment.

Feeling a presence behind her, Bea spun round to see a woman admiring the paintings. She must have stepped on board when Bea was serving the last customer.

'Good afternoon. If you want any help don't hesitate to ask,' Bea said warmly.

The woman nodded her thanks. Bea noticed that she was dressed immaculately, in a style that reminded Bea of a Hollywood superstar, with a lightweight head scarf and oversized sunglasses covering most of her face. The scent of her perfume delicate and classy.

'These are very impressive; are you the artist?' The

woman turned her head slightly to look over her shoulder at Bea.

'No, not me. The artist is Nolan. He's currently working over at The Little Blue Boathouse. We swapped jobs for a couple of days because I sprained my ankle.'

Bea couldn't quite place the woman's accent, but she was friendly and continued to praise the paintings as she walked around the boat.

'Do you live here?' she asked.

'No, yes … actually, I'm not sure.' Bea realised how confusing that must have sounded. She quickly added, 'I was here on a two-week holiday and I've extended it, but now I'm considering leaving everything behind to start somewhere new. Are you from Heartcross?' she asked. She loved finding out about people and their backgrounds.

'Once upon a time, but I was a little like you. Weighing up my options. Everyone told me what I couldn't do and for a moment I doubted myself, but after a family argument I upped and left and started a new life.'

'Any regrets?' asked Bea, then realised the question was a little intrusive. 'Sorry, I shouldn't have asked that, curiosity got the better of me.'

'That's okay.' The woman smiled. 'It was one of the hardest decisions I've ever made. At first there were no regrets but would you believe after all this time I'm beginning to feel a little homesick? As we get older we start to think about our time left on this earth. It's made me realise time is precious and I wish I could see my family more. Do you have family?'

'Just a sister, and a bossy one at that.'

The woman laughed. She carried on looking at the paintings, stopping in front of the painting of Morgan and Patsy. She lifted her sunglasses off her face and scrutinised it. 'Who is this?' she asked.

'That's Nolan's grandfather and his one great love,' replied Bea.

'Who is she?' prompted the woman.

'Unfortunately, all we know is that her name was Patsy.'

'You have a similar necklace,' observed the woman, placing the sunglasses back on the bridge of her nose.

'It's actually the very same necklace. We found it recently.'

'If you don't mind me asking, where did you find it? It's very beautiful.'

'It was inside a message in a bottle.'

'Really? That's unbelievable.'

'Yes, really. It's such a romantic love story.'

'Do tell me more.'

'This boat, The Hemingway, sailed into Patsy's life many moons ago and she and its captain fell in love and spent the summer together. That's really all we know.'

'And who painted this picture?'

'Morgan Hemingway himself. He was an artist too.'

'There's no price on it,' noticed the woman.

'Unfortunately, it's not for sale. It's the only painting I'm not allowed to sell.'

The woman nodded her understanding.

Noticing there was another group of tourists walking

towards the boat, Bea said, 'If you need anything or wish to purchase anything else, please give me a shout. I'm Bea, by the way.'

'Thank you,' she replied, not introducing herself.

Welcoming the tourists on board, Bea began chatting to them about their days and the excursion they'd just been on. Out of the corner of her eye, she noticed the woman had walked round and viewed all the other paintings and was now back in front of Morgan and Patsy. With her phone in her hand, she snapped a photo of the painting then left the boat and sat on the bench outside The Little Blue Boathouse.

It was fast approaching lunchtime and after selling one more painting Bea glanced over to see Nolan locking up and bounding towards The Hemingway like an excitable puppy.

'Lunchtime! I've been prepared again! This morning I picked us up some lunch from The Old Bakehouse and that fantastic chocolate shop next door.' Nolan didn't stop for breath. 'Look at you without crutches!' he enthused, pointing to her ankle.

Bea didn't react. She was looking over at the woman sitting on the bench. She'd taken off her headscarf.

Bea's mouth dropped open.

'What's up with you. What are you staring at?' Nolan narrowed his eyes.

'Not what. Who.' Bea pointed. The woman had now taken off her sunglasses and was looking up the river path.

Isla was walking towards her, holding the hands of both of her boys.

'Who exactly are we looking at?' asked Nolan, sounding a little confused.

Bea watched as Isla let go of her boys' hands and they began to run towards the woman. Her arms were stretched open wide, and a tsunami of tears was flowing down her cheeks. Having hugged both little boys, the woman stood up and embraced Isla, the two women clinging to each other.

Bea grabbed Nolan's arm. 'Nolan, the woman. It's the woman from last night I couldn't place.'

'What woman? What are you talking about?'

'She's been here, on the boat. I couldn't place her accent but it's New Zealand. That must Gwen – Isla's mum and Martha's daughter.'

'Ah, so the headscarf is a disguise in case Martha clocks she's back before the big reunion. That's a massive secret to keep. Good job it's not for much longer,' added Nolan.

Bea turned around and looked at the painting of Morgan and Patsy. 'Call it a hunch but I think Hemingway and Fernsby are back on the case.'

'You're talking in riddles. Spit it out,' encouraged Nolan, intrigued.

'Last night, I saw Gwen arrive at the B&B and she seemed familiar but I couldn't figure out why.' Bea walked over to the painting. 'She's been on the boat and asking questions about this painting and I see now that the reason she looks so familiar is because she looks like Patsy ... and I don't mean just looks like her, she could be her.'

'She can't be the woman in the painting, she's way too young.'

'I know, so think about it.' Bea looked back at Gwen and Isla, who were walking down the jetty and about to get a river taxi. 'Call yourself a detective? I think the woman in the painting is Martha.'

'But that's Patsy,' Nolan said, gesturing towards the painting.

Bea took out her phone and searched Google, then passed the phone to Nolan.

He read, '"The name Martha is biblical. First popular in France, then after the Reformation, in England. There, it evolved, being shortened to Matty as well as Patty. American colonists then transformed it further into Patsy." It's not that much shorter,' he remarked, 'just one letter, but anyway, you really think this is Martha?' He stared at the painting.

'Yes, I do and I think Gwen recognised her mother too. The question is – what are you going to do about it?' asked Bea.

'There's only one thing to do, ask her.'

After a day of selling paintings, Bea was sitting in The Little Blue Boathouse preparing for her meeting. People were due to start arriving at 7pm so for the next hour she would be full steam ahead.

Felicity and Rona would be arriving with refreshments

any time soon and Julia and Flynn were bringing chairs from the conference room at Starcross Manor. Bea wondered how everyone was going to fit inside the Boathouse but Nolan had pointed out that since it was such a glorious warm night, they could set up the chairs outside, which was a perfect solution.

Bea rehearsed over and over again what she was going to say at the meeting. After the conversation with Felicity, she felt a renewed sense of strength. If she could get the villagers on board with her idea, Heartcross would be a safer place for everyone. She knew it was all about the number of volunteers and the money they could raise to get the project up and running, but surely that would be doable with the likes of Flynn and celebrity chef Andrew Glossop living in the village. With the power of social media and the local press, surely they would be able to create awareness? All she could do for now was hope.

Hearing an engine sputter to a stop, she walked outside to see Julia waving at her through her van window. As soon as Julia jumped out of the van, she exclaimed, 'No crutches!'

'I know! It feels okay at the moment,' replied Bea, looking down at her ankle.

'We have the chairs,' said Flynn, opening up the back of the van.

'Perfect. Nolan has suggested we have the meeting outside, on the other side of the Boathouse.'

'Brilliant idea. Also, we thought this might come in handy.' He handed her a battery-operated microphone.

'Thanks, I think.'

'You'll be great. I'm looking forward to hearing what you have to say.' Flynn began passing the chairs to Nolan and Julia, who lined them up in rows facing the river. Flynn hammered a sign into the ground outside the entrance with an arrow directing the residents to the far side of the Boathouse, whilst Bea stood in front of the chairs, imagining the sea of faces that would be looking back at her in around an hour's time. Her heart began beating nineteen to the dozen.

Nolan appeared at her side and smiled warmly at her. 'You've got this. What you have to say is important and once you get in your stride, the nerves will disappear.'

'I hope so,' she said, placing the microphone down on a small trestle table that Julia had put in front of the rows of chairs, along with a jug of water and a glass.

'Shall we set up the tea, coffee and refreshments outside too?' asked Flynn, looking towards Bea and Julia. 'It might make it easier?'

They both nodded and Flynn and Nolan disappeared inside to bring out the aluminium urns.

'Here's Felicity and Rona now.'

They appeared around the corner carrying a basket of cups and saucers, which were soon laid out on another table at the side of the Boathouse, followed by assorted refreshments.

'I can't thank you all enough,' said Bea, overwhelmed by the effort that everyone had put in for her. She checked her watch and looked up the river path. Already there were villagers walking towards them.

'I'm actually feeling a little nervous,' Bea confided to Julia.

'You'll be great. It looks like it's going to be a fantastic turnout too.'

'You've got this,' encouraged Nolan, taking a seat next to Flynn.

'Let me point a few people out to you,' said Julia. 'Second row, we have Grace and Andrew. They live in Heartcross Castle.'

Immediately, Bea recognised the celebrity chef.

'Then we have Allie and Rory. Allie's parents own the pub, the Grouse and Haggis – they are Fraser and Meredith, sat over there. Rory is the local vet, along with Mollie, who is married to Cam, who owns The Old Bakehouse.'

'Woah! This is an overload of information.'

Julia grinned. 'Eleni, my assistant at the B&B, she goes out with Jack, the local builder. Then we have Ella and Roman, Callie and Gianni. Dolores and Hamish, from the village shop, et cetera. But here is a useful contact for you – come and say hello. This is Aidy Redfern, the local reporter. He worked with Felicity to support her fundraising for the bridge, and his articles and news reports helped to spread the word. Aidy, could I introduce you to Bea.'

Bea smiled and extended her hand. 'Pleased to meet you.'

'You too. I think what you're suggesting here is commendable and I'm really looking forward to hearing what you have to say. And if we can help at all through the news channels and the newspaper, I'm all for that.'

This was music to Bea's ears and she couldn't thank Aidy enough.

Everyone smiled in her direction and a quick check of her watch told her it was 7.30pm Bea exhaled. This was it.

As soon as she stepped to the side of the table and picked up the microphone the babble of voices in front of her died down. She noticed Emmie slip into a seat in the back row and give her a thumbs-up. Bea gave her a nervous smile. Trying to steady her hand, Bea switched on the microphone and brought it up to her mouth.

She dared a glance towards Nolan, who responded with a reassuring smile, giving Bea the confidence to take the plunge.

'Thank you all for coming,' Bea said, looking around at the community and acknowledging everyone with a nod of her head. 'I've invited you all here to talk about the river and our safety. Water is unpredictable. For some, the River Heart is a playground, for others it's a means of making a living. People travel here to Heartcross to enjoy your welcoming community and the spectacular scenery, but also the River Heart itself.' Bea stretched out her arm and turned towards the river. Thankfully, her nerves were slowly disappearing. 'In the summer months you welcome a colossal number of tourists to this area, so many that I've found myself wondering, how on earth does this small village fit that many people in it?' The crowd laughed. 'With the number of people that visit Heartcross, I assumed when I arrived that there would already be some sort of river rescue in place. There's no doubt it's needed. In the short time I've been here I've seen paddleboarders struggling to get back on their board, swimmers in difficulty and kayaks capsizing. It's so easy to go from having the time of your life to being in mortal danger – in a matter of moments.' Bea took a breath followed by a sip of water.

'What I'm proposing is a volunteer family of community members ready to give up some of their time to helping save the lives of others. I know Heartcross is a passionate community and I know I've only been here a very short time but I hope you think this is as important as I do.' Bea turned towards Julia, who placed a large flipchart stand next to her and mounted a couple of large photographs on it. 'To begin with, we would need two boats: one all-weather boat, and a fast response boat. We would also need pagers, and another piece of kit that is essential is a drone, which can be sent up in the air to help identify any danger. We would need one volunteer watching the river at all times, and the rest of the crew would be alerted by the pagers. When those pagers go off, the volunteers would need to be prepared for absolutely anything. But saving someone's life is phenomenal. There is nothing more rewarding.' Bea could see the whole community nodding in agreement with her.

'I know you're all extremely busy – you have families and businesses to run and it's a lot to ask you to commit on a regular basis, but that is what I am asking you to do. It will take time and money to build a team of lifesavers, give them the necessary training, obtain boats and the kit – not to mention build a small headquarters, for which of course we'll need planning permission. Establishing and building a river rescue will take time but I'm hoping you will all get on board this project. I want to support the community as best I can and it's my belief that if we can all work together we can make this dream a reality.' Bea took a breath and realised what she'd just said. She wanted to stay in Heartcross and see this project through to the end – and she'd just told the entire community.

'I think I've done enough talking so I'll invite anyone to speak who has anything to add, or any suggestions or questions about how we can carry this forward.' Bea picked up her glass of water and began to panic when everyone stood up at the same time, as if they were about to leave. She looked towards Nolan, who was standing next to Julia and Flynn. All of them were smiling broadly. Nolan began to clap, then, to Bea's surprise, the rest of the community followed suit and she was surrounded my rapturous applause. They weren't leaving – it was a standing ovation. Overcome with emotion, Bea's eyes welled up with happy tears. She'd never in her life felt such a sense of belonging. This meant so much to her. Emmie was also up on her feet, clapping and nodding at her. Julia stood up, hugged Bea where she stood, and took the microphone.

'Bea has only been here for a very short time but the second I met her she gave out such warmth that I knew she was going to be an asset to this community. She was the person who raised the alarm when Lucas went missing and didn't hesitate to go clambering over rocks in stormy weather to help rescue the little boy. I think this is a wonderful idea; it's what we need to make our water safer, and, like Bea said, if we work together, I'm sure we can make it work. Now, back to Bea.'

'Does anyone have any questions?' asked Bea.

'The boats, the kit and a rescue building will cost phenomenal amounts, surely?' shouted Hamish, who was sitting at the back.

'Yes, it will be very costly, but surely we can draw on our resources in the village, and businesses in Glensheil too. We have influential businessmen living in this village...' Bea looked towards Flynn and Andrew Glossop. 'I'm sure they'll have great contacts and perhaps even ideas about sponsorship.' Bea was hopeful she hadn't overstepped but both Flynn and Andrew were nodding. 'We also have builders amongst us. Would there be any chance of putting up a small building to house the boats and the kit? Right here, where you're sitting now, could be the perfect space – an extension to The Little Blue Boathouse.'

Eleni nudged Jack, who shouted to Bea, 'I'm sure my company can help out but we need planning permission.'

'I can take care of that,' offered Arthur, who worked at the council.

'We can raise money for the kit, pagers and the drones but what we also need is a person watching the river at all times. But that would need to be from quite a high building. I was thinking about the lighthouse, but is that too far away?'

'Possibly,' shouted out Flynn. 'But we've installed new security cameras at the hotel and they are brilliant. They're attached to a very tall mast and you can swivel them to survey all areas. It's operated from a TV monitor in the office and you can flick between different areas. Maybe something like that could be set up?'

'This sounds perfect,' enthused Bea, happy to see that all the villagers were getting involved. 'I don't mind taking care of the admin and the volunteer rotas and I can set up a system that we all have access to. This is going to take some organising and it won't happen overnight, but we've already taken a step forward with this meeting.' Bea bent down and pulled out a handful of paper from the bag at the side of the table. 'If anyone would like to be a volunteer lifesaver, or can offer a donation or help to raise funds, help to buy the kit – help with anything, really – then can I please ask you to jot it down on one of these pieces of paper and give it to me, Nolan, Julia or Flynn? That will give us a starting point. I'll then go through all the papers and devise a plan and get an update out to the community by the end of next week. I'll also see about opening a bank account for any funds that are raised, and maybe we could set up a committee that could be in charge of finances. Would that be okay with everyone?' There was so much to think about and this was a huge project to coordinate, but Bea was up for the challenge.

Everyone nodded. Bea began passing out the paper along with some pens, and people began to scribble down ways that they could help. The community was enthusiastic and Bea felt that if they all worked together, they might be able to create the rescue service within the next eighteen months to two years.

'Thank you all for coming. If anyone has any further ideas or suggestions then do let me know. In the meantime, please help yourself to refreshments. I propose we hold another meeting in four weeks' time, for an update.'

The crowd was nodding and Bea felt proud of her efforts as she stepped away from the table. Emmie walked towards her with her arms open wide. 'Bea, you were brilliant!'

'Thank you,' replied Bea. 'In a funny sort of way, I was enjoying myself.'

'This is a worthwhile cause and if anyone can get this up and running, it's you.' Emmie took hold of both of Bea's hands. 'I've never seen this side of you before. Standing up there … you were full of passion. There's something different about you that I can't quite put my finger on.'

'I'm happy. I feel comfortable and I can just be me here. I know you're very fond of him, but Carl is not my future. He didn't encourage my growth. He suppressed my personality. He never let me be me and never gave me the loyalty I deserve.'

'I'm sorry, Bea. I feel like I've let you down. I should have realised that you were unhappy and I should have been a better sister.'

'It's okay, honestly it is.'

'And what about Nolan?'

Bea looked across at him. He was busy collecting the pieces of paper from the community. Every time she looked in his direction her stomach performed somersaults. He was her type of perfect but she knew she had to try and keep a little distance to protect her own heart. 'Nolan will be moving on after the River Festival and I'll miss him but I'll always be grateful to him. He's taught me how to laugh and enjoy life again.'

Isla popped her head between them. 'Sorry to interrupt but there's a taxi for Emmie here.'

'A taxi?' questioned Bea, looking at Emmie, who pointed to her suitcase standing against the wall.

'I'm heading home. I came because I needed to see for myself you're okay, and you are. In fact, I think you already have this community eating out of your hands. I can see you're happy here and I really don't blame you if you want to stay.'

Bea could see that Emmie was holding back the tears.

Emmie continued. 'It will be a good place to bring the children on holiday and we'll look forward to seeing Heartcross Life Rescue up and running. And knowing that's down to our Bea…? I'm very proud of you.'

They hugged each other like their lives depended on it. 'I'll see you soon, I promise,' whispered Emmie. 'Take care of you.'

Bea watched her sister wheel her suitcase to a taxi and climb into the back seat. She waved out of the window as the taxi drove away.

'Are you okay?' asked Isla, who was still standing next to her.

'I will be,' confirmed Bea, blinking back the tears.

Isla passed her a tissue. 'I always have a tissue handy, that's one of the joys of being a mum.'

'Thank you,' said Bea, dabbing her eyes and taking a deep breath. She looked over her shoulder to make sure there was no one else in earshot. 'And was that your mum that I saw you with today?'

Isla's smile was wide as they took a few steps to the water's edge so they couldn't be overheard. 'It was, and it's the first time she's ever met her grandchildren. I've missed her so much. I know we FaceTime but it isn't quite the same. She's back for Mum's special birthday but I'm not quite sure what my grandmother's reaction will be. Believe it or not, they haven't spoken for many years, after a family argument.'

Feeling a tap on her shoulder, Bea looked round to see Nolan holding up the collected papers. 'Firstly, you were amazing, and secondly, wait until you see all of these. I can't see one villager that hasn't volunteered in one way or another – there's offers of financial help, ideas for fundraising... The whole community loved your speech and were singing your praises.'

'This is absolutely brilliant.'

'You smashed it out of the park!'

'I think I'm actually going to make this happen.'

'I think you are. What happened to Emmie? I thought I saw her.'

'Emmie has gone home. It's okay. *We* are okay. I think we had a moment ... a good moment.'

Isla touched her arm. 'You have made us all think and

each and every one of us will help to get this project up and running.'

'And I second that,' added Nolan, smiling at them both.

Flynn tapped Nolan on the shoulder and he left Bea and Isla standing alone. Bea brought the conversation back to where it was before Nolan appeared.

'If they haven't spoken for years, how do you think it's going to pan out?' asked Bea.

'I'm actually beginning to worry. I can still feel animosity on my mother's part, though I've got no clue what has gone on between them except that my mum moved thousands of miles away as a result.'

'That must have been some argument. Surely after all these years it's time to move on?'

'You'd hope so. At first, I thought it was a good idea to surprise Granny at The Lakehouse but now I'm not sure.'

'There's always two sides to every story, and sometimes when arguments have gone on for so long, people just push all the hurt to one side and it's harder to make things right. What does your mum think about surprising Martha?'

Isla looked sheepish. 'I've not quite told her that part ... or the whole truth. In fact, I've had to tell a white lie to get her here. I'm going to have to face the music very soon and I'm not relishing that thought, but, in my defence, she's my mum and I know, deep down, she wouldn't want to miss this.'

'Which is understandable. It's tricky,' said Bea.

'What's tricky?'

Both of them jumped out of their skin. They spun round

to see Martha standing behind them, staring inquisitively. They'd kept their eye off the ball and Martha had sneaked up behind them.

Isla was quick to think on her feet. 'We said sticky! We sampled Rona's sticky buns in the teashop at lunch, and they were delicious.'

'They were,' agreed Bea, but the look on Martha's face suggested she wasn't buying Isla's answer.

'Something is going on. I can feel it. Everyone is being weird around me.' Martha waggled her finger. 'You do know I'll find out what is going on.' She gave Isla a look that meant business before turning around and walking towards Meredith and Fraser from the pub.

'Yikes, that was close,' whispered Isla.

'Too close,' agreed Bea.

'Right, let's mingle.'

Bea spotted Nolan and made a beeline for him. 'Thank you for helping out. It's much appreciated.'

'You don't have to thank me. I want to see this project up and running as much as you.'

For a moment, Bea hoped he meant he was sticking around, but this project wouldn't be up and running overnight and she knew Nolan would probably be long gone by then. 'Refreshments?' she said, wanting a comforting cup of tea.

On the way towards the refreshment table Bea received praise and pats on the back from the villagers.

'They love you,' whispered Nolan.

'I wouldn't go that far but I have to say, standing in front of the community, it was lovely to see everyone taking on board what I was saying, and I quite enjoyed it. I'm going to spend tonight at the B&B but tomorrow I want to go back to my attic room. I'm going to upload all the information that we've collected tonight to my laptop. I need to arrange meetings with Flynn and Jack, and of course the council. I'll also need an architect to design the new rescue centre and hopefully within the next couple of months we can get the planning permission and set the wheels in motion for everything else ... and you –' she pressed a finger to his chest '– you better come back and check it out once it's all up and running.'

'You try and stop me. You do know I think you are remarkable, don't you?' Bea could feel herself blushing slightly. She wasn't used to anyone giving her compliments. 'You turn up here, distraught because your life became a sudden mess, and did you sit and wallow? Absolutely not. I know you're going to get Heartcross Rescue up and running no matter what it takes, and lives will be saved because of you.'

'Anyone would have done the same.'

'But they didn't. This was down to you.'

'And I second that.' Bea hadn't realised that Amy and Lucas were standing right behind them. 'What you did for Lucas ... we'll never forget, and I know it's not much but can I give you this? It's a cheque to start off your fundraising. I wasn't sure who to make it out to so I wrote it out to The Little Blue Boathouse.' Amy handed over the cheque and looked down at Lucas who was pulling at her top.

Bea was overwhelmed. 'I can't thank you enough.' She gave a tiny squeal as she waved the cheque in front of her. 'We are now off the starting blocks. This is brilliant.'

'And I think Lucas wants to give you something too.'

Lucas was wearing the cheekiest of smiles as he reached into the pocket of his shorts and pulled out a handful of empty sweet wrappers and coins. 'My pocket money.' He cupped it in both hands and held it up towards Bea. 'There's seventy-five pence,' he said proudly. 'There was a pound but the village shop had some gobstoppers and they wanted to be eaten.'

Bea laughed and bent down in front of Lucas. 'You're a very special boy. When I get these lifeboats up and running, I think you should come back and have a special trip on one of them, because if it wasn't for you looking for treasure then all this wouldn't be happening.'

'Can I, Mum, please?' Lucas looked up at his mum with the most adorable hazel eyes.

'Of course you can.'

'Yes!' squealed Lucas, high-fiving all three of them.

'Our holiday ends in the morning but thank you very much for all that you have done and all you're doing.'

Full of emotion, Bea nodded at Amy and smiled at Lucas. She didn't trust herself to speak, knowing she was close to tears. She watched them walk away with Lucas looking back over his shoulder one last time and waving.

'Those gobstopper sweets look just the business. I might take a trip to the village shop,' Nolan said.

Bea laughed, which was just what she needed. Looking around at the gathered community members, she slipped her arms around Nolan, who gave her a much-needed hug.

'Heartcross Rescue is going to save so many lives,' he said.

'And that's the reason I'm going to work so hard to get this up and running.'

'And you're going to see the project through. That's going to take more than a few weeks in Heartcross though, isn't it?'

Bea looked up at him. 'I am and it is.' For the first time in ages, she felt passion in her belly. She was raring to go.

'Bea, could we get a photograph for the local newspaper please?'

Nolan gave her a gentle push. 'This is the start of the publicity. Get in there and shout "Heartcross Rescue" from the rooftops. There's no time for shyness.'

'You're absolutely right.' With a smile on her face, Bea posed next to The Little Blue Boathouse.

'We just need a quick interview from you and then we can get this article written up,' Aidy said, pulling out his mobile phone.

'No problem,' replied Bea.

The next evening, Bea and Nolan were sitting at the table in the living room of the B&B. Yesterday had been a huge success and, browsing through the pieces of paper that the villagers had completed, Bea couldn't believe the amount of support that had been offered. 'I think we have a crew. There are enough volunteers to actually make this work, and look…' She gave a tiny gasp and tapped the piece of paper in front of her. 'Flynn and Andrew Glossop have said they will donate initial funds to put the crew through training.'

'You're going to be so busy. This is all amazing. Making the water a safer place is a priority and you've made everyone understand this. It's going to take some doing but I know with you behind it it's going to be a huge success.'

Bea looked up at him. 'Thank you,' she said.

'What are you thanking me for?'

'For building me up, encouraging my growth. Letting me be me.'

'You don't need to thank me for that, that's just how you are. You're brilliant. You do know that, don't you?'

'It's nice to hear compliments and be appreciated.'

'And that's how it should be. Come here.' Nolan stretched out an arm and pulled her in close. Wrapped in his arms she felt safe. He hugged her tight and she closed her eyes briefly and smiled.

'I think you're going to need a personal secretary with all your meetings,' he said, breaking the silence.

That was the furthest thing from Bea's mind at this

moment. All she could think about was that the River Festival was creeping closer and, with it, Nolan's departure.

As she pulled away, she placed a hand on his chest. 'Listen. What's that?'

'I can't hear anything.'

'Shush. That.'

There was a commotion in a ground-floor bedroom. They stood up and walked to the door.

Nolan gave Bea an incredulous stare. 'What's going on in there?'

Bea recognised the voices of Isla and Gwen, and, judging by her tone, Gwen was far from happy. 'That must be Gwen's room, Isla is in there.'

They loitered outside for a second before Bea nudged Nolan. 'We shouldn't be listening.'

'What are they arguing about? Gwen has only just arrived,' he whispered, eying her.

'Probably the fact that Isla has been a little deceitful in getting her mum here. Martha is going to find out that Gwen's back, very, very soon, but I'm not sure it's a secret that needs to be revealed on Martha's birthday.'

Nolan raised his eyebrows. 'You might be right but maybe this forced reunion is the push they need.'

'It still sounds a little raw in there to me,' admitted Bea.

'What was the argument about? Why won't you tell me?' Isla's voice was fraught. 'Surely whatever it is it can be sorted out. Granny isn't getting any younger. Have you ever thought you're both as stubborn as each other?'

Bea and Nolan heard a shuffle then the click of the door.

'Mum. Where are you going? This is your room – if anyone should be leaving, it's me.'

Closing the bedroom door and stepping out into the hallway, Isla noticed Bea and Nolan standing there.

'Sorry, we weren't being nosey, we were just—'

Isla interrupted Bea. 'It's okay, I've just admitted to my mum that I got her here under false pretences and as you can see…'

'Not quite the reunion you were expecting?'

Isla shook her head, looking close to tears.

'Fancy a drink in the communal bar?' suggested Bea.

'Do I ever.'

'I'm going to leave you girls to it. I'm no good in situations like this but if there's anything I can do…'

Isla nodded her appreciation and Nolan touched Bea's arm. 'I'll pick you up in the morning.'

'Thanks,' she replied.

Nolan began to walk towards the reception but Bea called out to him and caught him up for a moment. 'Am I allowed to share the case of Hemingway and Fernsby with Isla?'

'It's up to you, but it seems she has a lot going on at the minute.'

Bea nodded her understanding and two minutes later, with double gin and tonics in their hands, Bea and Isla made their way out into the garden. It was a perfect evening for sitting outside.

'You had a very successful night, last night,' said Isla warmly, taking a sip of her drink.

'I did, but I'm not sure yours is going that swimmingly tonight.'

'I only have myself to blame. I know I've been dishonest, enticing Mum over here by telling her Granny wanted to see her and put things right, but I was feeling desperate and time is going too fast. With it being Granny's eightieth birthday, I just thought if I could get Mum here... But now I realise I shouldn't have. As Drew says, whatever is going on with them is between them and none of my business.'

'Being a grown-up can be so difficult at times.'

'It's all a mess. It's not one of my better plans.' Isla took a breath.

'You have had the best intentions. You never know, when they clap eyes on each other, all might be forgiven,' Bea said hopefully.

'What would you do?' asked Isla.

'If it was me, I would tell Martha straightaway. Whoever was right or wrong all those years ago, let's hope that after the initial shock of finding out they are both in the same village...' Bea took a breath. 'You never know, a miracle might just happen.'

'Thanks, Bea. There's nothing else I can do except hope for that very miracle.'

'Always here if you need anything. Can I ask, did Martha ever marry? Where's your grandfather in all this? Could he maybe play peacemaker?'

'It's always been just Granny. Which isn't a bad thing because I could imagine her being a handful. Some things don't change.' Isla swigged back her drink and smiled.

'Dutch courage. I know Granny always goes for a walk at this time of night so I'll go and see if I can catch up with her. Wish me luck.'

'I really do and I hope you can bring your family back together. A walk at this time will be very picturesque. I bet Martha is delighted she found those binoculars and is putting them to good use.'

'I didn't know they were lost. She's had them almost permanently attached around her neck for many years.' Isla stood up. 'And thank you for the chat. I didn't mean to dump all this on you.'

'Sometimes it's good to get it off your chest to someone who isn't directly involved.' Bea stretched a leg and wiggled her ankle. 'I have to say, this ankle is feeling a whole lot better today. I might just take a small walk over the bridge and get some fresh air myself, before I settle down for the night.'

'If you walk over the bridge, you can catch the water taxi back.'

Bea was thinking that was a good idea and maybe she would get a glimpse of The Hemingway and Nolan on her travels.

'I'll walk out with you, and I do hope all goes well with Martha.'

'Me too. The wrath of my granny isn't something I'd wish on my worst enemy. Hopefully I can somehow get my mum and her in the same room, but there's only one way to do that … emotional blackmail.'

They walked down the path together and Isla held open

the gate. 'Be careful on that ankle. Don't overdo it,' she ordered.

'I won't.'

They parted company at the bottom of Love Heart Lane and Bea made her way towards the bridge. There were a couple of private kayaks out on the water but everywhere else was quiet. The Hemingway was still anchored where it always was, by the riverbank, and with numerous paintings sold today, Bea knew that Nolan would be busy replenishing his stock.

The water taxi was heading from The Little Blue Boathouse towards the far end of Glensheil and Bea knew she had time to walk to the nearby river stop at the end of the bridge. Enjoying the fresh air, she noticed a small aeroplane soaring through the clouds and a banner trailing behind it with the words 'Freya! Marry me!' When Carl had proposed, he had used a Moonpig card that he hadn't even written inside. She should have known at that moment it was never going to last.

She noticed a woman standing in front of The Little Blue Boathouse and realised it was Martha. Bea watched as she mounted the ramp and boarded The Hemingway.

Chapter Twenty-Three

Nolan was more than a little surprised to see Martha walking onto his boat. Glancing towards the painting, he guessed why she was here.

He smiled. 'How are you? It's a lovely night for a walk.'

'It is.' Martha looked over her shoulder and up the river path. There was no one in sight except the people on the river taxi. 'Have you got time to chat?'

'Of course.' Feeling a slight tension in the air, Nolan gestured towards the seat. 'Shall we sit?' he asked.

Martha nodded and sat down on a chair opposite him. There was silence and he followed her gaze towards the church, its steeple towering at the top of the hill. Her eyes were watery and she was visibly upset.

'Is everything okay?'

'Why now?' Martha asked hesitantly.

'I don't understand,' replied Nolan. He gave her a warm reassuring smile that whatever it was, was going to be okay, even though she looked like she had the weight of the world on her shoulders.

'Some things are better left in the past.'

The mood was sombre and Nolan could guess this had something to do with his grandfather. Taking a bold step, he asked, 'Martha, did you know my grandfather? The painting in your van of Castaway—'

'Yes, I knew Morgan.'

'Are you Patsy?' he asked, cautiously.

Martha nodded. She pressed her hand to her chest and her gaze fell to the floor. 'It's been a long time since anyone has called me Patsy. It was your grandfather's nickname for me, which was silly as it was only one letter shorter than my own name.' She gave a tiny smile.

'My grandfather always talked about you and that's one of the reasons I am here. I can't believe I've actually found you. I wish my grandfather was here.'

Martha's eyes lifted to Nolan's.

'When I was growing up my bedtime stories were mainly about the travels of The Hemingway. This boat has definitely sailed many seas.' Nolan looked around it fondly. 'I'm sure it brings back some memories for you too.'

'It does.'

'The stories almost always involved secret coves, The Little Blue Boathouse and Castaway Bay. Growing up, I thought it was a make-believe place, and it was only when the village of Heartcross was all over the news a few years ago that I Google searched the place. When I saw the images of the village I realised the stories that my grandfather had told me were true. He always spoke about his time here with you with great fondness.' Nolan got up from the chair, took the message in the bottle and handed it to Martha. 'Bea and I found this at Castaway Bay. There was a necklace too.'

'We threw this into the water on our last trip to Castaway Bay. The necklace is still as beautiful now as it was back then. I always regretted putting it in the bottle and I couldn't believe it when I saw Bea wearing it.'

'She was just minding it, until we found you.'

Martha turned the letter from the bottle over in her hand. 'I remember this day like it was yesterday. It was one of the best days of my life...' Her voice faltered. 'All through that summer we were inseparable.'

'I think my grandfather thought that too.'

Martha shook her head. 'I don't think so.' She handed the bottle and letter back to Nolan, who noticed her mood had suddenly changed.

He kept his voice soft. 'I don't mean to pry but I was excited about tracking down Patsy. I was on my own adventure in The Hemingway, retracing my grandfather's summer but...'

'Exactly what do you know?' Martha held his gaze.

'Just that he talked about you and his summer at Heartcross. Even when he passed away you were still on his mind. He spoke about you then too.'

Martha wiped away a tear with a tissue. 'I knew one day all this would catch up with me. It's just too painful. I can't do this.' She stood up.

'Please don't go. I'm not sure what's going on here but there's a box full of memories from your summer together … and a letter.'

'A letter?'

Nolan nodded. 'Yes. Please sit back down.' He gestured to the chair and quickly moved to retrieve the box, which he handed to Martha.

With the box resting on her knees, she looked at him. 'There's so much to share but without your grandfather here to give his side of this story…'

Nolan leaned forward and took the box from Martha, placing it on the floor. 'What happened, Martha?'

'I don't know where to start. Too much time has passed now. Believe it or not, I've mellowed in my old age, and I don't hold any animosity towards your grandfather, but seeing you and how much you look like him has brought back a lot of feelings I've tried to bury.'

Martha was talking in riddles but Nolan could sense by the pained look on her face that she was hurting deeply. 'Martha, whatever it is, there will be no judgements on my part. I promise. Shall I make us a strong cup of tea?'

Martha shook her head. 'Tea? I think I'm in need of alcohol.'

Nolan gave a small laugh. Standing up, he took the bottle that his grandfather had purchased back in Heartcross that fateful summer and handed it to Martha. 'I've no idea what it tastes like but be my guest.' While he collected a glass from the kitchen and a bottle of tonic, Martha uncapped the bottle and took a whiff. 'It smells about sixty years old.' She smiled. 'I was with Morgan when he purchased this from Glensheil Gin.'

'I'll get you a glass of wine from the fridge, shall I?'

Nolan returned with a full glass and placed the bottle on the table. He passed the glass to Martha, who swigged it down in seconds and refilled it.

She took a fleeting glance towards the painting before she continued. 'Without any judgements, you say?'

'I promise.'

Martha took a deep breath. Her lips were slightly trembling as she began to speak. 'Your grandfather was my life for that summer. I was working at The Little Blue Boathouse when Morgan sailed in and anchored by the bank. I watched him for about three days from the attic room before he came into the Boathouse. He was handsome, dressed well and had a wild mop of hair. You take after him.'

Nolan ruffled the top of his head. 'It is a little unruly at times,' he said, with a smile.

'I was quite surprised he took a liking to me. You see, I wasn't from an affluent family. In fact for most of my childhood we were on the poverty line, living hand to mouth. It was difficult at times. I also wasn't a fan of education and after school I spent my time running errands and helping to clean. Such a different way of life from today. My first paid employment was at The Little Blue Boathouse and when it came with the attic room, I thought I'd made it.

'When I met your grandfather, he made me feel like I'd

never felt before. Those flutterings in your tummy... The second we clapped eyes on each other it was an instant connection. We laughed, we had so much fun, everything was just so easy. People come and go in your life but in here –' Martha tapped her heart '– I fell in love with your grandfather, it's as simple as that.'

He knew exactly what Martha was talking about, when she spoke of those flutterings in her stomach. What Martha was sharing was exactly how he was feeling about Bea. They laughed, had fun together and she always put him at ease. Every time he saw her, he was drawn to her. Bea's smile was everything.

'I knew he was posh and I came from the worst street in the town but that didn't matter when we were together.'

'Was it class that kept you apart?' asked Nolan tentatively.

'I didn't think so, but I'm not too sure.' Martha looked at the painting. 'He never hid the fact he was leaving after the summer, but it didn't make it any easier.' She pointed to the cliff. 'The day he left, I sat up there for hours, watching The Hemingway and Morgan sail out of my life. My heart was smashed into smithereens.' Martha took a tissue out of her pocket and dabbed her eyes. 'I vowed I never wanted to feel hurt like that ever again but I did, six months later ... when I went looking for him.'

'I didn't realise you'd seen each other again. My grandfather never said,' Nolan replied, surprised.

'He didn't see me. I remember he'd talked about where he lived. Cornwall. It's a hell of a way from here. I took several trains and buses, along with Bonnie. It was like a mini holiday and cost us all of our wages and some.'

'If you travelled all of that way, why didn't you see my grandfather?'

'I did see him. It was the beginning of February. The weather was bitterly cold and there was snow on the ground. Even the church steeple was covered.'

'The church?'

'He was standing in the arched doorway of the church, looking more handsome than when I saw him last, if that was possible. His suit was exquisitely cut, his hat perched on his head and that was when I realised – he was getting married.' The colour had drained from Martha's face, the hurt still very much visible.

Nolan knew the marriage between his grandparents hadn't been one of love and passion, but more of being pushed together by two wealthy families. It was destined to not work out, and even though couples stayed together through thick and thin back in those times, his grandmother eventually upped and left, leaving his grandfather a single parent. He never remarried.

'Martha, I don't know what to say, except I'm sorry.'

'How could I speak to him then? It was his wedding day. He was laughing and joking with his best man and I watched him walk into the church as his bride arrived. I couldn't believe he'd moved on from me so quickly and my whole world came crashing down. I felt so alone and a fool. I thought about him every day and hoped he would come looking for me. When I saw The Hemingway –' Martha wafted her hand in front of her face and fought back a tsunami of tears that was about to freefall '– I thought…'

'I can imagine it must have been a bit of a shock. I know it's no consolation but over the years he always talked about you and this place and that's why I'm here now – to see how magical it is. And it's everything I imagined it would be, and more.'

'It is.'

'I don't want to upset you further and I understand if you don't want to read the letter but he did write it for you.'

Martha looked towards the box and slowly picked it up. Balancing it on her knee, she cautiously took off the lid. Staring at the memories in the box she placed her hand on her chest. 'The ticket to the bandstand. This was where we shared our first kiss. And these rocks and shells … we collected them from Castaway Bay.' Martha flicked through the sketchbook then picked up the pack of cards. 'We used to sit right here, on the deck, in the evenings and play – Morgan rarely beat me. And this is the small teddy bear he won for me from the fairground that was at the River Festival. We argued over who would keep it but I never imagined he would have kept it this long.' Picking up the letter, Martha stared at the handwritten scrawl in black ink.

'Maybe, if you don't want to read it now, you can take it away with you and read it in private?'

Martha traced the word 'Patsy' with her finger, then looked up at Nolan. 'I think I would like to read it now, if that's okay with you.'

'Of course, whatever you feel is best,' he replied warmly.

Taking a deep breath, Martha opened the envelope and unfolded the cream paper. 'It's dated three months after he left here,' exclaimed Martha. She began to read. 'This isn't true. He never came to see me...' She gave a tiny gasp and gripped the letter, the tears flowing freely down her cheeks.

Nolan reached over and put a supportive hand on her elbow.

'Morgan says he came back to find me, three months after he'd left. That was before he got married. He missed me and couldn't live without me but I wasn't at The Little Blue Boathouse. He wanted to talk to me, to tell me I was more to him than just a summer romance but—'

'Where were you?' interrupted Nolan.

'I had to go away for a short while.' Martha's eyes widened.

'Go where?'

'I was staying with Bonnie's auntie because I had to hide away and she was the only one who would take me in. It wasn't easy in those days.'

Martha was talking in riddles and Nolan didn't understand what was going on.

'I thought he didn't care but...' Martha picked up the train ticket in the box. 'He loved me. And here's the evidence. And he did come back. I thought he'd abandoned me... And now he will never know... Everything could have been so different.'

'What will he never know? What could have been so different, Granny?'

Martha looked over her shoulder to find Isla and Bea standing behind her.

Martha was trembling, her face pained and her eyes blurred with tears. Isla bent down and took her grandmother's hands.

'Whatever it is, it's okay, really it is,' she said reassuringly.

'The whole situation spiralled out of control, and it could have been so different for your mum.'

'What could have been different for Mum? Whatever the argument was about between the two of you, you can sort it out, I'm sure of it.'

'Do you want us to give you some time alone?' asked Nolan looking from Martha to Isla.

Martha shook her head. 'This concerns you and Gwen.'

'Me?' queried Nolan.

'Yes. And now I don't know what to do for the best.'

Isla was still crouched down at Martha's side. 'Granny, there's something you need to know. I'm not sure how you're going to react to this and I just want you to remember I've done it for the best reasons because time is going so quickly. I've told Mum that you want to see her. Please don't be mad with me,' she pleaded softly. 'I thought with it being a special birthday...' Her voice trailed off.

'Of course I miss her. I've always missed her. She's my daughter and if you only knew what I was up against, bringing a child into this world as a single mum... If it wasn't for Bonnie and all the support she gave me...'

Martha dabbed her watery eyes again. She looked fragile.

'Gwen agreed to come home,' Isla said softly.

Bea could feel the adrenalin pumping through her veins as she looked from Isla to Martha, then caught Nolan's eye. Judging by the look on his face, he hadn't worked it out yet.

Martha mopped her brow with a tissue. 'When is she arriving?'

Isla hesitated. 'She's already here.'

The silence hung in the air.

'Shall I make us all some tea?' chipped in Bea, knowing tea was always good in a crisis and this seemed like one of those. She didn't wait for an answer before heading towards the kitchen.

'Shall I go and get Mum?' Isla asked Martha.

She nodded.

Chapter Twenty-Four

I t wasn't the happy reunion that you'd expect if you haven't seen someone for many years.

Bea and Nolan had placed more chairs around the small coffee table and there was steaming hot tea in the pot. Martha was still looking distraught and clutching the teddy bear that Morgan had kept all these years.

Everyone on the boat was silent.

'You've got to believe me when I say that I never meant to withhold information from you. I was just frightened and I didn't want the situation spiralling out of control.' Martha looked at Gwen, her voice earnest.

When Gwen didn't speak, Isla placed a supportive hand on Martha's knee.

'There's no other way to say it and it's the information you have wanted to know for years. The man in the painting ... Morgan Hemingway...' Martha took a deep breath. 'He's Nolan's grandfather but he's also your father.'

Gwen and Nolan gave a tiny gasp at the same time.

'I wasn't expecting this,' Nolan said. 'My grandfather never said a word or even hinted that...'

'He didn't know, and I am sorry, Nolan. It must be a shock for you and I'm truly sorry for keeping it from you, Gwen, but please know I had my reasons.'

Gwen's eyes had welled up. 'It's the only bit of information I've wanted to know all my life. You were an amazing mum when I was growing up and I know how hard you worked to keep a roof over our heads, and the number of jobs you took, but why wouldn't you tell me?'

'Because I was scared. When Morgan left and I discovered I was pregnant I was living in the attic room of The Little Blue Boathouse. It wasn't as easy to be a single mum as it is these days. I was pregnant and unwed and the father gone. My morning sickness worsened and my own mother guessed I was pregnant. She was ashamed of me, called me the black sheep of the family and disowned me. Before I knew it, I was shipped off to a mother-and-baby home.' Martha's voice faltered. 'It was the worst time of my life.' She swallowed. 'You'd wake to haunted cries in the night from young mothers whose babies were taken from them minutes after giving birth. When my contractions started, I didn't want to give birth, not because of the pain, but because I knew they would take you away as soon as you were born. I could see the official papers on the side with a pen ready for me to sign you away.'

Gwen leaned across and touched her mother's knee. Both of them were engulfed in tears.

'My whole world plunged into despair and reality hit me. There was no one to help me. I was completely on my own. I had become an outcast in Glensheil, Morgan had married someone else and I was going to have to give you up. But what I didn't know at the time was that I didn't have to go through all this by myself.' Martha handed Morgan's letter to Gwen.

As soon as she read it, she closed her eyes in evident sadness. 'He came back for you.'

'Yes, and my mother sent him away, telling him I didn't want to see him. If only I'd got to see him, things could have been so different.'

Bea took Nolan's hand in hers, sadness bleeding between them. Martha could have lived a happy family life with the man she loved, if only her mother hadn't sent him away.

'When you were born, I was allowed to hold you in my arms. You were adorable and I loved you instantly with all my heart. But as predicted, the papers were thrust into my hand and I was forced to scrawl a signature. You were to be taken the next morning and given to a family who were going to collect you.' Martha wiped her eyes. 'The signature I scrawled was nothing like my signature, and all through the night I stayed awake watching you and planning. And then I took the biggest chance of my life. After only just giving birth, I decided to try and make a run for it.'

'Oh my gosh,' murmured Isla.

'It was like trying to get out of Fort Knox. Luckily, I was on the ground floor with a window we could squeeze through. I wasn't letting anyone take my baby and though I might not have my family or my baby's father, I had Bonnie.'

'Bonnie was Felicity's grandmother, Rona her daughter. They own the teashop,' shared Isla, filling Nolan in, in case he didn't know.

'I ran into the night, not knowing where I was going. It was pitch black. You were wrapped up tightly in a blanket and I had no money and no food. I was so scared.'

'What did you do next?' asked Nolan.

'I discovered a barn and bedded down for the night. Gwen had food because I quickly learned how to breastfeed. I remember there was an old horse blanket on top of the hay bales, which I pulled over us to help keep us warm, and I must have fallen asleep with you in my arms. The next morning, I was woken up by a very surprised farmer's wife and I begged her to help me. Luckily, she was a kind person. She invited us into the farmhouse. She fed me and gave me some clean clothes. If it wasn't for her...' Martha briefly closed her eyes. 'Her name was Gwen. That's who I named you after.' Martha looked up at a teary-eyed Gwen, who was listening attentively to every word.

'Gwen got in touch with Bonnie and it was Bonnie who arranged for me to go and stay with her auntie miles away from Heartcross and Glensheil. Bonnie's auntie Nora was amazing. She looked after us for twelve months and made me feel safe. For so long, every time I left the house, I thought I'd get a tap on the shoulder and they'd take my baby away. I was terrified. Nora helped me train to be a seamstress and she would look after you, Gwen. She gifted me a very old sewing machine and I began to make money. Before I knew it, I was mending people's clothes and able to stand on my own two feet.'

'I never knew that's how you learned to be such a good seamstress,' remarked Isla.

'I owe everything to Gwen, the farmer's wife, Bonnie and Nora and the reason I couldn't tell you about your father, Gwen, is because I knew he'd got married and I didn't want to put either of us through the pain of more rejection. I loved Morgan and it appears he loved me too. He was the one who got away and I will always regret the years that were lost because we didn't know the truth of one another's feelings.'

'He really did love you,' reassured Nolan. 'I know that from all the stories over the years. I just wish he was here with us now so he could tell you himself.'

'Me too,' replied Martha, looking at Gwen. 'I'm sorry I never shared all this with you before now. I know you got teased at school for not having a father, and the way people looked at us because I wasn't married. There was a part of me that felt a little ashamed you didn't have a normal family life and that we spent the whole time scrimping and saving. But there was no way I was ever going to be forced to give you up.'

Gwen stood up and opened her arms wide, pulling Isla and then Martha in, enveloping them in the biggest hug. Martha was sobbing and tears were running down everyone's cheeks. 'We've wasted a lot of time when we could have been a family, let's not waste any more,' said Gwen. Slowing pulling away, she looked at Nolan then took his hand. 'It looks like you have a new family.'

'It does,' he replied. 'It wasn't what I expected when I woke up this morning – but although there's a lot of emotion and pain in this situation, there's also happiness.' he said, joining the hug.

An emotional Bea looked on, happy that everyone had been reunited. There was one person missing, though, and Bea gazed up at the sky, wondering what Morgan would have made of all this. As they all sat back down, she unfastened the seahorse necklace and handed it to Martha. 'Strength and courage,' she said. 'You're a remarkable woman, Martha. Take this. It's yours.'

Martha gave Bea a watery smile. 'Thank you,' she said, clutching the necklace in the palm of her hand.

'I think we all need something a bit stronger than tea,' suggested Nolan.

'I agree,' Martha, Gwen and Isla chorused, causing everyone to laugh.

As Nolan stood up, Bea went to collect some glasses. 'Thank God my grandfather kept this boat stocked up with more than enough alcohol.' He raised a wooden panel on the floor and Bea linked her arm through his as she peered downwards.

There was a secret section underneath and Nolan lowered himself a couple of rungs on a small ladder. 'Should we have champagne?' he asked, unsure. 'I think we have many reasons to celebrate. Martha and Gwen have been reunited and as much as Martha and Morgan's paths should have been the same, at least now Martha has the comfort of knowing he came back for her ... and then there's you, Bea, a new addition to the family of Heartcross.'

'And let's not forget you. You have a new family.'

Nolan smiled. 'I have and it's all a little surreal.' He chose a bottle of champagne and closed the hatch. 'This was in the mini fridge so at least it will be chilled.'

'There's also something else to celebrate,' said Bea, giving him a nudge with her elbow. 'Hemingway and Fernsby have closed their first case.' High-fiving him, she pressed a kiss to his lips.

'I still think I did most of the work,' he replied with a glint in his eye.

'I dispute that wholeheartedly.'

Nolan popped the cork and everyone stood on deck with a glass of champagne. 'I think we should have a toast,' he suggested. All eyes were on him.

'Here's to new beginnings, family and The Little Blue Boathouse, where chance summer meetings took us by surprise in the past and present and have brought us all closer. Happy endings! And not forgetting, to Morgan and The Hemingway.'

They clinked their glasses. Even though they had started with an air of uncertainty and profound sadness, a lot of questions had been answered and everyone felt lighter and happier. Hopefully they could all now move on from the past.

'I can't believe I've got a new family,' Nolan said happily. 'I am genuinely chuffed.'

'You two need an invite to Granny's surprise dinner at The Lakehouse,' exclaimed Isla, then brought her hand up to her mouth when she realised what she'd said.

'I think the word "surprise" means we aren't meant to say anything,' said Bea, laughing.

'I don't need any more surprises at my time of life,' said Martha. 'Can we all just agree that everything is plain sailing from now on?'

'Agreed,' chorused everyone.

Chapter Twenty-Five

One week later

Bea didn't mind waking up to an empty bed, especially when she was greeted by the aroma of sizzling sausages and the sound of a kettle boiling. Already she could feel the warmth of the day filtering through the open window. It was finally the day of the River Festival and in the last twenty-four hours everyone had decorated their boats ready for the water parade. For the last week she'd spent every waking moment possible with Nolan and both of them had avoided the subject of what was going to happen after today. She knew the ball was in his court. He was still healing from his own past and she knew that if she had to let him go, as much as it would break her heart, that's what she would do. Life in Heartcross wouldn't be the same without him but his promise that he would be back gave her a little hope. And even though she felt sad that this was their last day together, she was going to try and savour every second.

Hearing him singing along to the radio in the kitchen she smiled as she picked up her phone to check her emails. Her eyes fixed on the top email – from Andrew Glossop. She opened it and scanned the text and then had to read it again. Not believing her eyes, she bounced out of bed.

'Nolan! Nolan!'

'Where's the fire?' he asked, popping his head around the kitchen door and cocking an eyebrow. 'And good morning!' he said, kissing the tip of her nose. 'What has got you so excited?' he asked, taking the phone from Bea.

'Andrew Glossop's email, read it.'

Bea excitedly shuffled her feet and waited impatiently for Nolan to finish reading it. He looked up with a beam and let out a low whistle. 'Holy moly! This is amazing news! Blooming brilliant!'

'Isn't it just? Andrew Glossop and Flynn Carter are going to fund the very first lifeboat as soon as the rest of the funds are raised. This is more than amazing!' Over the last few days the fundraising page on Facebook had been full of notifications and ideas from the community on how to raise the money, and everyone was pulling together to make this happen. 'Next week, I've got a meeting with the builders and the architect to design the headquarters. I've never project managed anything like this before. It's going to be hard work to coordinate everything.' For a second Bea started to doubt whether she could pull it all together, but then Nolan wrapped his arms around her and hugged her tight.

'You've got this! In years to come there'll be a statue erected outside The Little Blue Boathouse.' He grinned. 'Bea Fernsby. Founder of Heartcross Rescue. Thousands of lives saved because of her.'

'Can you imagine?' replied Bea, beaming. 'How cool would that be?'

'Very cool.'

'And that's not all.' Bea tapped the phone. 'Aidy Redfern has given this project a three-page spread in the local newspaper and wants to interview me on the local news next week, which he says hopefully will go out nationally too.'

'That's great! You will smash it. That's going to create more awareness and hopefully increase funds.'

'Which currently stand at a little over fifty thousand pounds. I know we still have a long way to go but by my reckoning Heartcross Rescue could be in full operation in eighteen months' time ... and do you know those sausages are nearly cremated?' said Bea, pointing to the frying pan on the stove.

'Damn,' replied Nolan, quickly switching off the stove and transferring the sausages to a plate. 'Go and have a look at the riverbank, the sight is amazing.'

Walking out onto the deck, Bea was astonished. The bank of the River Heart looked like a mini festival with pop-up stalls all in a line, and huge banners hanging from the bridge. The local radio station had set up a portable booth next to the jetty and was playing music. Hordes of people were walking along the path and positioning picnic blankets in various spots, ready to make the most of the day.

'Wow! Look at that view,' exclaimed Bea.

'Oh, I'm looking!' replied Nolan with a lopsided grin.

Bea attempted to swipe him but he caught her hand and pulled her in close, placing his lips softly on hers before pulling away slowly and cupping his hands round Bea's elbows. 'The Hemingway is leading the parade of boats today and I'm hoping you'll be up on deck with me?'

'Try and stop me! I would love to do that.' Bea flung her arms around his neck and hugged him tight.

'Now go and get changed, we're leaving in twenty minutes.'

'Where to? And what about the sausage sandwiches?' she asked, glancing towards the kitchen.

'They're coming with us.' Nolan placed his hands on her shoulders, spun her around and pushed her gently towards the bedroom. 'We're leaving for Martha's birthday meal at two o'clock so we need to be back before then.'

Twenty minutes later they had climbed into the rowing boat and manoeuvred their way through all the boats bobbing on the river. The weather was perfect, the sun was shining and only a few clouds dotted the sky. Bea knew exactly where they were going and as much as she looked forward to having breakfast at Castaway Bay, she felt sad and had to fight back the tears, knowing that after today she wasn't going to wake up in the attic room and see The Hemingway floating on the water anymore. Biting her lip, she filled her head with all the happy moments she'd had since she'd arrived – their first visit to Castaway Bay, the painting of her, the bike rides when her ankle hurt. The last month had been a blast and Bea didn't want the summer to come to an end.

There was a comfortable silence between them as Nolan rowed the boat, each of them lost in their own thoughts. Castaway Bay looked as beautiful as the first time she'd laid eyes on it. As the boat bumped along in the shallow water Nolan stood and tied it to the jetty. Placing the rucksack over his shoulder, he held out his hand towards Bea.

Wearing flip-flops, Bea stepped into the water and gave a tiny squeal.

Nolan laughed. 'It always feels cold at first.'

Still holding hands, they walked in silence to the spot where they'd had their very first picnic. Bea didn't trust herself to speak. Although this was a perfect moment, in a perfect setting, with the perfect man, her heart was already beginning to break.

Stopping in the same ideal spot as before, Nolan opened the rucksack, took out the food and laid it on the ground. They both sat down, stretched their legs in front of them and stared at the magnificent view. Nolan passed Bea a sausage sandwich and she unwrapped the foil whilst he poured them each a cup of tea from the flask.

'I know it's not as extravagant as our first picnic,' he said, handing Bea her drink. 'But I think this is my favourite place that I've ever visited.'

'Me too,' replied Bea. Taking a sideward glance towards Nolan, she said, 'I'm beginning to feel sad. I never wanted this day to come.'

Nolan stretched out his arm and Bea cuddled into his chest, taking in the familiar smell of his aftershave. She wiped a tear away with the back of her hand. 'I have had the best few weeks, I really have, and it's breaking my heart that you're going even though I knew that you would. Nolan, I can't cope with saying goodbye. I just want you to slip away.' Bea was shaking, her heart was thumping and the dull ache inside her was growing stronger. 'I know you have to do whatever you need to do to heal from the past and I know you're scared of getting close to anyone again after what happened with Hannah. I do fully understand. But please remember you're not alone. You have Martha, Gwen and Isla too. And you have me.'

'I know,' replied Nolan. 'Please don't cry. I knew today was going to be hard but I didn't know it was going to be this hard.' He paused, entwining his fingers with hers. 'I've brought you here because … I thought you might have worn that red bikini again,' he said, trying to lighten the mood. He gave her a wolfish grin with a glint in his eye and Bea shook her head and laughed.

He reached inside the rucksack and pulled out a bottle, a pen and a sheet of paper. 'I thought we could throw our own message in a bottle into the water.'

A smile spread across Bea's face. 'What a perfect thought.'

'And I wanted to give you this,' he said, reaching inside the bag.

'What's in there?' asked Bea, taking the object from him.

'Open it and find out.'

Bea's heart skipped a beat.

The contents were hidden beneath delicate blush-pink tissue paper, which Bea slowly opened to reveal three silver buttons. She turned them over in her hand. They were small and delicate and each button had something engraved on it. She spread them out in the palm of her hand for a closer look.

'H&F,' Nolan pointed out, as he took them from her and laid them out in order. 'Hemingway & Fernsby.'

'They are beautiful,' exclaimed Bea. He gave her back the H for Hemingway, kept the F for Fernsby, and placed the '&' in the bottle.

'Write a note,' he encouraged.

Bea took the paper and pen from him. In the top righthand corner, she wrote the date and replicated the heart that was on the letter they'd discovered from Martha and Morgan.

A Summer Surprise at The Little Blue Boathouse.
Hemingway & Fernsby, looking for another case to solve.

They both signed the paper and Bea placed the button in the middle of the page and folded it up into a small square.

Nolan pushed it inside the bottle and corked it securely. Joining hands, they walked the short distance across the sand to the edge of the water. Bea swallowed a lump and couldn't hold back the tears. Nolan pulled her in close and handed her the bottle.

'No, you throw it,' she said.

Nolan threw the bottle and then took Bea's hand again.

With a splash it hit the water and bobbed a little. They watched in silence for a moment.

'I wonder if anyone will ever find it,' Bea mused.

'You never know,' replied Nolan, turning to face her. Staring deep into Nolan's eyes, Bea held up a fist in front of her chest. Nolan did the same and they gave each other a fist bump.

'I declare this Hemingway and Fernsby cased officially closed,' murmured Bea, her voice cracking with emotion.

After hugging each other tightly, they turned back towards their picnic.

'Look!' Bea dropped Nolan's hand and began to chase away the cheeky flock of gulls that had landed on their sandwiches.

'It's too late, there's hardly anything left.' She shook her head in disbelief but deep inside was thankful for the light-hearted moment because all she wanted to do was break down and sob her heart out.

'Shall we take a walk by the festival huts on the riverbank? I'm sure we'll pick up some food there.'

'Sounds like a plan,' replied Bea, picking up the leftovers and wrapping them up in the foil again.

'And I've just had another thought – should I offer to sail Martha and the rest of the family and friends to The Lakehouse this afternoon in The Hemingway?'

'I think that sounds perfect. And if we time the end of the meal right, we could all join the parade as planned,' enthused Bea.

'Come on, let's get back.'

———

As they rowed away from Castaway Bay, Bea looked for the bottle but it was nowhere to be seen. People came into your life for different reasons, she thought. Nolan was someone who had taught her she could live again and change what she wasn't happy about in her life.

If only she could change that he would be leaving by the end of the day.

Chapter Twenty-Six

Bea and Nolan had spent a couple of hours packing away the floating gallery to make room for Martha and her guests. Martha was over the moon to sail on The Hemingway and thanks to Isla there were balloons and banners – left over from decorating The Lakehouse – adorning the deck. The boat looked magnificent and neither Bea nor Nolan could wait to celebrate Martha's special birthday.

Bea had then disappeared back to the attic room to get ready and was engulfed with pure panic. Searching through the rail of clothes she'd packed for her two-week holiday she realised there was nothing suitable for today's special occasion.

Julia picked the phone up after three rings.

'Julia! I need help and fast! Unless I'm going to Martha's birthday in a red bikini, I have nothing new to wear!'

Bea was met by laughter. 'And you will be the talk of the town.'

'Do you have anything I could borrow?'

'I'm actually just about to walk down to the river and have a browse around the stalls; I'll bring you a selection and if there isn't anything suitable, there's only one thing for it – you'll have to be the talk of the town. I'll see you in ten.'

Hanging up, Bea felt relieved. Anything that Julia could muster had to be better than the clothes she'd packed. At some point, she knew, she would have to travel back to Staffordshire to collect her belongings, but there was also excitement at the thought of starting afresh with all new belongings and clothes, and making her new life all about her.

Sitting in the window, waiting for Julia, Bea watched the River Festival in full spate. The river-bank was heaving. Set up outside The Little Blue Boathouse was a number of different carnival games, like hook-a-duck and ring toss. The Old Bakehouse was selling pretzels, chocolate-covered apples and mini doughnuts, Bumblebee Cottage was selling their wonderful homemade chutneys and honey, and Layers Treats, the chocolate shop, had a long queue of children who were holding their money in one hand and a colourful balloon tightly in the other. Bea smiled at the sight of the marching band and the flags flapping in the light breeze. Looking across to The Hemingway she noticed Nolan walking over the ramp towards the jetty where Flynn was waiting for him. They disappeared on to Flynn's boat and Bea wondered what that was all about, but she didn't think about it for long as Julia shouted up to her.

Bea poked her head through the hatch and was met by the sight of Julia laden with an armful of dresses.

'We have every colour under the sun!'

'You're not wrong,' remarked Bea, hurrying down the ladder. 'Look at these, you could open up a clothes shop.'

'I know,' she laughed, 'Flynn said exactly the same thing. If any of these fit, wear what you wish and I'll grab the rest back from you on Monday.'

'This is brilliant, thanks so much.'

'You're welcome, and I'll see you at the dinner. In the meantime, I need to track down Flynn.'

'I've just seen him disappear onto his boat with Nolan.'

'Oh, that's right, they're having a meeting. I'll catch you in a bit. I hope one of those fits.'

Julia left The Little Blue Boathouse and Bea racked her brains, trying to remember if Nolan had mentioned anything about a meeting with Flynn.

Climbing back up the ladder she laid the dresses out on the bed.

Each one was fit for the occasion but one in particular caught her eye and she knew it would look utterly gorgeous and be the perfect attire for a birthday meal at the world-famous restaurant The Lakehouse. The dress was a grey, shimmery satin, gathered at the waist and hanging just below her knees. As she pulled it over her body she gasped. It was a perfect fit.

'Cinderella *will* go to the ball,' she murmured, giving a

little spin in the mirror. After applying her make-up and tying her hair up in a messy bun with the loose strands framing her face, she slipped her feet into her ballet shoes.

Feeling a million dollars and grateful to Julia, Bea locked up The Little Blue Boathouse and made her way towards The Hemingway. She had never had girlfriends who helped you out at the drop of a hat. It was wonderful.

Stepping onto the ramp of the boat, Bea shouted out, 'Anyone home?' and looked around, but Nolan wasn't anywhere to be seen. Standing on the deck, she shouted again. Then the bathroom door opened and Nolan appeared, his hair soaped up into a wild-looking mass. He grinned. 'Why is it every time it's inconvenient people knock on the door?'

'Er, there is no door, and this wasn't the welcome I anticipated, but I don't mind it one little bit.' Bea ran an approving eye over Nolan's wet, toned torso and stopped at the towel wrapped around his waist. She leaned forward playfully and Nolan panicked, thinking she was going to whip the towel from him.

'Don't you dare! There's too many boats around and kayaks coming past.'

Bea laughed. 'You're no fun sometimes.'

'Go and pour yourself a drink whilst I get changed. By the way, can I just say you look absolutely stunning?'

Bea gave a little twirl. 'Why, thank you. You don't look too bad yourself,' she replied, giving him a cheeky wink.

'I'll be ten minutes max.'

Pouring herself a glass of prosecco, Bea stood on the

deck and looked all around. There were so many boats it was difficult to see the town of Glensheil in the distance. Each one was decorated in a carnival theme and they had begun to get themselves in a line ready for the boat parade that began in the early evening.

'Right, I'm ready,' Nolan stepped back on to the deck and Bea playfully whistled. 'Very impressive,' she said with a smile, tilting her head up to kiss him as he entwined his fingers around hers. With their eyes locked, he gave her the warmest, sexiest smile, and there it was again, that jittery feeling in her stomach of the first flush of love mixed with the dull ache of knowing he would soon be gone.

As Nolan straightened the birthday banner that had flapped over in the light breeze, Bea tried to ignore the ache in her stomach but it was still very much there. While she was getting ready, she had toyed with the idea of telling him how much she wanted him to stay, and that having him by her side made her feel like she'd won the lottery because he was everything she'd ever wanted. But her head and her heart were currently fighting each other, her head telling her that she needed to let Nolan do whatever he needed to do to heal, and her heart telling her to fight for him and tell him how she felt.

Her heart won. She owed it to herself to say what she felt. She'd spent the whole of her last relationship not being able to express her feelings. If she didn't say how she felt, how would Nolan ever know?

'Do you think Martha would like the painting of my grandfather and her for her birthday?'

'I think that's a great idea,' she replied, standing beside him and sipping her drink.

'That's good then because I've already wrapped it up.'

'Nolan,' she said, her heart beating nineteen to the dozen. 'Nolan.' Her chest heaved.

But Nolan was looking across at the riverbank and grabbed Bea's arm. 'Here they come. Quick, cue the music. Here's Martha!'

Bea looked up and there was the birthday girl walking alongside her family with her close friends following behind. With the moment lost, Bea did exactly what Nolan had asked and cued the music from the music player that he'd connected at the back of the boat, so that as soon as Martha stepped on to the ramp, 'Happy Birthday' played out. The surrounding boats began to cheer and clap, leaving Martha with a huge smile on her face.

'All aboard,' shouted Nolan, handing out the drinks as they all filed onto the boat. 'Here she is, the birthday girl!' he exclaimed, kissing Martha on both cheeks. 'Happy birthday!'

Martha looked radiant, her eyes sparkled and the smile on her face said it all.

'You look stunning. Happy birthday, Martha,' said Bea, air-kissing Martha, who gave a little shimmy in her dress.

'And so do you, my dear. I love that dress, it suits you.'

'Thank you,' replied Bea, giving Julia a thankful smile as she sipped her drink.

Close to emotional tears, Martha had her arm linked through Gwen's as they stood and admired the banners that hung from the sides of the boat and the clusters of balloons that were dancing in the light breeze. 'I can't believe you've gone to all this trouble for me.'

'It's our pleasure,' said Bea.

'And if you had told me when I was twenty years old that I would be travelling to my special birthday dinner on The Hemingway, I would never have believed you. It's a funny old world.'

'Isn't it just,' replied Nolan, shaking the hand of Drew as he stepped on board. 'If you'd told me I was going to travel to Heartcross and find a family, I would never have believed you.'

'And if you'd told me that my mother and I would be back on speaking terms, then I would definitely not have believed you.' Gwen nudged Martha lightly with her shoulder.

'All's well that ends well. And can I just say, with past troubles put behind us, it makes my life a whole lot easier,' added Isla.

'And mine,' chipped in Drew, giving Isla a wink.

'Have we all got a drink?' asked Isla, looking around at everyone. 'Because I would like to propose a toast.'

Stood in a circle with Martha in the centre, everyone raised their glass. 'Firstly, I'd like to say a huge happy birthday to my grandmother, Martha. You have filled my life with fun, laughter and despair on many occasions.'

Everyone laughed.

'You're the kindest and most compassionate person I know and in the past week we've all discovered how brave you were back in the past to keep your baby against all odds.'

Gwen leaned in and squeezed Martha's elbow. Her mother was close to tears.

'My granny, my best friend. We love you very much and you mean everything to us. We all hope you have a fantastic birthday. Having your family and friends standing here today, ready to celebrate with you, shows how much we all love you.'

'Or they are just after free food and drink,' Martha said to Drew, who pretended to look hurt.

'Happy birthday!'

Everyone echoed Isla's sentiments and clinked their glasses.

'Are we ready to get this show on the road?' shouted Nolan over the excited chatter.

'Yes, captain,' they cried in unison.

Nolan handed his glass to Bea as he detached the ramp from the riverbank and raised the anchor.

'How you doing?' Isla asked Bea.

'Not wanting this day to end if I'm truly honest.' She kept her voice low. 'I'm trying not to think about it. I've asked him to slip away when the time is right because I can't take goodbyes.'

'He'll be back. He has us here now and I think he would be mad to leave you behind. Anyone can see the chemistry between the pair of you could light up the whole of Scotland.'

Bea smiled. 'I hope he'll be back but I know he has to do

whatever is right for him.'

'And look around this boat. You arrived on a whim for a two-week holiday and now you're managing The Little Blue Boathouse, not to mention project managing Heartcross Rescue. We are all your friends and here for you no matter what. That's what I love about this community, it's like no other, even if I've never actually known any other.' She gave a small laugh.

'I love it too. This place is like a breath of fresh air. Thank you.'

As Nolan walked towards the steering wheel, he called over to Martha, 'Can I have the queen of the ship up at the helm, please?'

'Just a moment,' said Isla, whipping out a birthday sash from her bag and placing it over Martha's head. 'There you go, all ready.'

Martha made her way to Nolan and stood behind the steering wheel.

'Can you remember how to drive the boat?' he asked.

'Just like it was yesterday,' she said, smiling at him. 'Do you think Morgan is looking down on us?' She glanced towards the sky then back at Nolan.

'Without a doubt,' he replied.

Bea cued the music again as Martha turned the key and started the engine. She pushed the lever forward and The Hemingway began to slowly glide through the water. Everyone on board let out a cheer and Martha saluted; she was enjoying every second of it. With the breeze whipping their hair, their glasses full, everyone had a huge smile on their face. Cheers rippled along the surrounding boats as their occupants waved at Martha.

Bea slipped her arm around Nolan's waist and snuggled into his chest. 'I've never seen this part of the water.'

'Wait until you see The Lakehouse, it'll take your breath away.'

Martha enjoyed the next five minutes waving to every person on all the boats that bobbed on the River Heart. The atmosphere was electric, with people sounding their horns and shouting happy birthday. As soon as they glided into the open water, Martha turned to Nolan. 'Take over. I have fizz to drink and friends to talk to.'

'No problem,' replied Nolan, taking the helm. 'Go and have fun.'

'And thank you, I enjoyed every second of that.' She nodded her appreciation and joined Gwen and Isla, who were sitting down watching the view as they sailed past.

'Would you like a go?' asked Nolan, looking towards Bea. 'It's just like driving a car.'

'Would I? Yes please, I thought you'd never ask!'

Nolan stepped to the side but kept his hand on the wheel until Bea was standing in front of it.

'We're heading in that direction. This lever slows the boat, if you pull it towards you like this.' Nolan pulled on the lever and the boat slowed. 'Push it back up and we travel faster. Have a go.'

Bea's hand brushed against his as she took over the controls. She pulled back the lever and the boat slowed, then pushed it so it quickened up.

'Hey,' shouted Drew. 'You'll have me spilling my drink!'

'Sorry,' Bea shouted, with a giggle. 'This is so much fun. I can see why you love living on here.' She kept her eyes on the water, and successfully piloted the boat towards the trees.

'We're nearly there. When we pass through those trees The Lakehouse is just around the next corner.'

'Wow, look at those!' exclaimed Bea.

'Secret coves, but this next part will take your breath away. I'll help because it can get a little tricky around this next bend.' Nolan stood right behind Bea and reached for the control. She could feel his presence so close to her as he leaned forward and placed his hand on top of hers. 'We need to slow down completely now.' Nolan kept his hand on hers as Bea steered The Hemingway through the gorgeous weeping willows that hung over the water's edge, then around a cluster of rocks.

'This is just beautiful,' she exclaimed, keeping her eyes fixed on the water in front of her.

'You haven't seen anything yet.'

As The Hemingway moved through the calm water Nolan took over for the last stretch. Bea gazed up at the chalk-white rocks that overhung another tiny secluded beach, just like Castaway Bay. Nolan guided the boat to the jetty and pointed to the stop button. 'Press that,' he said.

The engine cut out and everyone on The Hemingway cheered. Bea was in awe. The Lakehouse restaurant stood in front of them with its old-fashioned shutters, purple wisteria and pink roses tumbling all around the doorway.

Up on the roof terrace there were tables and chairs overlooking the secluded water.

It's breathtaking,' she exclaimed.

'Isn't it just,' replied Nolan.

'Heartcross is the place that just keeps giving,' she murmured. 'And look!'

Standing outside The Lakehouse was Flynn, who'd ferried the rest of the villagers to the restaurant. He'd even laid out a red carpet under an archway of cream and gold balloons. As soon as The Hemingway docked, everyone cheered and Martha was the first to step off the boat. Greeted by Flynn, who popped the cork from a bottle of champagne and poured Martha the very first glass, she looked overwhelmed but incredibly happy.

Inside the restaurant, Bea was completely blown away. Members of staff were circulating with even more drinks and the room was decorated to perfection with birthday banners and balloons. Twinkly fairy lights and lilac roses filled every corner and Bea was momentarily lost for words. 'I can't imagine who would go out of their way for me like this when I reach this age.'

'Everyone would,' replied Nolan, taking her hand in his.

'Nolan, Bea, would you both like to join us at the family table? It would mean so much to me,' asked Martha.

'It would be our honour,' they replied at the same time, then laughed.

Martha was in her element, working the room and reminiscing with all her friends, until Gianni the chef came out and spoke to Flynn, who sounded the gong in the corner of the room.

'Dinner will be served in fifteen minutes.'

When everyone was seated, Isla stood at a microphone and the room fell silent.

'Thank you all for coming this afternoon to help celebrate my beautiful grandmother's special birthday. Apparently, I am banned from saying her age.'

The room laughed.

'Just before we devour the delicious delights of the three-course meal prepared by award-winning Michelin star chef Gianni, I thought it was only fair that we suitably embarrass my granny with a trip down memory lane. The Heartcross community began many years ago and, as the saying goes, once you arrive in Heartcross, you never want to leave.'

Bea dared to take a sideward glance at Nolan, who was looking in Isla's direction. She could have sworn he had tears in his eyes.

'It's an absolute privilege that I get to call you my granny, my family and my best friend. Family is everything to me and us. Not only will my granny be suitably embarrassed but there is a long list of wonderful folks who are taking one for the team this afternoon.'

There was a ripple of laughter around the room.

'If you look over towards this screen, you'll see that we have photographs going back to Granny's childhood, showcasing every step of her life. So, sit back and enjoy the journey ... the long journey,' she joked, giving a tearful Martha a cheeky wink.

The whole restaurant turned towards the screen as Martha's life began to play out to the soundtrack of her favourite song.

'Look, there's The Little Blue Boathouse.' Bea grabbed Nolan's knee. 'And a very young Martha.' She was posing against the door with her leg kicked back and her hands on her hips. 'You look like a right handful there, Granny,' whispered Isla.

Nolan stared at the screen as images of his grandfather and Martha were projected before his eyes. There they were paddling in the water at Castaway Bay, sitting on the deck of The Hemingway and dancing in front of the bandstand at Primrose Park. Nolan felt sad, knowing that if his grandfather had known about Gwen, everything would have been different. The way he and Martha looked at each other, they oozed true love and admiration. He glanced at Bea out of the corner of his eye. A lonely tear ran down her face and she discreetly brushed it away with the back of her hand, her eyes transfixed on the photographs in front of her.

Slipping out of his seat, Nolan took a breather outside and walked back down the jetty. His mind and heart were in turmoil. He never thought when he came on the hunt for Patsy that he would end up with distant relatives and a girl that he knew he was falling in love with. Looking up at the sky, he closed his eyes and took a deep breath. Deep down he knew Hannah would want him to be happy but he was so frightened by the prospect of experiencing such grief again.

He walked back towards The Hemingway and into his room. Locked in the bottom drawer of his bedside cabinet was an album full of photos of Hannah. He sat on the bed and turned the pages slowly, weeping as he looked over every photo.

When the slideshow came to an end, a ripple of applause coursed around the room. Martha, who had held on to Gwen's hand throughout, was full of happy emotion. It was at that moment that Bea turned towards Nolan and found his chair empty. Her heart began to pound as she looked around the room but couldn't see him anywhere. Martha was up on her feet giving a short speech and thanking her family and life-long friends for coming. The waiters then began to bring the food out, but all Bea could think about was that she'd told Nolan to slip away without saying goodbye.

'Are you okay?' whispered Isla, noticing Bea had paled.

'He's gone.' Bea took a deep breath and held out her hand. 'Look, I'm shaking. I'd hoped he'd wouldn't go.' Feeling the pain in her heart she pressed a tissue to her eyes. She needed to hold it together somehow. After all, this was Martha's moment.

'He hasn't gone anywhere, he's here.'

Bea's head swung in the direction of the door and relief

flooded her veins at the sight of Nolan. He held a huge bouquet of beautiful blooms. Her heart pounding, she couldn't take her eyes off him as he made his way to the microphone. He looked across at Isla, who gave him a nod of encouragement.

'What's going on?' whispered Bea.

Isla shrugged but gave Bea a warm smile. 'Everything is going to be okay.'

Nolan looked nervous as he took to the microphone and all eyes were on him. 'I won't keep you long as I can see a magnificent feast being brought to your tables. My name is Nolan Hemingway and I live on the houseboat The Hemingway, which once belonged to my grandfather, Morgan Hemingway. Many moons ago, my grandfather sailed into Heartcross and his boat paraded in the very first River Festival.

'My grandfather recorded all his travels in a log book, and I've been retracing his voyages since he passed away.' Nolan's voice cracked. His emotions were still very raw when he spoke about his grandfather and he pressed his fingers against his eyes. 'Sorry, I didn't mean to get upset, this is a joyous occasion.'

Martha stood up and walked over to Nolan, taking his hand. She nodded at him. 'You've got this,' she whispered.

'As a young boy my grandfather used to tell me stories of a place called Heartcross, with its towering mountain and the castle on the hill. It was the place where he met his Heartcross Princess, Patsy, at The Little Blue Boathouse. I didn't realise this place was actually real until a few years ago when I saw it on the news, and it took me by surprise. After I renovated the boat, I knew the place I had to visit most of all was right here, and what I stumbled across was a wonderful place filled with an amazing community, which has begun to help me heal after my own tragedy a few years ago. Heartcross is a special place that helps to mend broken hearts.' Nolan looked over towards Bea, who was on the verge of more tears. 'Even though I've not known Martha very long, I feel like I've known her all my life, and I can see exactly why she is so special to your community. I know that my grandfather would have loved to be here today, but unfortunately you've got me...'

Martha laughed and gave him a quick squeeze.

'And so, on behalf of myself and my grandfather, these flowers are for you, Martha, and I hope I got them right because in his stories he always talked about Princess Patsy's favourite blooms.'

Martha nodded, the tears cascading down her cheeks as she took the stunning bouquet of pink oriental lilies and large roses hand-tied with eucalyptus.

'They are my absolute favourites, thank you.'

'Now please enjoy your meal. Once again, happy birthday, Martha.'

There was jovial chatter all around as the guests picked up their knives and forks and tucked into their first course. Nolan returned to Bea, who had her hand on her heart. 'That was a beautiful speech and those flowers are gorgeous.'

'I left the birthday painting on the boat but I'll drop it off to her later in the week.'

Bea's eyes widened. 'Say that again?'

'I said I'll drop it off later in the week.'

'But just then … when you disappeared … I thought you'd slipped away without saying goodbye.'

'Hang on a minute, you *told* me to slip away without saying goodbye,' he said, grinning.

'I know but it's a woman's prerogative to change her mind.'

'And what about a man? Can he change his mind too?'

Bea's heart was racing. 'Are you trying to tell me something?' Under the table she had her fingers crossed.

'Since I arrived in Heartcross, life hasn't been quite the same. I wonder why that is?'

'Hopefully me,' said Bea, not holding back.

'I know I'm still a little way short of healing from my past but I think with your help that may become easier.'

'Are you telling me you're actually staying?'

Nolan nudged her elbow. 'Early this afternoon I had a meeting with Flynn…'

'About?'

'Opening up my own art gallery in the village. He's given me some ideas. Apparently the barns on this side of Foxglove Farm are going to be turned into small retail shops. One is already occupied – Buttercup Barn, which is a florist – but there are two more available. The other option would be to anchor The Hemingway outside The Little Blue

Boathouse and convert the whole boat into a gallery to display my paintings.'

'Are you serious? Does that mean you're staying?' Bea could feel herself tearing up. 'Because rumour has it that once you arrive in Heartcross, you never want to leave Heartcross,' she added, knowing she definitely had no intention of moving anywhere else any time soon. 'It's a magical place and has already captured my heart in more ways than one.' She nudged Nolan lightly with her shoulder.

'I think it's about time I stop sailing away from my past and hold on to the good memories. I think I'm happier now … and I mean, look at this place, who wouldn't want to be part of this community?'

Bea let out a squeal. 'This is brilliant. I was dreading today and now…' She closed her eyes and put both hands on her heart. 'But now, it's just the best day.'

Opening her eyes, she knew she had a huge grin on her face. Nolan kissed her on her lips.

'You gave me a reason to start believing in the living again. It's been a hell of a few years … but anyway, without Fernsby there's no Hemingway and Fernsby, and I think they go perfectly together.'

'You'll get no arguments from me on that one.'

Bea couldn't wipe the grin off her face as she smiled over at Isla, who gave her a wink and whispered, 'I'm so glad everyone is getting their happy ever afters. Granny and Mum back together, Granny at peace with Morgan, knowing he was in love with her… Life twists and turns in mysterious ways but I would say fate brought you and Nolan to the River Heart. All this is meant to be.'

'I agree,' mouthed Bea.

Three hours later, Bea was amazed to see the crowds of people lining the riverbanks. She'd never seen anything quite like it. Everyone had got into the spirit of the day, with flags waving high and cheers that rippled across the water.

There were photographers positioned along the bridge between Heartcross and Glensheil, ready to capture every boat in the parade; the radio station was broadcasting from the top of an open-air bus; and as soon as The Hemingway joined the front, the parade could begin.

'Where do we go now?' asked Bea.

Nolan pointed. 'We stay on the left of the river and head for the bridge, where we turn around and make our way back to The Little Blue Boathouse. Once all the boats are in position, I believe something spectacular happens.'

Everyone had assembled back on The Hemingway, Martha surrounded by all her family and friends, and after passing around some opened bottles of champagne they gathered in a group behind Nolan at the wheel. Nolan took Bea's hand then slipped his arm around her waist. She felt the excitement zipping through her body as the boat began to move towards the front of the parade. The atmosphere was electric as a voice over the Tannoy alerted the spectators and fellow boats to their arrival.

'Here comes The Hemingway leading today's River Festival parade. The Hemingway is a spectacular boat that frequented the waters of the River Heart at the very first Rival Festival and was owned by Morgan Hemingway. Today, the captain of the ship is Morgan's grandson, Nolan Hemingway.'

Beaming, Nolan stood still, acknowledging the crowd with a wave.

'Look at this turnout! I've never seen so many people,' exclaimed Bea, glancing towards the riverbank.

'They're all here to wish me Happy Birthday!' shared Martha, making everyone laugh.

'How do you feel, leading the parade?' Bea asked Nolan.

'Damn proud – and all the better for you being by my side.'

Feeling a tap on his shoulder, Nolan turned round to find Gwen standing behind him, her arms open wide. 'If it wasn't for you sailing back here then the past might never have been resolved. It's time for new beginnings for everyone.'

As Gwen hugged Nolan tight, he looked over her shoulder and locked eyes with Bea. 'New beginnings,' he repeated.

Gwen rejoined Isla and Martha, and Nolan turned towards Bea.

'My grandfather would have loved today.' His voice wavered as he took a quick glance towards the sky.

Bea swallowed. 'He's with us all in spirit.'

At that very moment, the brass band on the riverbank began to play. Horns sounded out continuously and the spectators began to wave at the boats from the banks and the bridge.

'And we are off!' hollered Nolan, nearly deafened by the cheers behind him. 'Cheers, everyone!'

'To The Hemingway,' cheered Martha. 'And everyone who has sailed in her.'

Everyone stood on deck waving their flags and drinking their champagne.

Nolan looked over his shoulder and fought back the tears. He'd sailed into Heartcross on a mission to find his grandfather's first love and what he had discovered was a brand-new family and friends and a girl who made his heart beat faster. Life couldn't get any better than this. He thought about Hannah. He knew she would approve of Bea. He turned to face her. 'I never planned to settle anywhere. I thought I would end my days sailing from bay to bay…'

'And now?' asked Bea.

'I've found happiness, a family, I'm about to start an exciting business venture… And that's all down to you.'

'You never know what's around the corner, but for me, I'm glad it's Heartcross.'

The spectators were still cheering and clapping as The Hemingway motored past the jetty and took its place in front of The Little Blue Boathouse. Martha's family and friends lined the side of the boat, waving at the crowd on the bank.

Nolan pulled Bea to him. 'I do think you're an absolute superstar and I'm so proud of you for making Heartcross Rescue happen. If there's a position available to be your right-hand man, do let me know.'

'You have the job!'

'Martha! Nolan! Bea! Look this way!' Aidy Redfern had brought photographers and a TV crew.

With their arms wrapped around each other's waist, they stood in a line, with the rest of Martha's guests standing behind them. As a line of photographers clicked away, Bea knew she was well on her way to cementing the future of Heartcross Rescue as well as her own.

'It's been a rollercoaster of a few weeks, hasn't it?' she said, swinging a glance towards Nolan.

'It has. Life is certainly not dull with you around!' he replied, kissing the top of her head. 'Look!' His voice rose as he pointed up to the sky above The Little Blue Boathouse.

Bea gasped as the ultimate firework spectacular burst into life in the sky. Vibrant colours shot straight up before a glittery silver shower fell over The Little Blue Boathouse, while others whirled in spirals and some shattered into thousands of sparks.

'The Little Blue Boathouse, where two love stories began,' Nolan whispered, his words melting Bea's heart. 'So, shall we officially reopen the Hemingway and Fernsby partnership?'

'Er, Fernsby and Hemingway still sounds better,' she insisted.

'I'm not arguing with you,' he replied, lowering his lips to hers and kissing her softly as another shower of sparks lit up the sky.

With her heart bursting with happiness and her eyes brimming with joyful tears, Bea knew that this was what love was meant to feel like. She had no intention of letting it go. Even though her goal was to save lives in the future, hers had already been saved, right here, right now. They stared at the sky for a little longer, Bea feeling the happiest she'd felt in a very long time. Heartbreak often led to beautiful beginnings, and that's what had happened for her. Heartcross was her future.

'Hemingway and Fernsby,' Nolan said once more.

'I thought you said you weren't arguing.' Bea hit him playfully.

'Bea Fernsby, I think we have an exciting future ahead of us.'

'I think we do, Nolan Hemingway.'

Today had been perfect. She'd found her reason for arriving in Heartcross and he was standing right next to her. This was exactly where they both wanted to be.

Acknowledgments

My eighteenth book is published! As ever this book is a team effort and the hugest of thank yous to my wonderful editor Laura McCallen – I have enjoyed working with you on my latest book from the Love Heart Lane series. This extends to the fabulous team at One More Chapter, HarperCollins for their ongoing support and especially the brilliant Charlotte Ledger, who without a doubt is the best boss and one of the loveliest people in the world of publishing.

A massive thank you to my children, Emily, Jack, Ruby and Tilly who of course are my greatest achievements in life. I'm proud of you all.

Big Love to Woody (my mad Cocker spaniel) and Nellie (my bonkers Labradoodle) who are the best writing partners in crime.

Much love to Anita Redfern. BMITWE. Always.

A huge thank you to Julie Wetherill. In the last two years we have been on so many crazy adventures and here's to many more!

Deep gratitude to all my readers, reviewers, retailers, librarians and fellow authors who have supported me throughout my career. Authors would be lost without you and I truly am grateful for your support.

This book was inspired by a very long chapter in life. Recently, I found the strength to walk away from a situation that had been hanging around in my life for over 30 years. This book touches on a storyline where the main character embraces her own self-worth and finally stands up for herself and what she deserves.

I have without a doubt enjoyed writing this latest instalment in the Love Heart Lane series and I really hope you enjoy A Summer Surprise at the Little Blue Boathouse. Please do let me know!

Warm wishes,
Christie xx

PS. I simply do have the best job in the world.

Don't miss *A Winter Wedding at Starcross Manor*

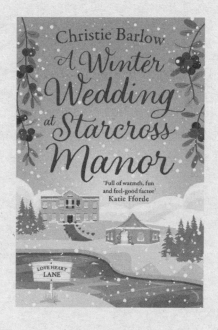

The next heartwarming instalment in the Love Heart Lane
series by Christie Barlow!

Where friends are there for you no matter what...

Love Heart Lane Series

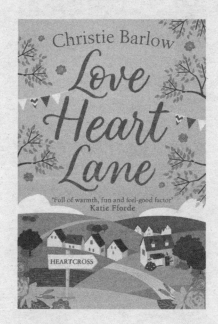

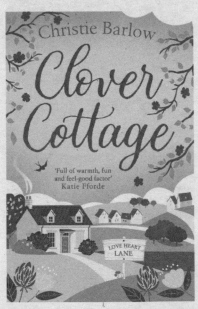

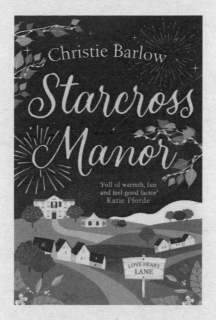

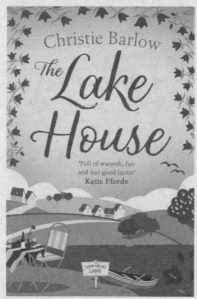

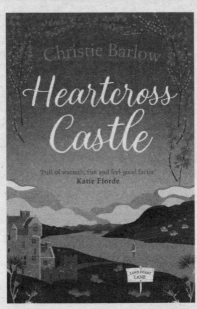

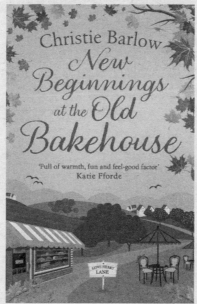

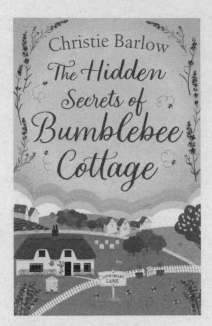

ONE MORE CHAPTER

One More Chapter is an
award-winning global
division of HarperCollins.

Sign up to our newsletter to get our
latest eBook deals and stay up to date
with our weekly Book Club!
<u>Subscribe here.</u>

Meet the team at
<u>www.onemorechapter.com</u>

Follow us!

 <u>@OneMoreChapter_</u>
 <u>@OneMoreChapter</u>
 <u>@onemorechapterhc</u>

Do you write unputdownable fiction?
We love to hear from new voices.
Find out how to submit your novel at
<u>www.onemorechapter.com/submissions</u>